1

His Britannic Majesty's Ship *Diana*, twenty guns, moved like a wraith through the pre-dawn sea smoke. Her canvas filled in gentle, pushing curves before the fitful breeze, moving the ship silently through the grey world. Beneath the long, steeving finger of the jib-boom the water whispered under the forefoot, adding its own sound to the slow creak of the ship's timbers, to be the only disturbance in the ghostly quiet that enveloped the ship.

It was mid-summer 1742, and the ship was no more than a half-league off the high-cliffed headland of Cap de Carqueiranne, to the eastward of the Grande Rade, the great bay which led into the French naval fortress of Toulon. The waters of the Golfe de Giens were a pale, milky grey, only slightly lighter than the thick mists which whirled around *Diana* in billows. High above the slowly moving maintruck of the British vessel, a dome of blue marked the sole promise that when the hot sun rose over the Hyères Islands astern of the ship, the grey murk would vanish and the ship would be lit with the full, clear glory of a Mediterranean summer day.

Diana was a ship-rigged vessel, a four-hundred-ton fighting craft of the Royal Navy of George the Second, classed by that institution as a sixth-rate. Five other 'rates' of warship preceded *Diana* in importance and size, ending with the enormous floating fortresses of the first-rate ships of the line. Somewhat more than one hundred feet in length, and with a greatest beam of thirty feet, *Diana* was none the less a formidable naval fighting machine for her size. She carried some one hundred and thirty officers and men to sail and fight, and was armed with twenty six-pounder truck guns enhanced by a clutch of swivel guns set in strongbacks on the quarterdeck rail. Above the mustard-and-black hull three tall masts pierced the encircling mists, and carried on their yards a cloud of sail, the dull-coloured seaworn British canvas easily distinguished from the bone-white flax of Spanish or French ships. Forward, the ship had set the foretopmast staysail, jib, and jib topsail; on the foremast, the forecourse, foretopsail, and foretopgallant. On the main, the course, topsail and topgallant were set as well, while on the mizzen, the mizzen topsail arched slightly above the spanker, a fore-and-aft sail set on the after part of an archaic-looking lateen spanker yard. At the foretruck, a British Jack hung limply; from the maintruck, a red pennant twisted off in a snakelike tendril before the teasing breeze; and from the ensign staff above the transom rail, a huge British ensign curled in vivid colour over the mist-dampened quarterdeck.

Below the gentle snap and rustle of the great ensign, the commander of *Diana* stood in sharp-eyed watchfulness. Lieutenant Edward Mainwaring, Royal Navy, was an American, a native of the seagirt Massachusetts island of Martha's Vineyard. He had entered the Navy of George the Second by blind luck, through an immediate and local need for his ship at the time, the Provincial schooner *Athena*, and a colonial officer to command her. Soon thereafter, Mainwaring had distinguished himself in the capture of Porto Bello under Edward Vernon, and gained a reputation in the years that followed for a number of bold and dashing exploits, at Cartagena during the disastrous British siege, and on a trek by boat and foot across the Isthmus of Panama to attack and burn the Manila Galleon. But if Edward Mainwaring was a bold officer, he was also one totally without 'interest', as the important and vital patronage of a senior officer or other influential authority was termed. And that had meant that, brave exploits notwithstanding, the rise to the security of post captain rank had eluded Mainwaring; he remained a virtually penniless lieutenant, commanding a vessel worthy of post rank but denied that distinction, a colonial favourite of no one except the increasingly discredited Edward Vernon. It was not lost on Mainwaring that he was, in fact, damned fortunate to have been left in command of such a vessel in the midst of a growing war and under the command

8

VICTOR SUTHREN

Victor Suthren is the Director of the Canadian War Museum, Ottawa, and has a wide range of sailing experience in traditional ships and small craft in which he has followed the routes of the eighteenth-century wars. He was commissioned in Canada's Navy Reserve and is a Board Member of the Canadian Sail Training Association. His novels featuring Edward Mainwaring, *Royal Yankee*, *The Golden Galleon*, *Admiral of Fear* and *Captain Monsoon*, are written with authenticity, an historian's eye for detail and a born storyteller's art. He lives with his wife and children in Ottawa.

Admiral of Fear

Victor Suthren

CORONET BOOKS
Hodder and Stoughton

First published in Great Britain in 1991 by Hodder & Stoughton
A division of Hodder Headline PLC

A Coronet paperback

10   9   8   7   6   5   4   3   2   1

A CIP catalogue record for this title
is available from the British Library.

ISBN 0 340 63840 0

Printed and bound in Great Britain by
Cox & Wyman Ltd, Reading, Berkshire.

Hodder and Stoughton
A Division of Hodder Headline PLC
338 Euston Road
London NW1 3BH

ADMIRAL
OF FEAR

of an admiral at Gibraltar who had his own clamouring favourites to reward.

He was tall, a touch under six feet, with an athletic grace marked by broad shoulders and narrow hips. His hair was a sun-dusted brown, tied back into a simple queue sheathed in eelskin. Below even, black brows and a forehead that bore the faint line of a jagged scar, his eyes were a clear, startling blue, and to the rest of his face there was a lean, aristocratic cast that was altered only by the prizefighter's break in his nose. A perceptive and intelligent face, suggesting at once a warm sensitivity and the capacity for hard-edged and resolute action, it was saved from severity by lines around the eyes and mouth which had been put there by laughter as much as by the weathering of sun and sea. In the heat of the Mediterranean summer he wore his linen shirt open at the throat, and a pair of loose-legged seamen's trousers above salt-rimed buckled shoes. A battered tricorne was crammed down over his brows, and he had his hands clasped behind his back over the tails of the simple, Spanish-cut white linen coat he wore, in deference to the need for pockets in which to carry his watch and a sheaf of penned notes on the coastline along which *Diana* crept before the zephyring wind.

Mainwaring spat thoughtfully over the rail and peered off to starboard, sure that at any moment a headland would appear as the thick haze lifted. His eyes shifted to the clutch of men around the ship's double wheel. The ursine figure of Isaiah Hooke, *Diana*'s sailing master, was standing beside the binnacle box, broad bare feet planted on the decking, his small blue eyes fixed on the almost motionless card. Hooke was powerfully built, with thick, peppershot blond hair hauled aft into a tarry pigtail, his heavily-muscled frame bulky inside a check shirt, sleeveless leather jerkin, and a pair of striped, wide-legged 'petticoat breeches'.

"Mr Hooke. A word with you, please."

"Zur." Hooke rolled past the wheel and approached Mainwaring's windward preserve.

"What's the current here, Mr Hooke? Any sense of it?"

Hooke's eyes crinkled. "It'd be 'bout a knot or two, zur, longshore westerly."

"Then we're still a cable or two away from having to tack up to weather Cépet."

Hooke scratched his thatch. " 'Ard t' say, zur. Ain't sail'd these waters since I was nought but a lad, an' if we're into th' mouth o' th' 'arbour, we'd 'ave t' turn seaward after Cap Brun came abeam, zur." He glanced at the helmsman, a formidable-looking figure whom Mainwaring remembered was a pressed Dorsetshireman named Garnet.

"Keep 'er clean full, Garnet. Eye on th' pennant, an' th' tops'l leech."

"Aye, Mr Hooke,' nodded the man. "Clean full."

Mainwaring's eyes turned to starboard, up to the grey tip of Carqueiranne, looming above the fog. He could see, he thought, the square-cornered ramparts of the Fort de la Gavaresse on its bluff, with the tiny pale square of the French ensign floating above it. There would be guns there, a battery facing to seaward, and likely gunners with linstocks smouldering while a glass was trained on the little English ship, careful for any sign that the sloop-o'-war was about to abuse the fiction of French neutrality. It was, of course, with Spain that England was legally at war; but the French were the barely-hidden allies of the Spanish, and it would only be a matter of time, Mainwaring knew, before open war was declared with the French.

It was difficult to explain simply the cause of the war – beyond the obvious and endless efforts of England to force open the colonies of other nations to her trade, and the equally obvious desire of the Spanish and their vast empire to prevent that. Nominally, England was at war with Spain because the beautiful young Queen Maria Teresa of Austria was under assault from a consortium of ungallant European nations determined to part her from portions of her realm, following the death of her husband. Spain, as a Bourbon nation, was all too willing to assault the Hapsburg Maria's holdings wherever they might be – in the present instance, the northern Italian lands of Lombardy. Allied with the Kingdom of Two Sicilies, the Spanish were embarked on a war of conquest, their armies under a certain General Montémar joined by a Neapolitan horde in the Lombardy assault. Their supply routes to

Spain by land were menaced only by hostile troops of the King of Sardinia, who supported the unfortunate Maria Teresa, and whose sturdy Piedmontese blocked the coastal roads from Nice to Conti, holding as well the coastal town of Villefranche against the growing threat of a French garrison at Monaco. To avoid the Piedmontese, Montémar needed supply and fresh troops from the sea – and the sea was the theatre where the weed-fouled and weatherbeaten ships of the Royal Navy, commanded by Vice-Admiral Thomas Mathews, hoped to bring an end to the Spanish adventure. From the Straits of Gibraltar to the Adriatic, Mathews' ships prowled the sea lanes and headlands of the Mediterranean coast, stretched to exhaustion in an effort to interdict the Spanish at sea, while watchful of the powerful French Navy. Should the French declare open war, and should the Toulon squadron put to sea without sufficient time for Mathews' squadrons to gather, the result would be the piecemeal destruction of the British presence in the Mediterranean. And that would threaten Minorca, Gibraltar itself, the vital trade to the Levant – far more than Their Lordships of the Admiralty were prepared to explain as a loss to Parliament and the King, not to speak of the even more volatile critics of the London mob.

Mainwaring watched tendrils of fog swirl over the blue-green sea face. Several ships were careening at Mahon, on Minorca; at Villefranche, where the port was open to British vessels by virtue of the Piedmontese control, there were four ships, including *Namur*, ninety guns, and *Royal Oak*, seventy. At least three ships were somewhere in the Adriatic, the sixty-gun *Pembroke* one of them; there were four on station off Cape Delle Melle, Corsica; five hovering between Villefranche and Cape Garoupe, watching Antibes; another, the *Dorchester*, fifty guns, was cruising alone between Barcelona and Majorca. Everywhere it was the same: foul and old ships, manned by exhausted, sickening crews, stretched in a thin line along hundreds of leagues of shoreline, waiting to pounce on Spanish vessels, determined to retain control of the Mediterranean, and thereby prevent the Spanish armies from succeeding in Lombardy, and British trade dying in the ancient Roman sea.

It was the French who were the unknown factor. The Spanish could be seen and chased, and with their set destinations and desire to protect their ships and cargoes, hounded as deer by wolves. But the French were an animal in its lair, still nominally a 'neutral' nation, but virtually at war with the English. Now Mathews had determined to concentrate more of his efforts on helping King Charles Emmanuel of Sardinia to reinforce the latter's garrison at Villefranche, while sending an ill-spared squadron to Naples to try, by fair means or foul, to pressure the Neapolitans out of the war. It was a moment of extreme peril, when the French, if they sensed Mathews' preoccupations and weaknesses, could strike a vital blow at Mahon or elsewhere. Mathews needed to know what kind of force lurked in the great French fortress-harbour of Toulon; and he needed to know what they were about.

And that particular task is ours, thought Mainwaring. He cupped his hands to call, clearing his throat.

"Mr Howe!"

"Sir!" The slim, straight form of James Howe, *Diana*'s first lieutenant, appeared round the foot of the mainmast. Howe was an impeccable dresser, almost the equal of the marine officer, Aston Millechamp, and was smoothly attired in a sombre brown suit, white hose, a small brushed beaver tricorne set at a Vauxhall rake over his eyebrows, and immaculate linen showing at wrist and throat. He had a clear, intelligent face, and over the last year or two had become Mainwaring's warm friend as well as a highly dependable second-in-command of the sloop.

"My best wishes to you on your birthday, Mr Howe!" called Mainwaring.

Howe grinned. "Thank you, sir! Another year too many!"

Mainwaring returned the grin. "Directly the watch below have lashed up and stowed their 'micks, Mr Howe, I'd be pleased if you'd call the ship to Quarters. But make it a silent call, mind. No drum, no pipes. I don't want to alarm our Froggy friends any more than necessary."

"Aye, aye, sir. I understand!" Within a moment Howe was speaking to Isaac Jewett, the boatswain, and the latter was knuckling his forelock and making forward, calling for his mates.

Hooke caught Mainwaring's eye and stepped closer.

"If ye'll pardon th' question, zur, what is it ye wish t' do?"

Mainwaring glanced up at the threatening heights of Gavaresse as the shadow of the ensign rippled round him.

"You know what our task is, Mr Hooke. Quite simple, actually. The admiral must know what the French have at anchor in there: how many ships, what rate, if there are transports, the lot. And I'm considering the best way to find all that out."

Hooke spat over the rail and shifted the plug of tobacco that bulged in one cheek to the other side of his mouth. "By comin' t' Quarters an' firin' a few round shot in at 'em, zur?"

Mainwaring smiled. "Nothing so pleasurable. But the simplest means are sometimes the best." His face grew serious. "Look. We're into the mouth of the Great Harbour, and if this fog lifts we might find ourselves able to see into the Little Harbour, where the French'll have the squadron. At least, Mr Hooke, that's what you've led me to expect. Haven't misled me, have you, Isaiah?"

Hooke frowned. "Well – no, zur. When I put in 'ere in thirty-seven, they'd all their ships rafted in the inner 'arbour, right enough. Snug as ducks, they were. But, Christ's guts, zur, there be batteries t' both sides o' th' mouth, an' we'd be well in the lee o' Cépet to boot."

Mainwaring nodded. "Indeed." He looked again up at the silent battery. "Perhaps we might add some confusion to the picture, then, in order to lessen the risk." He raised his voice. "Mr Pellowe? D'ye hear, there!"

Stephen Pellowe, the blond and boyish second lieutenant, was appearing up the after companionway, one of Jewett's mates at his heels. Pellowe was in a short linen coat similar to Mainwaring's, and had taken off his tricorne, his blond locks gleaming like straw in the morning sun.

"Aye, aye, sir!" he called. "Ready to bend on at your word, sir!"

"Very good. Set the new colours, then, if you please."

Pellowe nodded to the boatswain's mate, a short, muscular man named Cave in a striped shirt and stocking cap, and the latter moved on quick bare feet to the ensign staff at *Diana*'s taffrail. Within a few moments the British ensign had been gathered in, and the fluttering, emblazoned colour of His Most Catholic Majesty, the King of Spain, curled out over the quarterdeck.

"Ye'd best get the Jack down from the foretruck as well, Mr Pellowe,' said Mainwaring.

"Spanish colours, b'God!" breathed Hooke. "But sartin they'll take no notice, zur?"

"Perhaps not. But it might introduce an element of doubt that could prove of advantage to us. Mr Pellowe? I'll trouble you to have our true colour hoisted directly we open fire, should that happen!" Mainwaring turned back to Hooke. "The entire scene will be clearer shortly, I would think. The fog's lifting."

Hooke looked round. The grey tendrils were sweeping away as if before a fishwife's broom, and the English sloop was surrounded now not by a wall of impenetrable wet, but the shores of the Grande Rade, the vast outer harbour of Toulon. The shoreline was rocky and wave-splashed, with steep descents, and wooded, white-rocked hillsides rising to the *massif* behind the red-tiled roofs of clusters of villages. To the starboard side, Cap Brun was drawing abeam, Carqueiranne and the mass of the Fort de la Gavaresse now off the starboard quarter. Off the larboard beam, the low mass of the peninsula that formed the south arm of the outer harbour, the Presqu'île de St Mandrier, glimmered in the morning light, dotted with the red of the tile roofs and the silvery spires of three churches. But ahead lay the mouth of the inner harbour. To the right sprawled the white and red mass of the city of Toulon on the slopes of what Mainwaring knew was Mount Faron. A small bay, the Lazaret, appeared on the left, angled in just before the mouth of the Petite Rade, which was formed by another pair of points of land with the low shapes of gun batteries – Mainwaring's outdated Dutch chart showed these as the Balaguier and Eguillette batteries – and on the right by a long tongue of land reaching out from the city itself, cluttered with small buildings and a queer, low lighthouse: le Mourillon.

Mainwaring's heart began to thump in his chest as he realised just how close to peril he was bringing *Diana*. For a moment he wondered if the impulsive stand into the very mouth of the major French naval port in the Mediterranean was far less a matter of boldness than of thoughtlessness. But it was too late to ponder that question now. *Diana* footed steadily along over the placid waters of the Grande Rade, only a few distant fishing chaloupes and a worn-looking xebec, quite some distance inshore, sharing the broad, pale surface. Ahead, beyond the low roofs of the Mourillon, in the inner harbour, he could make out what seemed to be a veritable forest of masts and yards. He looked up, cupping his hands.

"Foretop lookout, there! What d'ye see?"

There was a moment's silence while the man aloft gathered his thoughts. The view from the ship's foretop must have been dramatic, for his voice was shrill with excitement when the reply came.

"Ships, sir! A bloody squadron of 'em, all at anchor close inshore, there, sir!"

"How many?"

"Dozens, sir! Christ, it's a fleet!"

"The Frogs be at 'ome, zur," rumbled Hooke at Mainwaring's elbow.

"Aye, that's clear enough. But I need more than a shrieked estimate from a lookout, Mr Hooke." Mainwaring tightened his lips. "Shape your course directly into the inner harbour, Mr Hooke. Right in amongst them."

The sailing master stared. "Are – are ye sure o' that, zur? Christ, it's puttin' our 'eads into a gun muzzle, sure."

"I'm aware of that, Mr Hooke. Carry on, ple—"

"Deck! Deck, there!" It was the same foretop lookout, his voice cracking in excitement.

"Deck, aye?"

"National frigate, sir! Spanish colours, an' standin' from th' anchorage towards the 'arbour mouth, sir!"

"Oh, Christ!" muttered Mainwaring.

"An' 'is guns is run out, sir!"

Mainwaring stepped to the waistdeck rail and peered forward, crouching to see under the maincourse foot. There it was: a smaller set of masts, with canvas taut and yards braced up sharp on a tack, moving against the backdrop of the still masts of the ships within.

Hooke was at his side, his eyes narrowed. "He's bigger'n us, zur. Thirty guns or more, beloike."

Mainwaring nodded. Inwardly he was beginning to feel very foolish indeed.

"Perhaps he's just coming out to chat."

A thump carried on the air to them, and both men looked up as a puff of smoke curled away from the bows of the emerging ship. The ball sent up a jet of silvery spray a little past half the distance to *Diana*.

"Damn. So much for the *ruse de guerre*," murmured Mainwaring. "There's our answer, Mr Hooke. Bow chaser shot, and a clear challenge."

"Come about and beat out, zur?"

Mainwaring narrowed his eyes. "That Spaniard's likely a proud fellow, Mr Hooke. And easily stung by the usual French contempt for the Spanish. I'd wager the Don wants to fight us and show his French hosts a thing or two."

"Aye, zur, but—"

"The lads have been putting up with months of this damned patrolling and skulking about, Mr Hooke. They need something to sink their teeth into. And I have a feeling the French'll not try to stir the brew. Not just yet." He bit his lip. "Stand by your sailhandlers, Isaiah. We're going to fight him!"

"Beggin' yer pardon, zur, but why not run fer some sea room? Draw th' bugger out some?"

Mainwaring looked at the shoreline, imagining the figures running to the ramparts to watch the drama unfolding below. "Because we have an audience, Mr Hooke. An audience that could do to be reminded what it means to be at war with England. The Spaniard would not let himself be lured offshore in any event, I'd warrant."

Mainwaring moved to the waistdeck rail. "Mr Howe!"

"Sir!" Howe's head appeared up the forward companionway.

"Belay my last order, if you please. Call the ship to Quarters, but by drum and call. And I'll thank you to ask Mr Pellowe to take down that damned Spanish rag and get our own true colours up!"

Howe's grin was bright in the sunlight. "Aye, aye, sir!" he barked.

Within a few moments the little sea-regiment drummer, a freckle-faced urchin almost lost under his tassled mitre cap, was standing with his back to the mainmast timber-bitts. At a nod from Howe the lad thumped away on the deep, unsnared drum, the rhythm sending as it always did a thrill up Mainwaring's spine. As it echoed through the ship, it was joined by the squeal of the pipes blown by Jewett and his mates as they pounded on swift bare feet through the depths of the ship, their cries of "D'ye hear, there! Hands to Quarters! Hands to Quarters! Move y'selves, aloft an' alow!" a keening counterpoint to the sudden thunder of running about the ship.

Diana's complement had been divided, as was the practice, into not only watches, but into teams and responsibilities which were listed on a Watch and Quarter Bill. This was nothing less than a list, endless copies of which had been penned by Moll, Mainwaring's clerk. The name of each man was set beside his duty or position in any one of a number of situations to which Mainwaring might call the ship. A man might be entered as a topman, or fo'c'sleman, for sailhandling duties; second stroke in the captain's boat's crew; second man, larboard-side tackle, number three gun, starboard battery, in gun action; and a boarder, to be armed with a pistol and a tomahawk, and to board from the foredeck area under the command of Mr Pellowe. As much as a man's mess number, the Bill dictated the confines of a seaman's life in *Diana* just as the Articles of War outlined what fate would befall him if he ignored those confines. Now the men in the little ship moved in response to those dictates with the quick but disciplined orderliness that was the characteristic of a British man-o'-war.

Diana's main armament was six-pounder guns; black-ened cast-iron weapons that threw a cast-iron ball weighing six pounds up to a distance of three miles. There were sixteen guns on the upper, or weatherdeck, of the sloop – as ships of *Diana*'s rate were frequently known – the pieces, or barrel, of which were seven feet long. On the quarterdeck, there were four additional guns, shorter in length by a foot. The black pieces of the guns rested in ochre-coloured, oaken gun carriages, and snouted out through gunports in the bulwarks, the inner surfaces of the latter painted in the same dried-blood tint of ochre. As well as the shorter six-pounders on the quarterdeck, there were four swivel guns, murderous little one-pounders, fixed by their pins into the caps of strongbacks at the ship's rail, two to a side.

The gun crews ran to these guns, urged on by the curtly hissed orders of their gun captains, who were the senior hands responsible for commanding each gun and crew, and were distinguishable by the large priming horns they wore over one shoulder. As *Diana*, in the manner of warships, sailed in reasonable weather with her guns shotted and wadded, the first action of the crews was to cast loose the breeching line and side tackles, so that the guns might recoil upon firing. Next was the leap for the vent covers and tompions, sliding the former – plates of thin lead – from over the vents and pans of the guns, and pulling the latter, like great wooden bottle corks, from the gun muzzles. With a sharp length of wire, the gun captain probed the vent, breaking open the flannel cartridge within – Mainwaring refused to use paper cartridges – and then shook his priming horn over the vent and pan, filling them with fine black gunpowder.

Behind the gun crews, the boys of the ship had pelted fore and aft, scattering buckets of sand across the whitely-scrubbed deck to give traction to running bare feet – and to absorb the blood that would otherwise render it slick and treacherous in action. On this gritty surface match tubs were thumped down by other men, a tub amidships behind each gun pair, the smouldering snakes of slow-match set in notches round the tub edges over the water within. The gun captains seized one of these matches and wound it expertly round the short staff of their linstocks, the glowing end held in a metal yaw at the tip. Then, with a barked order to the crews to stand clear, they crouched to one side of the gun, waiting for the command to fire from the pacing officer in charge of the battery.

The men swarming up *Diana*'s ratlines were engaged in other duties: clewing up and dousing canvas until the sloop was down to her fighting canvas of topsails and headsails; rigging chain lifts to the yards to prevent their catastrophic crash to the deck below if shattered in action; struggling aloft with the great net and then wrestling it into position, so that it hung suspended over the ship's weatherdeck to shield the men from wreckage falling from aloft; hefting boxes of tools to the tops, in readiness for any repairs that would have to be carried out even as battle raged. Other men were going aloft as well; men with shot boxes and cartridge buckets, to man the swivels mounted in the fore and main tops, other men, picked sharpshooters, carrying up with them shoulder-slung cartridge boxes and Sea Service flintlock muskets, the heavy weapons affectionately known by soldier and sailor alike as 'Brown Bess'.

The men who had spent the morning watch below in the cramped oblivion of sleep in their hammocks, had rushed on desk as it ended with those hammocks lashed neatly into long tubes. Forcing them into a U-shape, bend uppermost, they had thrust them into the double line of netting that circled the weatherdeck, thereby affording a kind of barricade against musketry. A thunder of heavier feet up the forward companionway announced the thick-shoed arrival of the company of sea-regiment soldiers, or 'marines' as they were coming to be called, driven ahead of the blasphemous, halberd-wielding sergeant, a brick-faced worthy named Pound. In a few moments Pound had harried them, like a border collie with his sheep, into a three-rank formation in the waist, facing forward, their dull-red, full-skirted coats and buff belting a slash of brave colour across the deck. They wore tall, tasselled mitre caps, and canvas gaiters rising from their square-toed shoes to above their knees. Eyes steady to the front, they stood in the regulation Position of the Soldier: feet twelve inches apart, primed and loaded musket on the left shoulder held by the comb atop the butt, right hand resting on the flap of the leather cartridge box that rode on the right hip, suspended there by a broad buff belt from the left shoulder. Their hair was unbound, wisping about their hard, pockmarked and tattooed faces as they awaited the passage along their ranks of their slim and elegant officer, Lieutenant Aston Millechamp. He carried a graceful little silver-hilted hanger and acknowledged Pound's whistling halberd salute with a languid touch of a slim hand to the front cock of his hat.

As Mainwaring watched in building tension, his eyes flicking repeatedly to the shape of the Spanish vessel, the remainder of *Diana*'s men reached their posts. Some ten minutes after the order had been given, the ship now sailed under reduced fighting sail; her tops were manned, sailhandlers and gun crews were alert and waiting. Pellowe and Howe paced in readiness behind the larboard and starboard batteries respectively, and on the quarterdeck, another man had joined Garnet on the wheel. Here and there, as the hubbub of preparation died away, and the murmuring sound of the ship's quiet movement through the sea could be heard again, faces turned aft to look at Mainwaring where he stood with Hooke on the windward side of the quarterdeck, just forward of the wheel. A few moments before the decks had been relatively clear, but now Mainwaring was conscious of standing in the midst of a crowd of men, their attention focused on him, and he could sense their apprehension and anxiety.

"Ten minutes, Mr Howe!" he called out. "Damned fine work, sir. I believe we have a fighting ship's company to unleash on the Dons, poor bastards!"

A quick laugh of pleasure ran through the ship, and whispers which were just as rapidly stilled by the bark of the gun captains and boatswain's mates. But Mainwaring's remark had broken the tension; there were cocky grins now, and confident, even eager expressions as they craned from their posts to try to see the shape of the approaching Spaniard.

"That 'uz a foine thing t'say, zur, if I may," said Hooke, at his elbow. "But ye know the lads'll follow ye, zur."

"Thank you, Isaiah," said Mainwaring quietly. "Every commander hopes for that. But I want them to know I believe in them, what?" He cleared his throat in some embarrassment and adopted again his formal quarterdeck posture, both hands locked behind his back.

"Now what the devil is the Don up to?" he said.

Hooke pointed forward. "'E just passed behind th' lighthouse, zur. Drawin' clear now."

Mainwaring squinted forward, making a deliberate effort to calm the fluttering in his stomach. *Diana* ghosted in towards the mouth of the inner harbour. To either side, Mainwaring knew, he was being watched by French gunners, and the realisation again of how perilous was the situation in which he had placed the ship and her men twinged in his vitals. The French, it was true, had not yet actually fired on an English warship, but that tenuous thread of neutrality was a damnably thin line to hang *Diana*'s survival upon. He swore silently, spat over the side, and scanned the scene again with meticulous attention.

Ahead, the narrows of the inner-harbour mouth were just a cable or so out of the reach of a ranging shot. To starboard, the forest of masts of the French squadron were clearly visible now. And before them, the tall rectangles of canvas gleaming in the sun, the Spanish vessel lay over slightly before a puff, tacking with her yards braced sharply up on a course that would put her across *Diana*'s bows just as the latter nosed into the harbour.

"Aye, aye," Hooke was muttering. "She's thirty guns at least. 'Alf again our weight o' metal."

"Take the glass out of its sheath, there, Mr Hooke. Put it on those batteries. D'ye see *any* twitch o' movement at all?"

Swiftly Hooke had taken the long brassbound telescope from its oiled leather sheath on the side of the binnacle box.

"No, zur," said the master, after a minute's squinting. "Nought. Either their 'eads is down or they be stayin' below decks until piped up."

Mainwaring narrowed his eyes. "They're up there, all right. And likely with their batteries loaded and matches smouldering. But I'll warrant you they're waiting. Expecting this Don to do us in while they watch."

Hooke snapped the long glass shut. "Hell, zur, effen we *sink* the bastard—"

"Right, Isaiah. The Frogs could put a storm of shot into us. They've done some wilful things, but they're not dishonourable for the most part. I'm wagering they'd honour their neutrality, and not open fire." He smiled lightly. "But then, if I'm wrong about that—"

"Deck, there! Foretop 'ere, zur!"

"Deck, aye?" acknowledged Mainwaring.

"The Spaniard, zur! 'E's alterin' course!" The man cried. "Looks to be 'eavin' to, zur!"

"The deuce you say," murmured Mainwaring, and peered forward.

The Spanish vessel was clearly out into full view now, and had turned into the wind, the tall, tapering rectangles of her topsails rippling in long, wavelike shadows before they went aback. Seen bows on, the graceful tumblehome of the hull was evident. White Bourbon pennants drifted lazily from the trucks, and in the clear morning light the hull's brilliant paint scheme of alternating bands of yellow and red stood out glaringly against the white and green of the shore behind. The white ripple of the bow wave faded away to nothing as the ship lost way.

"Hove to, well enough," said Mainwaring. "Either he wants to draw us in, or he's reluctant to fight." He glanced up at the Gavaresse battery and at the low, humped shapes of the batteries flanking the harbour mouth, and took a deep breath. "Very well. If he'll not come to us, we'll go to him. Set the maincourse again, Mr Hooke, if you please."

"Aye, aye zur!" rumbled Hooke. A few barked orders had the maincourse clewlines, buntlines and slablines eased away, and the sail dropped with a rippling thump from its yard, billowing immediately in slow, ponderous beauty to the light breeze. There was a lifting to the hull's motion, and *Diana* hurried forward.

"Now, look at that whoreson buntline, there, Watkins! Ye'd not overhauled it, proper-like, did ye?" Hooke was booming. "Christ's guts, wot kind o' King's 'ard bargain be ye? Worse'n a sowjer! Lay out an' slack it off, lively, now!"

Diana moved in, the sea whispering under her forefoot. Mainwaring felt the trembling in his stomach and cursed it, forcing himself to keep a calm and emotionless expression, making every movement in almost deliberate slowness, conscious of the eyes of the gun crews on him.

No more than a thousand yards ahead, the Spaniard was waiting, the great foretopsail aback against the mast, figures visible now rushing about the decks and clustering at the rails, the glint of sunlight off gun and blade winking here and there. A lull came in the wind, and with it a faint sound of a distant squeal and rumble.

"Gun trucks, zur," declared Hooke. "'E's runnin' out."

"Which side?"

Hooke extended the long glass. "Both, zur. Must 'ave more men in 'er than Portsmouth Poll."

Mainwaring nodded, gauging *Diana*'s speed as she floated in, conscious again of the eyes on him, of the tensed, waiting figures at the nearest six-pounder, of the tap-tap-tap of the reef points on the mizzen topsail over his head. Now the Spaniard was about six hundred yards ahead of *Diana*'s bowsprit, and with the course drawing again the sloop was closing the distance rapidly. Once more he looked ashore, seeing still no movement, no tiny figures rushing to guns behind embrasures. It was almost as if the French were deliberately ignoring the incident unfolding before them. But that, Mainwaring was sure, was not the case.

"Th' Frogs are watchin', zur, never you fear," said Hooke, reading his thoughts.

But Mainwaring did not reply. His narrowed eyes were on the Spanish vessel, looking for the scarlet-clad figure who would be the commander on the quarterdeck, trying to sense the man's thinking. *Why are you waiting, señor?* asked his mind. *Are you afraid? Or do you have some other plan? One that requires you to lure me in?*

"Steady on this heading, Garnet," said Mainwaring, stepping quickly to the helm. "But stand ready for rapid helm orders. You'll have to respond the instant they come. Clear?"

"Aye, aye, sir," replied the muscular Garnet, with a nod. "Jes' yew gives th' word, sir."

"Good. Mr Hooke! You'll stand ready for some rapid sailhandling, if you please. Our course and tack may change unexpectedly."

"Zur," rumbled Hooke.

"Mr Howe! Mr Pellowe!" called Mainwaring through cupped hands. "I hear your crews can knock a bung out of a barrel with a six-pounder! Is this the case?"

"Aye, sir!" came Howe's cheerful call. "But the lads say you'll have to give 'em a barrel full of Dons to shoot at, sir!"

"I believe I shall oblige you presently, then, Mr Howe. Stand ready to fire, both batteries!"

Mainwaring turned to the youthful seaman whom Howe had sent to him to be a runner.

"Ellison, isn't it? Good. Lay below to my cabin. You'll find a pair of pistols on my desk, and their case with powder and shot. Charge 'em, prime 'em, and bring 'em to me. And mind you don't shoot yourself in the foot. I'll need you as well as them all in one piece."

"Aye, aye, sir!" grinned the lad, and leaped off down the companionway.

Mainwaring peered forward. The Spaniard still lay like a great waiting seabird, drifting slightly astern, the brilliant white canvas outlining in relief the foretopmast as it was pressed aback.

"Steer small, Garnet," said Mainwaring, in a low voice. "Keep the ship's head a point or two to starboard of him. I want him to think he'll face the larboard battery."

"Aye, aye, sir. Point or two to starb'd, sir."

Mainwaring cupped his hands. "A touch or two on that larboard foretops'l sheet, I should think, Mr Hooke!" he called.

"Aye, zur! Lively, there, yew two. Down slack on that sheet, now!" Hooke's voice croaked in the otherwise quiet tension of the upper deck.

Diana ghosted in. The Spaniard was large on the larboard bow, now. Garnet was doing as he was told. And now Mainwaring could see the flash of sun on bayonets and musket barrels, as white-coated Spanish marine infantry moved in a mass to the side along which it seemed *Diana* would pass.

Hooke was at Mainwaring's side again, squinting up at the canvas, his eyes hard points.

"'E's took th' bait, zur. It'd be what ye did in th' Caribbees, beloike?"

Mainwaring nodded quickly, his mouth a tight line. His heart was beating so rapidly in his throat that he wondered if he could speak clearly. He willed the trembling in his legs to stop, and spat over the rail, the dryness in his mouth making him long suddenly for a pewter mug of cool small beer. He wondered if Hooke perceived his nervousness.

"Aye. A moment more, on this heading. Pray Christ he doesn't think about raking fire, now."

The Spanish vessel was looming very close now, taller than *Diana*, a clear, detailed picture of towering masts and sails, red and gilt hull, a slowly pitching figurehead of a robed religious figure in white and gilt, a mass of closely packed men, faces turned towards the English vessel, the sun glinting anew off musket barrels, bayonets, and pike heads. Below, the red-painted muzzles of the run-out guns gaped obscenely in the dark gunports. And in the next instant, *Diana*'s jib-boom would draw abreast of the Spaniard and the pounding, fearful destruction of the Spanish guns, twelve-pounders by the look of them, would begin.

But then the moment came.

"*Now*, Garnet!" barked Mainwaring. "Helm hard a-starboard! Sheet home, starboard side, Mr Hooke!"

Garnet's hands slapped the wheel over, and blocks rattled aloft as Hooke's sailhandlers eased the larboard sheets and braces while hauling with frenzied energy at those to starboard. With a dipping grace, the water curling and hissing under counter and forefoot, *Diana* swung in ponderous beauty across the bows of the waiting Spaniard.

"He's all yours, now, Mr Howe!" cried Mainwaring. "*Fire as you bear!*"

And as *Diana* swung on, crossing the bows of the Spanish vessel at a distance of not more than fifty yards, Howe's first

25

gun bore on the target. His gun captain's portfire arced down, and a sudden pottering and flash of musketry on the Spaniard's foredeck was lost in the tremendous bang of the gun, as it fired with a flash of flame at vent and muzzle, leaping back against its breeching line like a living animal. A cloud of boiling, acrid smoke punched out, suddenly obscuring all view of the Spanish ship except the topmasts. In the next instant the second gun fired, with an ear-splitting concussion, then the third and fourth, a half-moment's interval between each thunderclap of sound and licking, twenty-foot tongue of flame, each gun blasting out its own billowing gout of smoke to add to the roiling, wind-whipped wall obscuring the Spaniard. Below, in the waist, Millechamp had faced the marines smartly to starboard, and in a solid crack almost as loud as the bang of the six-pounders they delivered a volley of musketry into the cloud in the general direction of the Spaniard's upper deck.

The rippling sequence of firing reached the quarterdeck, and Mainwaring winced in spite of himself as the quarterdeck guns detonated. And then the gunnery had ceased, and *Diana* dipped on as the swirling cloud of smoke swirled and cloaked the Spanish vessel like a shroud.

Mainwaring forced himself to move, shaking himself against the stunning, numbing effect of the guns' blasts. He was deafened, and the reports had punched at his chest like blows from a powerful fist.

"Stand by to go about, Mr Hooke! Take her right round to larboard through the wind and put her on the starboard tack! We'll give him the larboard battery and work up to windward!" He swung on Garnet. "On my command, Garnet. Look lively, now!"

"Sir!" said the spread-footed man, his eyes alight.

Mainwaring glanced rapidly at the Spaniard, gauging the angle, and aloft at the sails and the pennant streaming from the maintruck. "Now! Helm a-lee, Garnet! Tack ship, Mr Hooke!"

"Helm a-lee, zur!" cried Garnet, the broad wheel spinning in his hands, the single spoke that had a brass cap to it flashing in the sun.

As *Diana* swung away, the wind suddenly more tangible now as it came forward of the beam, Mainwaring sprang to the taffrail, peering at the Spanish vessel. Even as his eyes found it, the vast cloud of smoke was being whipped clear of the enemy.

"'At's done fer 'im, zur!" offered the nearest gun captain.

"Shut your damned mouth and stand to your gun!" snapped Mainwaring. But the man was right. The Spanish vessel, free of the smoke entirely, was a shocking sight in the clear morning air. She still lay aback, but now several yards canted crazily with barely a sheet or tack secure, the clews snapping and thumping as ripples passed across the uncontrolled faces of the sails like waves in a wind-pushed sea. The jib-boom hung at a sharp angle from a tangled snarl of rigging at the bowsprit cap, and the headsails were a sodden mass of canvas trailing down like a bride's train into the sea under the forefoot. The vessel's old-fashioned bulkhead was shattered and splintered, gaping holes showing into the dark within where flying shot had wreaked untold horror. Here and there missing sections of rail, and great, splintery rents in the bow-hull planking close to the waterline below the catheads showed how effectively laid and trained *Diana*'s broadside had been.

But it was on the weatherdeck that the most appalling damage was visible, even at this distance as *Diana* swung smoothly into the wind. At least a third of the round shot flung by the sloop's guns had struck at upper-deck level, and a horrid welter of scarlet and white-clad forms were strewn in a bloody litter over the deck amidst a rubble of up-ended guns, shattered deck fittings, and hanging fragments of shroud and rigging. A haze of smoke was drifting over the deck from a fire raging by the bowsprit's knightheads, and through its pall knots of men were stumbling and pulling at the wreckage and the forms of the dead and wounded, voices raised in a jabber of alarm and fury carrying to *Diana* over the wind.

Diana came into the eye of the wind, canvas rippling in slow, thumping waves aloft, blocks banging and sheets snaking as the headsails were sheeted aback to urge the bows round. The foretopsail went aback with a sonorous whump as Hooke's sailhandlers braced round the other yards. Then the ship was round, and with a cry of "Let go and haul!" the headsail weather sheets were let fly, those to leeward hauled smartly in, and the great surface of the foretopsail swung as its yard was braced round, filling again with a punch of sound as *Diana* lifted smoothly ahead on the starboard tack.

Mainwaring was at the rail, his head turning sharply as he glanced along Pellowe's larboard battery to see if the gun captains were ready, then ahead to judge when *Diana* would cross the bows of the stricken Spaniard. It would be no more than a minute or two. Why in God's name had the Spaniard not fired? Why now was his starboard battery, which would bear on *Diana* with even the most elemental sailhandling, not returning any fire?

"Deck! Deck, there! Ahead, Cap'n! Look!" A voice was shrieking from aloft, one of Hooke's sailhandlers, pointing forward from amidst the packed knot of seamen and marines in the top.

"Dear God!" came Howe's cry, from forward.

Mainwaring stared ahead to where the man was pointing, his eyes followed by virtually every other gaze on deck. From out of the breeze-riffled water, barely thirty yards ahead of *Diana*, a shape was rising, dark and slime-coated. A shape that emerged like a long, thin line of ripples at first, like a tide rip, from the shore at le Mourillon to the opposite shore at Balaguier. A shape that, as Mainwaring stared, resolved itself as huge logs linked by massive sections of chain, being lifted to the surface in ponderous surges, as if by the hands of hundreds of men hidden in the distant fortifications and buildings, toiling at huge windlasses to heave the great iron links and the logs to the surface.

"In the name of Christ; a *boom*!" Mainwaring spat. *And the Spaniard was bait*! cried his mind. He spun on Garnet. "Helm down, Garnet! Hard! Put her into the wind!"

But Mainwaring's order came too late. Even as *Diana* began to turn into the wind, her forefoot was at the boom. The impact sent a shock like that of an earthquake through the ship's deck as *Diana* struck hard, riding up over one of the great logs until, with a sudden, unbalancing jolt, she stopped her forward progress with a fearful sound of grinding, snapping timbers.

The whiplash effect of bringing to an abrupt halt a four-hundred-ton warship and its carefully set and tuned web of slender masts and rigging was catastrophic. As Mainwaring stared upward in horror, the foretopmast and foretopgallant mast toppled forward with a sickening snap and a bowstring-like hum of parting rigging. The men aloft clutched at handholds in vain efforts to save themselves, falling with bitten-off shrieks into the sea alongside or down to impact horridly like a child's broken dolls on the deck. The jib-boom, its supporting upward tension gone, curved under the pressure of the bobstays and gammoning, and snapped downward, the headsails floating like collapsing tents over the bows.

There was a warning cry, and Mainwaring was conscious of a sudden shadow. More in instinct than in thought, he flung himself to one side against the rail, as the mizzentopmast, trailing a nest of cordage, smashed down with a splintering crash to the quarterdeck. A brief wail rang out as it crushed Garnet where he stood, the wheels shattering into flying fragments, one salt-rimed buckled shoe spinning away from the ghastly impact to strike against Mainwaring's shoulder where he lay.

Diana slewed around, broadside to the wind. The air was full of the creaking and groaning, almost human in sound, of wood bending and giving way under tremendous strain. A moment before, *Diana*'s decks had represented a warship about its deadly and disciplined work; now it was a chaos of wreckage, with sections of masts and yards, snarls of brace and sheet, crumpled shapes of canvas, splinters and a welter of rope and cable lying over the decks in a vast tangle. The gun crews and sailhandlers struggled to free themselves and their mates, pulling and hacking at the wreckage to get at the forms that writhed in pain, some silent, some moaning or crying out in agony while others lay in still, broken silence, the dark blood spreading from them in pools over the deck. Freed from its stabilising tophamper, the hull was rolling now, the mast stumps grinding and squealing against their wedges.

A mass of tarry cordage from the mizzen shrouds had fallen across Mainwaring, pinning him against the rail. The cries and screams of the men and the ghastly din of *Diana*'s disintegration filled his ears as he fought in a kind of elemental fury to free himself, kicking and clawing at the thick, black cable.

"Mr Hooke!" he cried. "Isaiah! Where—?"

And then in enormous relief he saw Isaiah Hooke clambering over the mizzen-mast wreckage, a boarding axe in his hand. A cut on his face was bleeding in a long scarlet line down one cheek.

"'Ere, zur! Thank Christ, ye're alive!"

Mainwaring tore his arm free from a coil of ratline and pushed himself to his feet. He grasped Hooke's burly shoulders.

"Work your way forward again, Isaiah! Look after the hands first! When you've got everyone clear that you can, cut away this mess over the side! If any spars are intact, stream 'em alongside so we can jury rig after! Understand?"

"Aye, zur!" croaked Hooke, and stumbled away.

Mainwaring clambered over wreckage to the waistdeck rail, scanning the chaos with a despairing knot in his stomach. He cursed and cupped his hands.

"Mr Howe! Mr Pellowe!"

"Here, sir!" came Howe's cry. He was in the midst of a knot of men struggling to free a comrade trapped under the topyard, forward of the smashed wreckage of the longboat on its gallows.

"Thank God!" breathed Mainwaring. "Where's Stephen?" he called, concern overcoming his sense of formality.

A gun captain called from the far side of the waist. "'E's 'ere, zur, caught under a mess o' gear! Took a knock on 'is 'ead but says 'e's orright! We'll dig 'im out, no fear, zur!"

"Good lad! Get him out as quickly as—!"

There was a familiar, terrible sound in the air, like ripping linen. Two enormous geysers of water hissed up beside *Diana*'s starboard quarter, the glittering columns toppling back as the dull boom of distant gunnery reached Mainwaring's ears.

"Dear Christ," he gasped. "Not now. Not that."

He spun round to stare shoreward. Clouds of heavy gunsmoke were rolling away from the gun embrasures of the battery on the tip of le Mourillon, and farther along the shore from the grey mass of the fort at la Gavaresse. Even as he watched, a pink flash showed in one of the embrasures of la Gavaresse, and seconds later a third geyser leaped up in silvery splendour, barely twenty feet from *Diana*'s side, as forward a horrendous, splintering crash and a shriek from a wounded man told of another impact that had found its mark.

"The bloody Frogs 'ave opened fire on us, zur!" Hooke was bellowing from forward, his voice carrying over the shrieks, the calls, the hammering at the shattered wood, the deep creaks and groans within the ship's hull. Then, even as he spoke, another shot struck *Diana*, scattering a halo of flying fragments as it burst through a foredeck bulwark and lodged, half-imbedded, in the foremast footing. It glowed cherry-red in the surrounding wood which hissed, crackled, and burst into flame.

"*Hot shot!*" Howe was shrieking. "Water, lads, quickly!"

As men scrambled to obey, feverishly seeking the leather gunners' buckets under the rubbish on the deck, more thunderous impacts sounded from forward, the decking leaping under Mainwaring's feet with each impact. In the next instant the rail Mainwaring had been gripping was torn from his hands. He stared down at his feet and the great furrow in the white planking where the ball had missed him by inches. A cry behind him made him spin round to see the man who had been standing at the helm with the luckless Garnet now trapped himself, lying on his back under a piece of the cro'jack yard and pushing weakly against the heavy spar. In a kind of daze, Mainwaring stumbled to him, picking up one of the six-pounder handspikes, and jammed it under the yard. With all his strength he pushed upwards, grunting with the effort, and then two other men were there, tugging the broken man free before Mainwaring let the great thing fall back with a crash.

"Get him below, lads!" gasped Mainwaring. "By the after—"

The decisive round shot struck at the mizzen shrouds, propelling a spreading mass of wreckage snarl ahead of it in an arc of disintegrating rigging and wood splinters. A ten-foot section of shroud and ratline, spinning like a thrown fisherman's net, swept Mainwaring off his feet and pitched him towards the side. But this time the restraining bulwark that had stopped him before was not there. It had been smashed away by the ball that had gone on to thrust up another shimmering tower of water that collapsed back in a hiss of white spray and froth on the sea-face, into which Mainwaring fell amidst the tangle of rigging.

Tumbling through the air in a twenty-foot fall, the wind whistling through his hair, he abruptly struck the water with a sharp impact, the breath knocked from his lungs. The panic was upon him immediately as he sank into the dark, and he fought to break through the clinging shrouds, his lungs screaming for air until suddenly he was free, the dark green before his eyes turning to pale green, then to a froth of bubbles, and he burst to the surface, gasping in almost a sob for air. He was not more than a stone's throw from *Diana*, and he stared in riveted horror up at the ruin that the ship had become: only the mainmast was still standing, hung with shot-holed canvas all aback, and a mass of snarled rigging trailing into the sea alongside.

And smoke. Curling from two gunports, forward near the magazine. Now, from three gunports.

Dear Christ! cried his mind, and he was cupping his hands, kicking furiously to stay above the water's surface, hoping one of the figures struggling above would hear him.

"*Fire*!" he shrieked, his voice cracking. "She's *afire*!"

For a moment he saw faces turn, hearing his voice, peering down at him in alarm and uncertainty. The faces still stared at him as more howling rounds hurtled in, one striking the ship with a splintering crash, another punching into the water near the stern, a huge geyser jetting up into the bright morning sunlight.

The gunports were lit from within by a brilliant, pink-orange flash that seemed to expand up and out until the gundeck itself was lit by the same expanding mass of flame, and the sides of the ship lifted in a kind of slow, steady motion upward and outward towards Mainwaring. It was all taking place in a half-second of time, before the thunderclap of sound could develop and move with the shock wave and flame, and gout of black smoke outward in a ball of appalling violence. But it had been enough for Mainwaring to know that *Diana*'s magazine had exploded.

Then the cataclysm reached him, and swept him up in it, and he knew no more.

2

Mainwaring sat up with a start, eyes wide in the blackness around him, the echo of *Diana*'s explosion pounding in his ears over the shaky sound of his breathing. He could see nothing except a small, pale rectangle of light from a window perhaps a foot above him. Then the weakness washed over him, nausea rose in his throat, and he fell back, turning a little to retch. He was on some kind of cot, covered in rough ticking, with a single woollen blanket over him. A basin was providentially there, he could see. But his stomach was empty, and after a few moments' fruitless gagging he fell back, waves of chills putting a chatter to his teeth. Suddenly, he was unutterably cold and he pulled the rough wool up to his chin, moaning a little through his rattling teeth. As he lay there trembling, he realised he was naked. The chills were shaking him like a wooden puppet on a stick, and he felt wretchedly ill.

Where? asked his mind. *Where in Christ's name—?*

A figure appeared in the deep shadow at the end of the room, as if coming through a small and narrow doorway; the skirted form of a woman, moving noiselessly to beside his cot, peering down at him in concern as he lay shivering.

"*Pauvre matelot,*" she whispered. "*Si jeune—*"

Through his pain and uncontrollable shaking he saw her hands, white and small in the dark, move to the fastenings of her bodice. In a moment the clothing had slipped away to the floor around her ankles, and the curves of her full figure shone like dull ivory. She bent over him, moving aside the rough coverlet, and lay down on the little bed. A smell of roses, and of fresh bread, and a delicate, small-animal warmth enveloped him. With soft, cooing sounds in her throat she gathered him against her, stilling his shivering, the heat of her body and her silken skin breaking down any resistance in him. He burrowed against her like a child, his cheek on the warm mound of her breast, conscious only of the refuge she offered. Her hand stroked his hair, her warmth soothing away the pain and the dreadful shivering until they gradually faded to nothing, and he slept in a wondering, grateful oblivion deep in the haven of her.

He awoke, for a moment unsure of where he was. Then he sat up, staring round him, a little dazedly, at the bare room. It was no more than a whitewashed garret beneath a rough planked roof, with the one narrow, dusty window high on the wall, through which warm sunlight beamed down through floating dust motes. He felt lightheaded, but the pain and the dreadful chills were gone. He looked down at the small pillow and the rough, woollen coverlet, remembering now the woman. But had that been a dream? He could not be sure.

From somewhere below came a sudden pounding, and then a splintering crash. Voices sounded in harsh orders, another man's voice rising in voluble protest, abruptly cut off. A woman's scream rang out, clear and piercing, and heavy-shod feet pounded up the stairs outside the low door.

Mainwaring looked around wildly, suddenly conscious of his nakedness under the coverlet. Then he spotted his clothing, the stained white linen carefully folded on a small ladderback chair in the far corner of the room, his salt-rimed shoes beside. Flinging back the cover, he lurched unsteadily over to the chair, clutched at his trousers and began wrestling them on.

The thundering of the shoes on the stairs grew louder, and in the next instant the door was smashed open. Sunlight flashed on the steel of weapons as three men burst into the room, all wearing the grey and blue of the ubiquitous French naval infantry, the *Troupes de la Marine*. The leading figure was an officer, small and wiry, with white gaiters rising to over his knees and a gilt-and-silver gorget gleaming in a shaft of the sunlight where it lay against the gathered white lace at his throat. His eyes were dark and intense below his large tricorne with its black silk cockade, and from one lace-cuffed hand a slim infantry hanger was levelled at Mainwaring's chest as the latter stood, half-dressed, by the chair. Two marines, short and swarthy with rat-tail queues and a sallow, fevered look, followed sharp at his heels, hefting the long, three-banded *fusil-grenadier* with fixed bayonets.

"*Et bien*," said the officer. "*Le voilà.*" The sword point flicked to Mainwaring's clothing. "*Habillez-vous! Vite!*"

Mainwaring made himself smile slightly. "By that do you mean I can at least get my bloody clothes on?" he asked.

The officer's brown eyes flashed in impatience, and the sword tip moved to within an inch of Mainwaring's throat.

"*Ce n'est pas drôle, salaud. Vite!*"

"Your meaning is quite clear," Mainwaring replied, and concentrated on pulling on his clothes. His shoes were hardened and curled by the salt, and his linen coat had one pocket torn away. But before he could dwell too much on the raggedness of his appearance, the officer seized his shoulder and thrust him towards the two marines, who bundled Mainwaring roughly off down the cramped stairwell, their bayonets banging and ringing against the beams. Mainwaring tried to keep from losing his footing as he half-fell down the steps, smelling for the first time the heavy aroma of tobacco smoke and garlic that surrounded the men, mixed with the reek of sweat and the added tang of wet, dirty wool and gunpowder. The experience of being packed into the fetid squalor of a French gun deck with a hundred men like these would be a unique experience indeed.

They erupted into the lower level of the house, a large, open room with a fireplace to one side, rough, spare furniture, a splintered doorway gaping open, bright sunlight streaming in through it and several open-shuttered windows. The floor was scattered with straw, and a few chickens pecked about industriously, while a very large and pregnant goat stood impassively chewing in a corner. On the floor in front of the door sat a thickset, balding man in the ticking shirt and petticoat breeches of a fisherman, holding his hands to a bloody forehead and moaning. Kneeling beside him was a plump, darkly pretty woman of about thirty in a housewife's apron and mobcap over striped woollen skirts. She was wringing out a cloth in a bucket of water to give to the man, and as Mainwaring was pushed into the room she looked up, her eyes flashing fear. They were brown and dark-lashed, and from the corner of her full, sensuous mouth a thin trickle of blood ran, below the welt on her cheek where the back of the officer's hand had struck.

For an instant her eyes met Mainwaring's, and he knew it had been she who had come to him in the night and healed him with her body. He opened his mouth to speak, but there was a blow in the middle of his back from a musket butt, and he was wrestled to the doorway and thrust out, momentarily blinded by the dazzling sunlight, feeling the heat of it on his face. Then his eyes adjusted, and he saw that he had been in a small fisherman's cottage. It was a humble whitewashed building with a red-tile roof and doubled, in the European way, as a barn for several animals as well. Before him, he realised, lay the waters of the Petite Rade, or inner harbour, of Toulon. Opposite was the red-and-white mass of the town itself, before which, across the sun-dappled face of the harbour, a mass of ships rode at anchor, their masts a forest of black spars and white canvas in tight harbour furls. If he visualised the chart accurately, he was on the south shoreline of the Rade, at la Seyne. And just there, to the right, would be where *Diana*—

"Cap'n! Be that yew, actual, zur?"

Mainwaring spun around, staring. It had been the voice of Isaiah Hooke. He was gazing at a throng of ragged, bare-headed men, flanked by several marine guards with fixed bayonets, each Diana linked to the next by a rope which was lashed to their wrists in a chain.

"*Isaiah?*" croaked Mainwaring. "Stephen? James?"

In the next instant he was amidst them, the men grinning at him like apes, and he was laughing with them, a tightness in his throat, looking at each sunburnt face in turn with a feeling of enormous affection. The French marines stood

37

apart, leaning on their muskets, as if granting the English their moment of reunion. Isaiah Hooke, a still-livid cut across the top of one cheek, was beaming at Mainwaring like a bear, his small blue eyes twinkling points of delight. Stephen Pellowe, his youthful blond locks whipping in the hot wind, wrung his hand wordlessly, his eyes moist. Now James Howe had his hand in a firm grip, concern and relief written large over his dirt-smudged features. In the ragged remnants of his coat and with his hair unkempt, he was a far cry from the fastidious James Howe who had paced *Diana*'s decks in such elegance.

"Thank Christ, sir. Thank Christ, you're alive. When the shot carried you away over the side, we thought—" He did not finish.

Mainwaring shook his head, laying a hand on Howe's slim shoulder. "Christ's guts, James, how can all of *you* be alive? I saw the ship go up like a bloody great mine!"

Hooke was beside him, and spat into the dust. "She did, right 'nough, zur. But th' magazine blew queer-like, zur. Th' blast went out through th' ports, like, but th' upper deck lifted clear, of a piece. An' most of us wiv it, zur."

Mainwaring swung round, scanning the ragged figures with a ghastly sinking feeling in his heart. "Who *is* here? How many?" he managed, hoarsely.

Howe's eyes were steady on his. "Besides you, sir, there's Stephen and myself, and Mr Hooke. We've Jewett and Shanahan, Evans, Winton, Sawyer and Slade. And Williams, too, sir. That – that's all we know of so far."

Mainwaring looked around the grim faces, meeting each steady look. They were so pitifully few, and from a ship's company of over a hundred.

Howe had caught another man's eye. "Oh, and a marine, sir. Private Price."

"Millechamp?"

Howe shook his head.

"Then that makes twelve. Twelve of us left."

"Er – yes, sir."

"Oh, my God," breathed Mainwaring. For a moment he could say nothing more.

"It were terrible, zur," said Hooke. "When yew went over th' side, a few o' th' lads made t' save yew. Then th' magazine blew, an' most of us were in th' Oggin, next we knew, hangin' on t' whatever gear there was floatin' about. Some o' th' lads as can swim helped them as couldn't. An' then a few Froggy fishin' dories, or whatever, were about, haulin' us out an' takin' us ashore. Mostly we were together last night in one place."

"Is that what happened to everyone who survived, as far as you know, James?" said Mainwaring. "Fishermen pulled you out?"

Howe nodded, and for the first time Mainwaring could see that he was holding one arm cradled against his side.

"Just a sore rib, sir. It'll be better presently. There were longshore fishermen out, watching us fight the Spaniard. When *Diana* went up, they rowed out and did what they could for us. Wouldn't be alive if they hadn't. I think we're all that's left. The fishermen saved our lives."

Mainwaring thought briefly of the Frenchwoman's body in the gloom of the attic.

"Yes. What did the Spaniard do?"

Hooke spat. "Beggin' yer pardon, Mr Howe. 'E did nought, zur. Left us t' die, 'e did, an' put back in t'that anchorage yonder. Ye c'n see the bastard, moored just fine t' starboard o' that French sixty-gunner."

Mainwaring peered briefly at the distant mass of anchored ships. Then his eyes swung to where *Diana* had met her end.

"There's nothing left of her, is there?" he said quietly.

Howe's face was gaunt with fatigue and pain.

"No, sir. Not a spar or keg. 'Longshore current's carried most of it out to sea, now that the boom's been lowered again. And the fishermen were picking over it."

Mainwaring nodded. It was a moment before he could trust himself to speak. "Is – is anyone else hurt other than you, James?"

"Mr Hooke has a gash on his head. Jewett took a splinter in the guts, but he's—"

"*Assez, alors! Alignez-vous, là. Caporal!*"

The *Troupes de la Marine* officer had come out of the cottage and was gesturing at the two marines who pulled themselves to attention with a surly kind of obedience, Mainwaring thought, and stepped towards the Dianas. One marine slung his musket and pulled a length of light line from his waistbelt. Roughly, he seized Mainwaring's wrists and bound them to the long central rope, beside Howe.

Mainwaring turned to the French officer, who would have known by the cut of their clothes, however ragged, that Mainwaring and Howe were not simple seamen. The Frenchman met Mainwaring's gaze and smirked.

"Not too gentlemanly, I'm afraid, sir," muttered Howe under his breath.

Mainwaring nodded. "The honour of a French officer, James, is a selective affair." He kept his face expressionless as the little marine finished the knot with a tug, stepped back a pace, and pointedly spat in the dust at Mainwaring's feet.

"*Allons! En avant, marche!*" barked the officer, and the leading man in the line, the powerfully-built Jewett, was prodded into movement with a bayonet. Watching to see that they did not trip over each other's feet, the rest were tugged awkwardly after, trudging in an uncomfortable shamble through the rising cloud of dust along the rocky track by the water. Sawyer, a whippet-thin little Yankee from Martha's Vineyard, was just ahead of Mainwaring, and the man turned and gave Mainwaring a quick, gap-toothed grin of reassurance as they fumbled along.

"Our turn'll come, sir! Reckon 'twill!" he said.

"Good for you, Sawyer. Watch your footing, now," said Mainwaring. Beside Sawyer was the dark-haired Shanahan, his striped shirt already dark with sweat.

"Bearing up, Paddy?" said Mainwaring. He flashed a look at the guards, one trudging at the head of the little column with the officer far out ahead, the other marine presumably behind them. "Keep your voice low."

"Aye, sorr. They'll not see me flinch. What d'ye think they'll do wiv us, yer honour?"

Mainwaring swore as he twisted an ankle on a stone. The dust was clinging to them as it hung in a choking cloud and their faces were quickly turning into harlequin masks of white.

"Can't say, Paddy. We're damned lucky to be alive. And these gentlemen seem less than happy to have us on hand." He forced himself to grin at him. "Don't worry. You'll see Dublin again."

"That I will, sorr," grinned back the youth.

For a time they stumbled on, moving as far as Mainwaring could tell along the narrow coastal track — no more than a rutted donkey-cart track — that led out towards the grey walls of the battery at l'Eguillette, where the southern end of the boom that had destroyed *Diana* was likely anchored. With the clinging cloud of dust and the difficulty of the shuffling march it was hard to see where they were going. But then after a moment or two they came round a bend in the track past a stand of low, weathered pine, and approached a whitewashed building that sat perhaps a hundred yards from the heavy wooden doors in the masonry of the battery that marked a gate or sally port. The building faced the harbour, and across the track, on the harbour edge, a ramshackle wooden jetty thrust out into the still, aquamarine waters. A longboat was made fast to the jetty, its twin lugsails brailed up against their yards. The building had a low verandah, and two doors in its front face. There was a single window, shuttered and barred.

"*Halte!*" cried the officer, and the prisoners shuffled to a halt, coughing in the thick dust. The sun was burning down with the intensity of a shot furnace, and Mainwaring's throat was parched. A certain lightheadedness made him reflect that he — and likely all the others — had not eaten since the morning of the day before. One of the marines, the *caporal*, appeared out of the swirling dust brandishing a wicked-looking knife. He went along the line, cutting the Dianas' bonds with deft strokes, and the heavy rope that had anchored them together dropped into the dust as they chafed their wrists. From somewhere behind him, a voice that Mainwaring thought was likely the British marine, Price, muttered an inventive obscenity about the little *caporal*. There were several sniggers in support.

The *Troupes* officer went in through one of the doors in the low building, into what appeared to be a small office, and slammed the door.

41

"Bars, zur," muttered Hooke, who was standing beside Mainwaring. "It be a bloody brig."

"Not quite, Isaiah," said Mainwaring. "I've seen its double in Louisbourg up on Cape Breton. It's a guardhouse, the French call 'em a *corps de garde*. Officer stands his watch in the smaller room. The other's for the sentries. These lads likely are posted here."

"Think this'll be—?" began Howe.

Before Howe could finish, the little *caporal* with the knife had materialised in front of Mainwaring, squinting up at the tall American and gesturing with the knife towards the door through which the *Troupes* officer had gone.

"*Vous, rosbif. Le capitaine veut vous parler. Vite, alors!*"

There was a blow in Mainwaring's back from a musket butt, and the other marine thrust him roughly ahead with the weapon. Mainwaring felt a quick, sudden spasm of anger and only at the last moment kept himself from spinning on his heel and decking the swarthy little man with a fist. He let himself be pushed up on to the plank verandah and through the low doorway. The interior of the building was dark and cool after the dust and glare of the sun, and as the door banged shut behind him he realised he was in a small, bare office, furnished with a few rough chairs, an *armoire* against one wall – and a plain desk in dark wood behind which sat the officer who had led them here, regarding him over steepled fingertips. The Frenchman had a dark, thoughtful face, more serious now than sneering. He had taken off his tricorne, revealing a neatly dressed wig in the Cadogan style, and the cuffs of his grey uniform coat – hellishly hot in this climate, Mainwaring thought – were heavy with lace. As Mainwaring waited, the Frenchman gestured towards a single chair that stood before the desk.

"*Et bien,*" he began, as Mainwaring sat. "You are the officer of this piratical rabble?" His accent was faint with an oddly Irish lilt.

"This 'rabble', as you put it, are the survivors of my ship's company," replied Mainwaring evenly. "And I am an officer of His Britannic Majesty's Navy."

"An easily refuted fiction," said the Frenchman smoothly.

42

"I beg your pardon?"

"You are not a King's officer, and you and your men are pirates, no more."

Mainwaring's eyes narrowed. "You are fully aware of who and what we are. You have no right to treat my people as felons, nor to—"

"*No right?*" The Frenchman's mouth lifted in a thin smile. "Where, by the Virgin, do you think you are?"

"Clearly not in the hands of a gentleman."

The Frenchman paled. "Be uncivil with me, *salaud*, and you will regret it. I can just as easily have you shot out of hand. Or would you prefer to be hanged?"

Mainwaring levelled a steady gaze into the dark, hostile eyes. "You threaten poorly. I am Lieutenant Edward Mainwaring, commanding His Britannic Majesty's Ship *Diana*. Engaged in lawful action against a vessel of the Spanish Crown until *un*lawfully trapped behind your boom and sunk by fire from your shore batteries. In total disregard for the policy of neutrality you claim to observe—"

"Don't quote your childish rules of engagement at me, *rosbif*," interrupted the Frenchman. "You deny your piracy?"

"Do you deny your dishonour?"

The Frenchman's eyes became hard, small points. "What were you doing within the waters of the Grande Rade? What were your orders?" His voice rose at the end almost to a shout.

A corner of Mainwaring's mouth lifted. "Interesting. I was not aware pirates acted under orders," he said.

"*Sacristi!*" swore the Frenchman. He stood up and strode to the door, pulling it open. "*Caporal!*" he bellowed, and then turned back to Mainwaring. "You English and your stupid games and posturing! You and that pack of louts are pirates, and will meet a pirate's end!"

The swarthy *caporal* appeared, a plug of tobacco bulging in one cheek. He spat into the dust beside the door and idly touched a hand to the small of his musket butt. "M'sieu'?"

"*Je les ai condamnés. Il faut qu'ils soient fusillés. Demain matin, à l'aube. Compris?*" The officer's voice was harsh, his words final.

43

The swarthy *caporal*'s eyes looked at Mainwaring, a mocking little smirk crossing his features. He nodded. "*A vos ordres, m'sieu'*."

The officer regarded Mainwaring and smiled mirthlessly.

"Sleep well, *rosbif*. Prepare your little band of brigands to meet their God on the morrow. If they have one."

Mainwaring's knowledge of French was rudimentary, gleaned from a few childhood voyages to Louisbourg in Seth Pomeroy's pink, the *William and Anne*. But it was enough to know that he and the others had just been sentenced to be shot at dawn the next day. A cold stone seemed to have materialised inside his body, and he looked at the French officer with a mixture of rising dismay and anger.

"You really are a contemptible swine, aren't you? Hardly better than those grubby little soldiers," he found himself murmuring.

The French officer's face flamed red, and he was out of the door in a swirl of the skirts of his uniform coat. The *caporal* swaggered in and levelled his bayonet at Mainwaring's midsection, pointing with his chin towards the door.

"*Marche!*" he hissed, the smirk still there.

Within a moment Mainwaring was standing before the low door that led in to the other two-thirds of the guardhouse. The *caporal* turned a massive key in the door, kicked it open, and gestured with the bayonet for Mainwaring to enter. As the American ducked his head under the low beam, the *caporal* drove his reversed musket butt into the small of Mainwaring's back. With a grunt, Mainwaring fell on his knees into the darkness inside and lay gasping as the heavy door slammed shut behind him. The blow had driven the breath from his lungs and there were little points of light dancing before his eyes. A sudden scuffle of movement sounded around him.

"Winton! Help me lift him up!" That was Howe's voice.

"Aye, sir!" Strong hands fastened on Mainwaring's arms, lifting him gently to a sitting position. He could sense the concerned faces all around him.

"Steady, zur," growled Hooke. "That were a hard blow."

44

Mainwaring grunted in reply, his eyes adjusting to the light. He could see the Dianas, kneeling or squatting around him. Howe and Pellowe were at one side, Hooke the other. He rubbed his lower back and swore.

"I'm all right. Are we all here?" he said.

"All of us, sir," said Howe. "They just pushed us in and left us."

"Beggin' pardon, zur, but wot did th' officer want wiv ye, zur?" Hooke's voice was full of concern.

"He wanted me to admit we were pirates of some sort. Deny that we are British seamen."

The room was nothing more than a cell with a single barred window, darkly shuttered. The floor was beaten earth, and there was no furniture, not even the wooden, shelf-like guard bed usual to such places. In the shadows, the men squatted with their dust-whitened faces like apes in a cave.

"I don't follow, sir," said James Howe.

Mainwaring laughed lightly. "It really is very simple, James. The French opened fire on us and sank *Diana*. In violation of their neutrality; a neutrality they've used to justify the interdiction of English shipping and flaunt their transportation of Spanish soldiery to Italy under the admiral's nose. So far we've not retaliated, although I gather Newcastle's latest orders to the admiral say something about that. In any event, if they admit we are Royal Navy seamen and officers, and that they wilfully destroyed a British warship in an act of war, the charade of neutrality isn't worth tuppence. Once word got back to the admiral, he'd be justified in standing in here and sending every hull he found to the bottom!"

Stephen Pellowe cleared his throat. "Is that why they were treating us like convicts, sir?"

"Exactly, Stephen. Prisoners of war have certain rights. Officers have the right to be granted parole. Very inconvenient. Pirates, on the other hand, can simply be done away with."

There was a moment of silence as this last observation was digested. Then, unexpectedly, it was the boatswain, Jewett, who spoke next.

"Yer pardon, zur, but does that mean th' little garlicky bastards mean t' do fer us?"

Mainwaring nodded in the gloom. "I'm afraid that's what they intend. But don't think the fight is over yet, 'swain."

Hooke spat into a corner. "Wot do they mean t' do, zur?"

"Shoot us. At dawn tomorrow."

Howe was the first to break the stunned silence. "Why, those pox-faced, dishonourable little—!"

"Steady, James! Listen to me, all of you!" barked Mainwaring. His voice rose over the outbreak of anger that had followed Howe's words. "We've a day, virtually: a day to plan how to get out of this. And we're not bound or chained. Remember that damned little cage we were in on the coast of Panama? Or the cable tier in the *San Josefe*? Right, then. We've got our wits and our hands, and that gives us a fighting chance!"

"It ain't fair, sir, beggin' yer pardon," broke out Jonas Slade, the little Cockney seaman who was the close friend and messmate of the Vineyarder, Sawyer. "We 'ad a go at th' Spanisher fair and square, sir. Nuffin t'get a musket ball in me guts about, sir!"

"I agree, Slade. Now listen, I say again." Mainwaring's voice was steady. "We've all got to keep our nerve. I want no man wallowing about in self-pity. We'll all need each other's strength to find a way out of this. And there will be a way!" He paused. "There is one other thing, and this affects you all."

"Wot's that, zur?" said Hooke.

Mainwaring sighed. "You all know a captain's authority over a ship's company ceases if the ship is lost. I have no right to give orders and expect you to obey 'em." He paused. "There may be a way to get us out of here, and there may not. But I'll need your loyalty if we are to have any chance—"

Isaiah Hooke's deep *basso* interrupted him. "Pardon, zur, but ye needn't say a word. The lads know th'custom. An' ye be cap'n."

"Aye, sorr," came Shanahan's voice. "We're still Dianas."

"Aye, sir! Aye!" A chorus of voices rose.

Mainwaring wondered if they could see the crooked grin that he could not keep from his face. "Very well. And thank you all. Now," and here he stood, "what do we have to work with? Has anyone got his knife? Anything at all. Each man search himself, although I damn' well know you're in rags."

Most of the men simply shook their heads. The seaman's petticoat breeches or wide-legged duck trousers had no pockets, and neither did their rough shirts. The French had taken every visible knife worn on a belt. Only Howe, Pellowe and Mainwaring had coats, and the pockets of Mainwaring's revealed nothing but his watch, ruined by the seawater, and a soggy paper mass of notepaper, which once held his handwritten sailing notes. Howe found the bowl of a broken clay pipe in one of his pockets. But Pellowe had a grin of triumph on his youthful features.

"Sir? I've got my clasp knife. The Frogs missed it. It was in my coat-tail pocket."

"Good lad!" breathed Mainwaring. "It'll be worth its weight in gold. Anyone else?"

A few leather waistbelts were reported, a few thongs or chains worn around necks with lucky charms. But most were empty-handed. It was not much to work with.

Mainwaring nodded. "All right, lads. Let's get some rest for the moment. You've had no food or water, and we may have some desperate work ahead. Get your heads down for a bit."

"Hard to do when we're facing a bloody firing squad, sir," muttered Howe.

"I know, James. But be assured we're not going out there tomorrow morning to let 'em shoot us down like dogs. Get some rest."

Howe's eyes were questioning in the dark. "What d'ye plan to do, sir?"

Mainwaring looked round the cell, at the men who were curling up to rest as best they could on the beaten earth.

"James, I haven't the foggiest idea," he whispered. "I'm simply trusting to luck at the moment. If we can keep the lads' spirits up, they'll be able to respond quickly if some opportunity does present itself!"

Howe nodded, looking at the quiet forms. A few were snoring already. "They trust us to come up with something, sir," he said.

"And we shall, James. We shall!"

Mainwaring squatted between Hooke and Howe, resting his head back against the clammy stone of the wall. His eyes found the thin sliver of light that edged the heavy door, and then closed in fatigue. Unbidden the face of a beautiful, dark-haired girl floated before him; sun-browned skin, clear blue-green eyes, and a wide, happy grin that lit his heart with a glow of sunlight. He felt the pang of separation and distance from her, wondering where she might be at this moment in far-off, rainy London.

Oh, Anne, dear girl, he thought. *How I wish I was with you now. How I wish the darkness was surrounding our bed, and I was holding you against me in it!*

Anne Brixham was the warm, vital daughter of a Caribbean planter and Mainwaring had fallen thoroughly in love with her. A headstrong girl of fire and spirit, she had stood with him on the quarterdeck of his ship, fought alongside him in the steamy hell of Panama, and lain locked in lovemaking with him on the moonlit deck of his great cabin. Now she was in London, where her father, Richard Brixham, was seeing to the liquidation of his plantation holdings through his solicitors in the City. Mainwaring found it hard to imagine Anne, whose hair had streamed in the wind and whose figure had moved unrestricted in baggy seamen's clothing as she worked like a man in her father's vessel, being trussed and powdered and patched like a London belle. That she would be a revelation with her smouldering beauty was certain; less certain would be her tolerance of the aimless posturings and foppishness of the drawing-rooms, and the sheer wastefulness of days spent in idleness. Richard Brixham was not without wealth, and hoped to obtain a seat in Parliament with the help of several well-to-do friends; Anne was certain of entry into a far different world from the barefoot, adventurous one she had inhabited until now. The image of her, the memory of her in his arms was so strong and poignant that he bit his lip urgently at the last second to prevent himself from calling out her name. If it pleased God, he would see her again; gaze into those shining, blue-green eyes, feel her dark locks tumble round him, feel the heat of her small, muscular body pressed hard in passionate lovemaking against him—

"Cap'n, zur!" It was Jewett, by the doorway, hissing a warning. "Somethin's afoot outside, zur!"

Mainwaring rose to his feet, the others stirring round him, as the scuff of leather sounded outside the cell door. A voice issued a few terse orders, and a musket butt thumped down as if a sentry was taking up a post. A key rattled in the heavy door, and then with the kick of a boot the door swung wide, the glare of light brilliant and blinding, and a slim figure stepped through into the gloom.

"Your officer! Who is he!" asked the figure. The English was clear, with virtually no accent.

Mainwaring stepped forward, recognising the figure as another officer of the *Troupes de la Marine*. Slimmer and somewhat more elegant; a hand rested on the hilt of a small hanger as he looked at Mainwaring with grave eyes in a long, aquiline face.

"I am," said Mainwaring simply. And was astonished when the Frenchman grasped the front cock of his tricorne, doffed it, and inclined his neatly-coiffed head in a courtly salute.

"*Enseigne en pied* Saint-Luc de Guimond. At your service, m'sieu'."

Mainwaring exchanged a quick glance with Howe, and then looked back at the Frenchman. He inclined his own head.

"Lieutenant Edward Mainwaring, His Britannic Majesty's Navy. At yours, sir. You speak English remarkably well."

De Guimond replaced his tricorne. "It is a little thing. My family is from the Bretagne, and I know London well." He looked round the cell. "These are your men?"

The American nodded. "They are. But I'm sure you are aware of that."

De Guimond had a peculiar expression on his face. He had not moved from where he stood, and his hand still rested on the little hanger hilt.

"*D'une certitude*. I – many of us witnessed your engagement with the *San Pablo*. It was a brave thing. And the results unfortunate."

"Thanks to your boom. And your batteries. You attacked us, and we are not at war, m'sieu'."

De Guimond looked down at his shoes and then up at Mainwaring, a kind of pain showing in his face.

"I wish you to believe that men of honour in the service of His Most Christian Majesty do not enjoy the dishonourable subterfuge of this 'neutrality'. And you are entitled to an apology for the treatment you have received as an officer and a gentleman. It has been inexcusable."

Mainwaring's eyebrows rose.

De Guimond glanced over his shoulder towards the doorway, as if watching for something.

"We – we cannot countermand the orders of the *capitaine* of my company, m'sieu'. He is in turn supported by the *major*. Neither is a gentleman. But I must obey their orders. It – it will be myself who will arrive at dawn tomorrow with a half-company. I have orders to march you to the cove just past l'Eguillette, towards the Balaguier fort. On the beach there I am to execute you and – and throw the bodies in the sea."

Mainwaring's eyes were hard. "Not a task for an honourable man, indeed. Why do you tell me this?"

De Guimond's face was pale and it was evident that he was struggling with the humiliation of his situation.

"I will carry out my orders, m'sieu'. I will arrive with my men at precisely six o'clock. The drummer atop the ramparts of l'Eguillette beats his first stand-to a half-hour before then."

"And?"

De Guimond cleared his throat. "The sentries are posted at the doors of this building. Two in the front, and two more who march a beat of the grounds. A fifth sentry is posted at the foot of the jetty, where I am sure you have seen a chaloupe is made fast," he said meaningfully. "At midnight I shall withdraw these sentries so that they may have a few hours' sleep, and prepare for the difficult duty the dawn will bring."

50

"*Enseigne*, what are—?" began Mainwaring.

"Please, m'sieu', listen! I shall be presuming that the door of this cell is firmly locked, providing sufficient restraint for you and your men. It would indeed be most unfortunate if, by error, the sentry departing his post at midnight should forget to ensure your door is locked. And doubly unfortunate if that door had become unlocked prior to his departure. Escape would virtually be a certainty between midnight and dawn, would it not?"

Mainwaring looked carefully into the young man's eyes and saw the message there.

"Yes, virtually a certainty," he said slowly. "And, of course, with what I presume is an unguarded but seaworthy boat nearby—"

"Exactly my train of thought, m'sieu'" said the French marine officer. "I would be most astonished to arrive at dawn and find this cell empty, and that boat gone. But then, such are the fortunes of war, *hein*?"

"Indeed," replied Mainwaring. "And one would respect and salute the honour of a gentleman who would concern himself with such a possibility; one which might have serious consequences for him."

De Guimond's chin lifted imperceptibly. "Some principles must be defended, m'sieu'. At whatever cost. I am sure you would agree."

A look of understanding passed between them, and Mainwaring nodded, admiring De Guimond for what he was risking for those principles.

"I must warn you, m'sieu'," said De Guimond. "Upon my arrival here at dawn, I will, of course, be in the service of my King. My duty would require me to pursue his enemies, and engage them, if found, to the limit of my ability and the forces at my disposal. I hope that is quite clear."

Mainwaring nodded again, a slow smile on his face. "I would expect nothing less from a courageous officer and servant of his King. And a gentleman of honour and principle. And I thank him."

De Guimond nodded, and then shrugged. "War is a foul business, is it not, Lieutenant Mainwaring?" he said, and held out his hand.

Mainwaring took it, feeling the firm grip, and returned the grip in kind. "Yes, *enseigne*. Most foul."

In the next instant, with a swirl of the skirts of his uniform coat, De Guimond was gone, the great door banging shut with a crash behind him.

"Lor' lummee!" breathed Hooke. There were incredulous murmurs from the other men, who had watched the little drama in motionless silence.

"D'ye think he meant what he said, sir?" asked Stephen Pellowe, wonderment in his eyes.

"Aye, zur!" put in Hooke, before Mainwaring had an opportunity to reply. "C'd be nought but a trap, zur! They'd lay in wait an' broadside us as we made a run fer it, fer sport!"

"What would that serve, Isaiah?" said Mainwaring. "They plan to shoot us in any event, and with a good deal less discomfort to themselves than what you are suggesting."

"You believe him, then, sir?" said Howe quietly.

"Aye. Aye, I do. I think he is what he appears to be: a French officer and gentleman doing what he feels is the honourable thing." He paused, regretting the ruin of his watch. "What time d'ye make it, James?"

Howe went to the door and put his eye against the seam of light. "Hard to tell, sir. I can see a bit of shadow line from some kind of stone bollard. I'd say it's damned near noon."

"D'ye think they'll feed us, zur?" asked Hooke.

Mainwaring grinned at the ursine sailing master. "I wouldn't have thought so, before the Frenchman came in. Now, I—"

There was another series of footfalls outside the door, and the dull thunk of pewter or tin.

"A timely question, Isaiah," said Mainwaring. "I think we're about to find out."

Again the door was unlocked and kicked open – an event happening with monotonous regularity, thought Mainwaring – and one of the sentries stepped in, his musket slung. He gestured behind him and as Mainwaring watched, the figure of a woman came quietly through the door, a broad straw hat tied down with a bandana on her head, and a heavy basket in one arm to which several tin cups were tied with cord. Under her shawl and apron she was wearing a familiar bodice and skirts of striped wool.

Mainwaring stepped forward to her as her eyes came up, dark and lustrous, wide now with concern as she looked round the circle of dirty, shadowy figures. Then her eyes fell on Mainwaring, and the twitch of a smile touched her lips. She offered the basket to him.

"*C'est pour vous,*" she said, "*et l'équipe. Un déjeuner très simple. M'sieu' De Guimond l'a commandé.*"

Mainwaring took the basket from her, meeting the dark gaze with his own, seeing now that she had the fullness in her body and face of a mature woman. She was past thirty years of age, and her small hands were workworn. Lines were forming about her eyes, and he could tell it would not be long before her beauty had faded forever. He saw the simple, unquestioning giving in her eyes, and his heart went out to her. He touched her shoulder, hoping she could read the gratitude in his eyes.

"Thank you, madame," he said, "for everything. Thank you."

The message had been read, and she flushed and looked down, gathering her skirts. Then she was gone, giving him a last, lingering look as she paused for a moment at the door. In the next instant the sentry had clumped out behind her, and the door thudded shut, returning them to darkness.

"A remarkably delicate woman for a fishwife, sir," said Howe, offhandedly. "One wonders—"

Mainwaring peered at him in the gloom. "Quite. Shall we see what our conscience-stricken young De Guimond has sent us?"

He sank down with the basket, the men crowding close. It was a bulky wicker container, and he pulled away the square of linen that obscured the contents.

"Ah. Two bottles of wine. To you for safekeeping, Jewett. Mind you do!" He added, to a ripple of laughter.

"No fear, zur. 'Tain't nuffin' but blackstrap, an' not good Jamaica, zur," said the burly Jewett.

The basket revealed a good deal more. Five heavy loaves of hard-crusted bread were soon being torn up and divided by Hooke and Pellowe. There were several pieces of strong-smelling cheese, of which Mainwaring gave one to Howe to apportion out fairly, putting the rest back as a resource for the future. A few dried fish lay wide-eyed in their waxed paper, and were avoided. Mainwaring untied the tin cups. "I'll have one of those bottles, 'swain, if you please. Mr Howe, I'd be grateful if you'd give each man a tablespoon or two of this. No more for the present."

"Aye, aye, sir," said Howe. "Here, Stephen, give me your knife for this cork. Price, you've a steady hand. Hold these cups. First tot to you, Shanahan; you're the youngest of this lot."

As the men munched on the bread and cheese, taking in turn their mouthful of wine, Mainwaring felt in the bottom of the basket for anything he might have missed, for it seemed oddly heavy even allowing for the cheeses he had kept. Then he touched something metallic.

"Well, I'm damned," he breathed, and he pulled out a slim and delicately-fashioned flintlock pistol.

Howe stared at it, his cheeks puffed out comically with bread. "Good Christ," he said through his mouthful. "I wouldn't have thought that Frenchman's honour would take him *that* far!"

Mainwaring turned the pistol slowly in his hands. It was beautifully crafted, with the balance and intricate carving that marked the work of a master gunsmith. On impulse he felt in the bottom of the basket again, and his hand closed on a small brass powder flask and, beside it, a leather bag of lead shot. "I don't think we have our gentlemanly young marine to thank for this, James," he said.

Howe's eyebrows rose. "The woman, you mean? She did it?"

Mainwaring remembered the clear dark eyes, the meaning deep in them. "Yes, I think it was her. In any event, we're armed!"

Hooke was grinning at him. "'Ere, zur, drink up yer tot. When do ye plan we'll slip an' proceed, zur? Wiv that pistol, why, we c'd do fer that Froggy meathead – no offence, now,

54

Price, there's a good lad – once we c'd lure 'im below decks in 'ere, like, an' 'ave 'im look down th' barrel. 'E'd be proper accommodatin', I'd wager, zur!"

Mainwaring gave him a grin. "Aye, Mr Hooke. That he would. But we'd be shot like fish in a barrel by the other sentries if we tried to force our way out. I think we'd best trust the Frenchman to live up to his word. And we wait for dark to see that he does. If he fails us, then we cross that particular bridge when we come to it. But I have a feeling he won't. Let's lay low, and be ready to move as soon as we can." He looked round at each man's face. "Clear, all of you? Speak up now, if ye've doubts."

No one spoke except Hooke. "Ye know the lads'll mind ye, zur," he said.

"Thank you, Mr Hooke," said Mainwaring, and hefted the pistol again. "Now, James, is it in fact my turn for a bit of that damned 'blackstrap' as Jewett there calls it?"

3

The day passed long and tediously in the dark cell. The eyes of the British seamen became somewhat accustomed to the gloom, and the whitewashed stone walls kept the hot sun from turning the prison into a stifling hell. Evans and Williams, the dark-haired, stockily-built Welsh lookalikes, amused everyone by singing bawdy jettyside songs – at sea, Mainwaring knew, they were called 'forebitters', and were the only singing allowed in a Royal Navy man-o'-war besides hymns, for the merchantman's 'chanteys' were not tolerated – and alternating these with soulful, incomprehensible Welsh songs in which Evans' baritone blended with Williams' tenor in a surprisingly moving way. The duo had launched into a raucous fourth verse of a sea-regiment alehouse song entitled 'How Stands the Glass Around' when the sentries ended the effort with thuds of musket butts on the door and barked threats which needed little interpretation. Muttering darkly, the two performers slumped down with the others and raised helpless hands at Mainwaring.

"The heathens don't know good music, sir, look you," said Evans, with a patronising air.

"True enough, Evans," said Mainwaring, grinning. "And they can't judge good voices worth a damn, either. Thank you both in any event. Well done."

"'Ere, Jacko, whyn't yew try t'warble us a tune?" piped up Slade, where he lay in one corner, idly pitching tiny pebbles at his friend Sawyer. "Scare us 'alf t' death, whyn't ye?"

"*Me*?" whinnied Sawyer. "Christ, I reckon I'd carry a mule a hannert yards sooner you c'd crack a note. Course, I'm sensible 'nough not to try, ay? Not like yew. Not pushin' m'self for'rard, an' takin' airs, an' thinkin' t' hisself that he oughta sing, him what sounds like a cat bein' a-strangled of."

Slade sat up, indignation writ large on his thin-cheeked, dusty features.

"'Ere now, yew split-arsed little Jonathan, ye mind where ye pitch yer slops ay? Oi've sung me 'eart out wiv th' loikes uv gennulmen, an' ladies of *quality*, loike—"

"Yer damned Vauxhall rangers, be more like—!" interjected Sawyer.

"An' sung 'The Roast Beef of Old England'," went on Slade, rising above it all, "more'n yew c'n count th' words t'yer damn'd Yankee hymns, what be all doom, an' hellfire, an' th' curse o' God, an' whatnot." Slade folded his arms, nodding for emphasis.

"Leastwise I sings hymns," sniffed Sawyer. "Better'n th' unseemly trash yew always be a mouthin'."

"*Trash*?" Slade spat in the dust of the floor. "Why, yew coot-nosed Yankee—!"

Mainwaring worked to keep his voice steady and betray no hint of the laughter. "Belay that, you two! Christ save us, you're worse than a parson and a fishwife, the two of ye!"

"It be *his* fault, sir," sulked Sawyer. "Ain't got the sense of a squirrel, he ain't!"

"Me? Leastwise oi knows when t'clap shut me mouth when an orficer tells me to —" began Slade.

"Enough, enough!" cried Mainwaring. "I'd let you two go at it hammer and tongs for hours, if we had the time. But unless you've noticed that we can't see our hands in front of our faces, you've missed the fact that the sun's gone down!"

Mainwaring was right. The quick Mediterranean sunset had passed in a few moments, and the rectangle of light round the heavy door darkened, turned orange, and then faded entirely, making the darkness virtually complete.

Mainwaring sat with his knees drawn up and his back to the wall, listening to the quiet breathing of the other men, who had sensed, without a word from him, that now they needed to be silent and attentive. But with no way to tell time, it would be difficult to know when—

"Zur? Summat's up. Listen!" whispered Hooke.

Mainwaring sat up, opening his mouth and turning his head a little to one side to catch the faintest sounds.

57

He could hear a faint clink-clink of metal. There was a slither of hard leather on stone as the sentry outside the door moved about, and then other footfalls which halted before the door. As the Dianas held their breath, a key was inserted slowly in the lock, turned, and then withdrawn. In the next instant the footfalls began again, fading away into the distance. But there was no slouch and thump of the sentry relaxing.

"They've done it, sir," said Howe, in the silence.

Mainwaring drew his feet under him and rose slowly, like a cat. He moved silently to the door and put his ear against it.

"Nothing," he said, after a moment. "I think you're right, James. Mr Pellowe, I'll trouble you to give your knife to Slade, there. He's a bit of an authority in its use."

"Aye, sir." Pellowe dug in his pocket and handed over the knife. The little Cockney took it and snapped it open, felt the edge, and nodded at Mainwaring, his eyes bright.

"Right. Here we go. And not a sound, any of you!"

Mainwaring grasped the latch and gave a gentle tug to the heavy door. With a slow creak it swung in on them, a gust of cool night air washing in behind it.

"By Christ, the Frog was as good as 'is word, zur!" breathed Hooke.

"Aye. There are gentlemen everywhere, it seems. Not a move yet, any of you. Slade, come for'rard here, by the door. When we look out, I'll look right, you to the left. Duck back in immediately. Now."

The two men peered round the doorway. To where Mainwaring looked, the sea shimmered under a half-moon, the grey mass of l'Eguillette huge and intimidating, the pinpoints of lantern light moving here and there slowly on the ramparts. Behind and beyond the harbour the town spread, under the shoulder of the dark mass of Mount Faron. The anchored ships of the French lay in a clutch of dark hulks at the far end of the rivulet of moonlight, their stern and anchor lanterns like a necklace of firefly light along the face of the shore; each tiny point of light putting a shimmering trace along the water beside the silver of the moon across to the beach before the guardhouse. A few glowing clouds drifted across a sky alive with stars. It was, Mainwaring found himself remarking, a truly beautiful night. Pity one had to be preoccupied with a damned war.

"Back in!" Mainwaring pulled back into the cell, looking at Slade. No blast of musket fire had greeted them, but, they had not yet moved out of the building. What would happen when they stepped into the moonlight?

"Your side, Slade?" asked Mainwaring.

"Empty cart-track leadin' off where we wuz picked up, zur. Nought on it. Fair clutch o' ships anchored inshore. An' just in front o' this place, the jetty an' that longboat, or whatever, sir. Nary a Frog t' be seen, zur."

"And none on mine. It seems our Frenchman has kept his word indeed. Mr Howe?"

"Sir?" Howe was at his shoulder.

"The moon," said the American. "Any idea of time?"

Howe pondered the rivulet of light. "About an hour left in the first watch, sir."

"Seven hours, then, till our friend De Guimond comes after us. It's time to move." He rose, turning to look at the faces waiting in the shadows behind him. "We'll make for the boat, lads," he said, his hand resting on the pistol thrust in his waistband. "Slade, you'll go first, like a kind of sacrificial lamb. I know how fast you are on your feet. Get half-way there without getting a ball in your guts and the rest of us will follow. Clear?"

Slade gave a ferret grin. "Aye, zur. Go now, zur?"

"Just a moment. Price, you carry the basket. Any girl on a picnic would be proud of you. Don't let those cups rattle, mind. Jewett, you be last man out and keep an eye out astern as we run. Sing out if you see muskets levelled at us."

"Aye, aye, zur," said the muscular boatswain.

"Good. Slade, you look for the bow line of that boat. Sawyer, you take the stern line. Evans and Williams, get the rudder in place on its gudgeons, and see the tiller bar's shipped. Winton, you'll clear away the brails on the main, and Shanahan, you'll do the same for the fores'l. Mr Hooke, you'll coxswain. Mr Howe, I'd appreciate it if you and Winton would clear away the mainsheets. Mr Pellowe, you'll get the foresheet, with Jewett. Understood?"

"An' me, sir?" put in Price.

"Stand by to repel boarders, like a good marine, Price," grinned Mainwaring. "When we get to the boat, keep a sharp eye out all around. Watch for any movement or sign that the French are moving on us. Then pitch in wherever I direct."

"Yes – er, aye, aye, sir," said Price.

"That's the spirit. Ready, lads? Not a sound now." He took a deep breath.

"Go!"

Slade was out of the door like a weasel, scampering through the moonlight, Pellowe's knife flashing in his hand as he ran. Waiting to check that no burst of musketry rang out, Mainwaring ducked out of the door and darted after the little man, his shoes thudding on the hard earth. The night air was sweet and soft, the sky a mass of brilliant stars, the lights of the ships a warm garland of light far across the harbour. The air rushed in his hair, and behind him he could hear the pounding feet and heavy breathing of the others running with him. A wild excitement gripped him, and he exulted like an animal in the sensation of freedom, only realising now how crushing to the spirit the dark confines of the cell had been.

Then he was there, clattering along the loose boards of the jetty, watching Slade as he crouched over, tearing at the longboat's painter where it was made fast to a ringbolt. He scanned the boat quickly, seeing its good length and stable beam, the oars laid fore-and-aft on the thwarts, the dark lugsails moving idly in the clutch of their brails with the light offshore breeze.

Offshore! cried his mind. *To sail out, directly to sea!*

Then, in the next instant, the others thundered on to the jetty, the ramshackle structure shaking, and all was thump and clatter as the Dianas sprang into the boat and began their tasks. Mainwaring waited until he saw that every man was aboard, save Slade and Sawyer on the lines.

"Ready, Sawyer? Into the boat with you! Shove us off for'rard, there, Slade! Mind the tiller, there, Mr Hooke!"

He leaped for the boat, landing off balance in the sternsheets and tumbling heels up into a heap at Isaiah Hooke's feet.

"Welcome aboard, zur," grinned Hooke. Slapping the cap atop the rudder post, he checked that the pin was in place and worked the tiller to see it played clear. Evans and Williams had already scrambled forward, ready to help with the sailhandling.

"Thank you. So much for bloody dignity." Mainwaring wrestled himself upright. "Lively with the brails, there! Get us clear, Slade! Isaiah, as she swings out put her bows into the wind."

The boat made gentle sternway as Slade thrust it with a grunt away from the jetty, clambering in at the last moment, and Hooke put the tiller over to swing the big boat's stern out away from the jetty. Mainwaring sensed the wind. It was setting in from the west, a bit north, from the cool mountain slopes of le Gros Cerveau.

"Wot d'ye want t' steer, zur?" said Hooke. "Wiv this wind, we c'n damned near run right out t' sea!"

Mainwaring bit a lip. "Think she'd point up enough to beat over to where those ships are anchored, Mr Hooke?"

"Aye, zur. Beloike. But what—?"

"We can't leave without some idea of what numbers of ships are here, Mr Hooke. And what rates. And whether they are Spanish, or merely the French. The admiral's got to know. We'll tack across and make a count of 'em, then run out. Follow?"

Hooke nodded. "Aye, zur. Guardboats'll be out, zur, is all."

"We'll deal with that when it happens." Mainwaring looked forward. The boat had turned and was sitting with its bows into the wind. "Shake out those brails, quickly! Good! Sheets, now, Mr Howe, Mr Pellowe. Larboard tack, Mr Hooke. Flat that fores'l out till she comes round. That's it. Very good. Sheet in, there!" He turned to Hooke again. "Steer for that double light to the right of the main mass of ships, Isaiah."

Hooke steadied the helm, and the two broad lugsails, shaken out from their constricting brails, turned from

61

idly-flapping tarpaulins into curved faces of power as the hands planted their feet on the leeward gunwale and hauled in the weighty sheets. The heavy craft lifted ahead, lying over slightly to the breeze, and began to draw magically away from the land, a sweet splash and gurgle sounding under her bows and round the rudder as the wind's force worked on her.

"Ease the sheets a touch. There. Now mind you don't jam 'em down. We'll need to let fly quickly, and I want 'em ready. All of ye, now, down off the thwarts and on to the floorboards. Let's give her a chance to fly."

The boat swept smoothly out into the rippled path of moonlight, and Mainwaring looked up at the two big sails, seeing the leeches flutter slightly, knowing again the sense of peace and fulfilment he always experienced at that moment when, in boat or ship, the tie to the land was broken.

"It be where we b'long, zur," murmured Hooke, as if reading his thoughts.

"Aye. Where we belong," echoed Mainwaring.

"Where all of us do, sir," came Winton's voice, a murmured assertion rising on the lips of the other men.

Mainwaring nodded. There was no more he could say. And the odd tightness in his throat – what on earth could be bothering him? – suggested it would be unwise to attempt speech. But his mind could not afford to rest. They were, he estimated, about a quarter of the way from the shore at la Seyne, where the jetty lay, to the mass of ships that were anchored in close to the town, in the inner basin of the Petite Rade. Their bows bore now almost dead on the hump of Mount Faron, behind the town. Guardboats would be out and perhaps a night fisherman or two. He had to decide very little now, really; it was simply a matter of getting in close enough to make some kind of rough estimate of the warships at anchor, and then quietly sailing for the open sea, providing this wind held and they could be well out before dawn. But another scheme was formulating in his brain, a scheme that came in two parts: one that promised merely a satisfying bit of revenge – and another that sent a premonitory chill through him. A part of him cursed

himself immediately for concocting rabbit-brained schemes
that would cause men to risk their lives. Then another voice
took over, one that he knew he would listen to, and which
said, *Be damned to caution!*

"Mr Howe?" he said, his heart pounding in his chest.

"Sir?" Howe was hunched down on the floorboards just
aft of Evans, on the larboard side.

"The ship we fought when we lost *Diana*. The Frenchman
mentioned her name. Can you recall it?"

"Yes, sir. The *San Pablo*, I think."

"That's it. You recall seeing where she was moored, as
well."

"That wuz me, zur, beggin' yer pardon," put in Hooke.
He shifted his grip on the tiller and spat into the sea. "She
were moored well t' th' starb'd side o' th' inner 'arbour,
zur. That'd be – hell, zur, that'd be damned near dead
ahead, zur!"

Mainwaring nodded, a slight smile on his face. "And
likely those are her riding lights?"

Hooke tugged gently on the tiller as the boat heeled
slightly to a freshet. "Why, aye, zur! I'd think that stern
lantern – there, t' starb'd o' that double one – could well
be 'er, zur!"

Mainwaring cupped his hands to direct his voice.
"Shanahan. You've sharp eyes. Climb for'rard and act
as bow lookout. Sing out if ye see any boats on a constant
bearing to us."

"Aye, aye, sorr," said the Irish youth, and began
clambering forward over the thwarts.

Crouching aft on the floorboards in the stern sheets,
Howe and Pellowe could see that Evans and Williams had
control of the sheets. Now they looked at one another
meaningfully.

"What is it you plan, sir?" asked Howe, after a moment.

Mainwaring's mirthless smile was lost in the darkness.
"The *San Pablo* owes us something, James. She lured us
in, helped us risk and destroy *Diana*. And now she sits at
anchor, right in there."

"Yes, sir. But with anywhere up to a hundred and fifty
Dons in her. Christ, d'ye mean—?"

"Exactly, James. I'm aware of the numbers of men normally in her. But I'm also aware of Spanish peculiarities, particularly when in port. They don't like to sit in their ships, not when there's land to walk or a *cantina* to carouse in. I'd wager a flask of good Jamaica White Rum that there could be no more than a corporal's guard in her. The rest could be ashore disturbing the good citizens of Toulon. That's not certain, mind, but it is a possibility." He paused. "That does raise the odds more in our favour."

"I'm not sure I follow, sir," said Stephen Pellowe.

"We're going to see what we can do to make life uncomfortable for the gentlemen of the *San Pablo* before we leave, Stephen," said Mainwaring. He grinned. "You might say we're going to repay a debt of sorts!"

The men silently digested this announcement, and Mainwaring turned his gaze ahead. Oddly enough, he was now completely calm, all the more surprising since he had no idea how to achieve what he intended; he had merely established the objectives in his mind. The dark mass of the anchored fleet, lit like a penitents' procession with its uneven rows of winking candlelight in their lanterns, loomed forebodingly ahead. Even in the darkness Mainwaring could see that most had the bulk and towering rigs of line-of-battle ships, and he frowned. The French squadron at Toulon was large, but not this large. Where had all these other ships come from? Were they more Spanish? Was *San Pablo*, instead of being a Spanish frigate taking shelter alone, merely one of an entire Spanish squadron that was hidden here, sheltering from the British until the fiction of the 'neutrality' was no longer useful, when the combined fleets would emerge to smash Mathews' ships aside and control the Mediterranean?

Mainwaring shivered. Before they left the harbour, they would have to find out what to tell Mathews. They would have to know what lay at anchor here, however that could be achieved.

He squinted forward. That a smartly-rowed guardboat bristling with *Troupes de la Marine* had not yet found and challenged them was a matter of luck, although the boat was familiar to the harbour. What on earth could he do with a handful of men in an open boat, armed with one knife and one pistol, against scores of ships and thousands of French and Spanish? The *San Pablo* might be chock-full of men. Why had he not simply steered for the open sea, where with this light wind and low, almost non-existent swell, they might have been two leagues out, well beyond Cap Cépet into the Golfe de Giens when the dawn came? Sooner or later one of the other British picket vessels would have seen them—

"Zur?" came Hooke's whisper.

"Aye?"

"There she be, zur! Ye c'n see she's still got some damage not repaired to 'er topm'sts an' whatnot! There, against that cloud, now that we're close in! That'd be 'er, right enough, wiv th' lantern aft an' anuvver 'oisted on 'er foretopm'st stay. Hell, she's no more'n a good musket shot off!"

Mainwaring hunched down on the floorboards to see under the foot of the foresail, The wind had almost died, and the boat ghosted along towards the glittering, endless line of lanterns, which looked like a vast, floating city. The Dianas sat in silence, eyes white in the darkness, looking aft at Mainwaring as if to find reassurance as they moved closer. The water gurgled lightly round the rudder, and now from the ships ahead came the muffled, over-water sounds of clumping footsteps, the rattle and creak of tackles, voices raised distantly in song and the oddly Moorish sounds of a fiddle and bagpipe drifting in tinny, atonal echoes.

The *San Pablo*, if that indeed was her, loomed ahead now, the silhouette of the hull and the masts standing out against the sky, the mastheads making slow circles under the blazing arch of stars. The lantern at the stern revealed the great, pale Bourbon ensign, idling and curling over the quarterdeck. From the leaded windows of the stern cabins and from a few gunports right forward, warm orange light spilled out on to the harbour surface to find its way in snake-like ripples over the still water to the men in the small boat that crept noiselessly closer. The ship was very near to *Diana* in size, but at this moment to Mainwaring she looked enormous.

"Evans! Williams! Brail in! Lively, now." He pointed to the long oars. "Winton and Slade, put an oar out to starboard. Sawyer, Price, do the same to larboard. Use some of that cloth out of the basket to muffle the locks!"

With a faint rustle, the sails collapsed in against their yards, while with much grunting effort, two of the long oars were wrestled over the side and set in place in their thole pins. The four oarsmen – Price having his instructions whispered in his ear by Sawyer – sat ready, the blades clear of the water, eyes on Mainwaring.

"Good lads," he muttered. "Mr Hooke, call an easy stroke. And steer for her stern."

"Aye, zur," growled Hooke. "Ready, oars. Give way t'gether. Stroke, stroke – gently, Price, it ain't required t' break th' damned thing – stroke, stroke—"

The oars dipped and swung, dripping, with a faint creak and thump against the pins. The Spanish ship was no more than fifty yards ahead now, that slap and gurgle of the water under her overhung counter audible. Only light showed from the glowing quarter-gallery window, even though it could be seen now that the window was propped open. No sound came from within. Far forward, where several gunports gaped open, voices could be heard over the clink and thump of glasses, voices raised in tremulous, high-pitched singing in a minor key, punctuated by many cries and rapid hand-clapping. The singing was so penetrating that Mainwaring knew the noises of the boat would not be immediately noticeable. The danger, rather, was that an alert pair of eyes on deck watch would glimpse its shape approaching in the darkness.

But then he realised that they might be virtually invisible, remembering how vision at night is blinded if a single, hypnotic source like a lantern is nearby. And they *were* in a French boat, after all.

He cupped his hands. "Shanahan!" he whispered hoarsely. "D'ye see any watchmen on deck? Sentries?"

Shanahan had been standing up, clinging to the foremast for support, a black shape alongside the misshapen finger of the mast and its brailed-in sail and yard.

His arm came up, pointing at the ship's bows. "There, sorr!" came his low reply. "On the fo'c'sle! One man with a musket, just for'rard o' th' bell!" He paused. "She's clear otherwise, sorr!"

Mainwaring waved a hand in acknowledgment.

"One man," he said. "Isaiah, we'll come in under her quarter gallery. Gently, now!"

Hooke nodded. By gestures, he made it clear to the oarsmen that he would call the stroke with a hand signal now. The boat moved in, ghosting over the oily, still water towards the overhung gallery, the cavelike hollow of the counter beneath it echoing the wavelets that slapped against the seemingly unmoving hull. They were very close now.

Mainwaring touched Hooke's arm. "Way enough, Mr Hooke. Hold water before we strike her. Fend off there, Williams, as we turn alongside!"

The oars stopped the boat's momentum, and at a nod from Hooke they were hauled inboard and placed, with much effort and cursing, on the thwarts amidships once more. Williams sprang to his feet, and as Hooke swung the boat neatly alongside the wall of the Spanish hull, the Welshman used his powerful arms to keep the boat from thumping and grinding into the ship. In a moment it sat motionless under the quarter gallery, the noise of the music from the celebration forward ringing around them, and even echoing off the dark walls of ships moored farther inshore.

Noise, thought Mainwaring. *Noise to mask other noise*.

He rose and moved forward, stepping gingerly from thwart to thwart, until he reached Williams.

"That was well done, Williams, now walk us along the hull until we can hook on at the mizzen chains. Winton, stand by that boathook, and hook us on as soon as you can reach it!"

Williams grunted, pushing against the rough, painted surface of the ship's planking. Then Winton was reaching with the long boathook, and in the next instant he had hooked on.

"Good!" hissed Mainwaring. "Shanahan, pass him the painter. Make us fast with one turn so that we can cast

67

off quickly if we have to!" The American turned and made his way back to the stern sheets, looking up at the quarter-gallery window ten feet behind them. He hoped against hope that whoever was in there had not seen the dark shapes of the two masts glide by in the darkness. He reached the stern sheets and crouched down, pulling off his shoes, while gesturing for Howe and Pellowe to come closer to him.

"What is it ye plan to do, zur?" asked Hooke.

"James, Stephen, I'd suggest you do this barefoot. Isaiah, in answer to your question, it depends on what we find aboard this hulk."

"Don't follow ye, zur," Hooke replied, puzzled.

"You will. Slade? Come aft here, will you. Do you remember that privateer's trick you showed me at sea that time, in the *San Josefe*? Walking along the wale of the hull?"

The little Cockney grinned at the officers. "Aye, sir. An' she was in a bleedin' seaway. This'd be a lark, 'ere!"

"We can hope," said Mainwaring. "Now, James and Stephen. The sentry on the foredeck could spot us at any moment, so I shall only have once to say this. We're going to divide into three parties. The first will go with me, the second with you, James, and the third with Stephen. Isaiah, you'll remain with the boat, with Jewett and Price. Sawyer and Slade are yours, James. Stephen, you'll have Shanahan and Winton. Evans and Williams will be with me." He pulled his pistol from his waistband and dug the ball pouch and flask from the tail pockets of his linen coat. "Isaiah, here's the pistol. Slade, you've still got Mr Pellowe's knife? Good."

Howe looked pale in the gloom. "What – what is it ye plan, sir? The Dons could have a hundred or more hands in this ship."

"Not by the look of her, James. We're not going to risk our lives for nothing. But the Dons do funny things at anchor. At the very least I want to finish the job we began out there." Mainwaring pointed with his chin. "Simply put, you and Stephen will secure the deck while I take my lads below, aft. If I can, I'm going to set fire to the ship. You've got to command the forward and midships companionways and not let a single Don on deck!"

"*Fire!*" Howe stared. "Good Lord!"

Mainwaring went on. "James, you and your lads will get up on the wale, there, and walk along it, forward. Slade and Sawyer can show you. It's not as difficult as it looks, and you can thank Christ the ship's not rolling in a seaway, as it was when I learned. Lean into the tumblehome of the hull and keep pressed against the ship's side."

" 'E'll get the knack, sir," grinned Slade. "I'll show 'im."

"I'm sure you will. James, I want you to work your way for'rard to the foreshrouds. Slade is good with a knife. Pick the right moment, and go over the rail. I want that sentry disposed of."

Howe nodded.

"Stephen, you and your lads will go forward along the wale to about midships. As soon as you see the sentry out of the way, get over the rail and on deck."

"But, sir—" began Pellowe.

"Wait for it all, Stephen. When you're on deck, both your parties, you're to arm yourself with whatever you can find, likely pins out of the fife or pin rails. Let lines go adrift if you have to. James, you'll watch the fo'c'sle companionway, where that party seems well underway. Stephen, you have the midships. I don't want a single Don to make it on deck. Cosh every bugger who shows his head."

Pellowe nodded. "For how long, sir? If they make a rush to get up, we may not be able to hold 'em for long."

"It will depend on what devilment these Welshmen and I can get into down the aft companionway. But I'd ask you to hold for five minutes, no more. After that, get over the side to the boat as quickly as you can. Jump if you have to. Mr Hooke, you'll defend the boat, and when everyone comes pelting back after those five minutes, you'll hoist sail for the harbour mouth and get clear of this place. Is that clear?"

Hooke stared. "What about yew, zur? If—"

"If we don't come up after five minutes we're likely not ever coming up. You'll get clear, whether we do or not. You must promise me to obey this."

Hooke nodded, looking troubled. "Aye, aye, zur," he said. Then he paused. "I don't like it, zur. Too damned risky. Why not pull fer th' wind an' get t'sea? We'll 'ave a chance t' cross swords wiv th' buggers anuvver day, zur."

"I know, Isaiah. But we've a score to settle with these Spanish bastards. And I want to let 'em know that they pay a price whenever they try a tussle with British seamen. It's a risk, but I think it's worth taking." He looked round the faces. "Are ye still with me on this?"

"Of course, sir," said Howe firmly, and the others nodded.

"Very well. Let's get moving. And remember, after we've gained the deck, *five minutes*. No more." He looked up at the wall of the ship's side. The gunports, some of which were open and some shut in an offhand manner that would never have been tolerated in a British warship, were set so that a man inching along the wale could pass beneath the ports while crouching.

"Right. Away you go, James. And get him!"

"Aye, aye, sir." The slim first lieutenant stood up, kicked off his shoes — his hose had gone to muffle one of the oars — and watched as Slade and Sawyer monkeyed up on to the wale and inched forward along it, shuffling like sweeps atop a town house, reaching for the mizzen chainplate irons as a first handhold.

"Dear Lord," Howe muttered. But in the next instant he had clambered up on the narrow ledge of the wale, and was inching his way forward.

"Your turn, Stephen. Shanahan and Winton, just mind your step and you'll do well. Keep flat against the hull."

Shanahan rose, swallowed hard, crossed himself, and was up lightly on the wale. The burlier Winton gave Mainwaring a grin that reminded the latter of all that they had been through together, and then followed, teetering briefly with a heartstopping windmilling of his arms, and then forging along, his feet white in the darkness. Stephen Pellowe, a determined look on his boyish features, scrambled up after Winton and seemed to have the knack immediately. Within moments both parties of men had inched themselves forward into the darkness of the night and the shadows along the ship's side.

"Now for us," breathed Mainwaring. He looked up at the ship towering over him. Barely six feet up and to the left, the quarter-gallery windows glowed with candlelight. What ever might be taking place there it was clearly not a gathering of Spanish officers; that would have set off a din and voluble jabber audible for miles. With the sheer of the hull, the wale rose near the stern, and he would have to leap for it. From forward, the music and song were still loud from the gundeck, but Mainwaring sensed that there were only a handful of voices. He wondered if Howe and Pellowe were having any problems. The moon had gone behind a cloud, and in the inky blackness no shapes at all were visible forward along the hull.

"Ready, Evans? Williams? Come on, then," he ordered.

Mainwaring reached for handhold, the boat rocking under him. The splintery, red-painted planking had a salt grit to its touch, and he scrabbled for a moment until he caught the lip of a gunport and levered himself up. He clambered on to the wale and then shuffled his way along it to the mizzen chains, his heart pounding in his throat. He could hear Evans and Williams behind him, moving, it seemed, with considerably less difficulty. Then he was at the mizzen channel, and paused there, judging the next move in the dark: to swing up on the channel itself while clinging to the shroud lanyards, and peer over the quarterdeck rail. What he might see in the darkness, he had no idea. Again he had the odd premonition that *San Pablo* was almost deserted; but then, he might swing up and look for the last seconds of his life into a levelled musket barrel.

Clutching at one of the hard, tarry lanyards, he pulled himself up, thrusting his toes between the *lignum vitae* deadeyes through which the lanyards were rove. Gingerly, he rose from his monkeylike half-crouch to hang outboard until he could see *San Pablo*'s quarterdeck. Lit by the warm light from the flickering oil lamp in the great stern lantern, it was empty.

Empty!

He glanced forward in time to see Pellowe, with Shanahan and Winton, vault over the rail and scuttle into the shadows at the foot of the mainmast. For a moment he thought they had forgotten about the foredeck sentry. In the next instant he saw the two locked figures, writhing on the deck in a terrible, soundless struggle, just abaft the bowsprit knightheads. Slade's arm rose up, the little knife flashing dully in the yellow light. Then with a thump and a choked-off cry from the sentry, it was over. Immediately, Sawyer and Howe were with Slade, dragging the body to one side, Howe scooping up the musket, tugging the cartridge box off the limp form.

Mainwaring looked behind him, where Evans and Williams waited on the wale, pressed in against the ship's side and peering up at him with white, excited eyes.

"They've taken the sentry. On deck, quickly now!" hissed Mainwaring. With a pull of his arms he was upright on the channel, swung to the rail, and dropped lightly to the deck. A second later, Williams and Evans thumped down on either side of him.

"Damned near a duplicate of poor old *Diana*!" muttered Mainwaring. With a quick look forward, he darted to the mizzen fife rail and tugged out an unencumbered belaying pin while beside him Evans threw off the coils of a pennant halyard and took its pin, and Williams seized a pin out of the pin rail by the shrouds. The pins were little better than foot-long clubs but they did provide a weapon.

With a nod to the other two, Mainwaring leaped down the ladder leading into the waist, and then turned aft, seeking the companionway leading aft into the great cabin. It was there, where *Diana*'s had been. He crouched by it, the others silently at his heels, and cast a last look around the deserted deck. He could see the white shapes of Howe and the others, half-hidden forward, but that was all. How different was the thinking in the Royal Navy where the deck would have been paced by a brace or more of alert anchor watchmen, with the hawk-eyed boatswain's mate of the watch likely vigilant as well. "Let us see if the Dons are at dinner!" Mainwaring whispered, and as the other two grinned at him he went over the companionway lip, the pin hefted and ready. Noiselessly he padded down the ladder into the warm orange light below, the two Welshmen after him, to crouch in watchful readiness at the foot. He looked quickly round, his heart pounding so hard in his chest it seemed the others must hear it. He was in a small, narrow passageway very similar to the same space in *Diana*: a corridor leading aft to the door to the great cabin, but flanked by smaller, louvred doors that led into the cabins of the ship's officers.

Mainwaring held his breath. There was no sound. No movement, no snoring, only the distant wailing of the singing far forward on the gundeck.

Christ, have they abandoned her? ran through his mind.

Moving swiftly on silent feet down the corridor, with the others following, he halted before the great cabin's door. Gingerly, he grasped the latch, nodded to the other two men, readied himself, and ducked through the door.

The next instant he paused, gazing about him. There was no astonished row of Spanish gentlemen finishing a pleasant dinner as guests of their captain; no document-bedevilled captain sitting alone at his desk and penning endless reports. The cabin was virtually the same in size as his own in *Diana* but in place of his sparse, mean furnishings this cabin was fitted with ornate, dark-wooded furniture: a heavy desk, tall, velvet-cushioned ladderback chairs, an intricately-carved *armoire* against one bulkhead, and beside it a weapons rack holding half a dozen slim Spanish muskets, cartridge boxes, and several cutlasses. From an opposing bulkhead hung a rich tapestry and across from it a canopy-draped box bunk swayed in a darker corner, to one side of the broad stern lights and the russet-leather settee beneath it.

"Bugger, sir!" breathed Evans. "It's a bloody pigsty!"

For all its rich furnishings, the cabin was a chaos of rumpled clothing and scattered rubbish, with piles of books, papers and charts strewn about aimlessly. On the deck, cutlery and dishes with the remains of meals had been thrown down, and a dark glass wine bottle lay in smashed fragments in a spreading pool of its contents.

"Look there, sir. In the bunk," said Williams, pointing with his belaying pin. Among a welter of coverlets, lay the obese, heavy-jowelled figure of a man, scarlet breeches and waistcoat half-undone and spotted with wine and food stains, shirt sleeves dirty with food and grease, and hose half-rumpled to his ankles. A wig badly in need of powder lay askew on a sweaty, bald head. The man's face had a horrid blue mottling, and a repulsive drool tracked down from one corner of his mouth. His eyes, which were small and dark, seemed to be staring in surprise right at Mainwaring.

But then Evans had moved to the bunk. He looked back at Mainwaring, and shook his head.

"Dead, sir," he said. "Choked on his own drink, likely."

Mainwaring grimaced. The cabin reeked with the foul smell of stale drink and vomit.

"Then that's one less to worry about," he said. "And the captain himself, I'd warrant. Evans, smash open that weapons rack. We'll use those muskets. Take those cartridge boxes as well, all that you can. And the cutlasses. Quickly, now. Help him, Williams!"

"Aye, sir!" In a bound Evans was at the rack, and smashed the locking bar with one powerful blow. Quickly the two men began pulling the weapons free.

Mainwaring ran to the desk, pushing aside pewter plates laden with rotting, half-eaten food. He leafed rapidly through the piles of paper, scanning the documents, not knowing exactly what it was he sought – and then felt his heart leap as he found himself staring at a piece of stained foolscap that had been pinned to a chart of Toulon harbour. In a fine hand, it bore the carefully-penned outlines of tiny ships in an anchored formation, with distances to the shore and the mouth of the Rade inked in. Beside each small ship's image was a name and a number; a number that, Mainwaring suddenly realised, was the quantity of guns carried by that ship. He stared at the drawing. There were literally dozens of ships, and many of them were Spanish.

"Good Christ, they've got damned near the whole Spanish and French Mediterranean *fleet* hidden away in here!" he murmured.

"Got 'em, sir!" grunted Evans, slung with muskets and cartridge boxes. "Do we set 'er alight now, sir? Them lanterns an' sheets an' whatnot w'd do th' trick, sir."

Mainwaring quickly folded the foolscap in two, and was about to thrust it into his shirt when he paused, staring at the paper again, and looked up at the waiting men, his mind racing. It was filled with a sudden, almost frightening thought. But an irresistible one.

Is a piece of paper all you take to the admiral?

"Listen to me carefully, both of you!" he said, with sudden resolve. "Take a good musket each, and a cutlass. Prime and load, and get for'rard to the main and fo'c'sle companionways. Station yourselves there and kill any Don who tries to come on deck. Give the other weapons to Mr Howe and Mr Pellowe, and ask them to run aft and meet me by the wheel! Follow?"

"Aye, sir. But—!"

"No questions! And leave me one of those cutlasses. Quickly, now, the both of you!"

"Aye, sir!" said the powerfully-built Evans. "Here, sir!" He threw a cutlass hilt-first at Mainwaring, who managed to catch it. "Come on, Bungy!" Evans cried, and the two men were out of the door, banging and clattering their way down the corridor with their load of weapons.

Mainwaring set the cutlass down on the desk, his mind leaping from thought to thought. Then he spied the grotesque body in the box bunk.

The first thing that needs doing, he said to himself. He reached over the settee and thrust open one of the broad windows of the stern lights. Then, with tight lips, he wrestled the man off the bunk, dragged him to the window, and with grunting effort forced the body, like a sack of rubbish, out through it. There was a half-second of silence, and then a heavy splash in the darkness below.

He spun to the desk, and found the broad chart of the harbour and the immediate coastline outside. *San Pablo* was moored almost directly across from la Seyne, on the north side of the inner harbour, the Petite Rade. The wind was out of the west-nor'west, from the mountain slopes. But *San Pablo* was moored with her head to westward; the wind, once it could be got abaft the beam, could carry the ship right out into the open sea if it held, even if all he could manage to set was a single topsail. But he would have to solve the problem of getting her off the mooring and turning her to bring the wind almost dead aft at the same time. There was no room for manoeuvre, and *San Pablo* would have to be underway quickly if she was to have a chance of getting out through the narrows where *Diana* had died before the alarm reached the batteries that had killed her. And how many hours had elapsed since they had left the guardhouse? De Guimond may have been an honourable officer trying to make the fighting odds more fair, but he would arrive ready for hot pursuit. If he reached the battery at l'Eguillette before Mainwaring could get *San Pablo* underway, and knew or suspected that the hand on *San Pablo*'s wheel was not Spanish or French—

Press on, my lad, Mainwaring thought, a little wildly. *Press on, and do it!* Scooping up the cutlass, he made off through the door towards the companionway.

The great cabin of His Most Christian Majesty's line-of-battle ship *Normandie*, ninety guns, lying at jettyside in Toulon itself, glowed with the light of the two great candelabra which stood on the broad table in the centre of the cabin. Sparely but exquisitely furnished in black-lacquered *chinoiserie*, the cabin possessed an exotic quality. The summer heat had made the atmosphere thick and oppressive, and the air was growing rapidly more stale as the candles burned down. The two sentries, one to each side of the cabin doorway, were sweaty *fusiliers* of the *Troupes de la Marine* who leaned their weight surreptitiously on their long muskets and blew drops of sweat from their noses. To one side a thickset *sergent* stood, cradling a heavy drill cane, the expression on his red face under his tricorne showing no sympathy for the sentries' plight. At a small desk beside the great table, a thin, sallow-faced clerk sat in sweat-drenched misery in stock and full-skirted coat, dipping his quill, adjusting his tiny spectacles, and scribbling quickly to keep up with the words being uttered.

Behind the table, and alone at it, a slim and darkly handsome officer in the resplendent dress of a *capitaine de vaisseau* sat, his linen and lace immaculate and unwilting, his full-bottomed *perruque à circonstance* beautifully powdered so that it cast a fashionable dusting of white over the shoulders of his dark blue uniform coat. He appeared unaffected by the heat and not a drop of perspiration could be seen on his smooth brow.

Not so fortunate was *enseigne en pied* Saint-Luc De Guimond, who stood at uneasy attention before the great table, his tricorne under his left arm, sweat trickling down inside the wool of his full-dress uniform. He fiddled with the hilt of his small sword in an effort to distract himself from the discomfort of the heat – and of the evident direction in which his interrogator was taking the 'interview'.

"Let me ask you once more, *enseigne*," said the *capitaine de vaisseau*. "You and your half-company were able to find about a dozen men only from the English vessel?"

"*Oui*, m'sieu'. As I've already explained—"

"Be good enough merely to answer the question," interjected the *capitaine*, in a silken voice.

"M'sieu'. The English captain had been taken up by a fisherman, as had the others. He was ill, and the fishwife tended to him, it seems. Her oaf of a husband put up a resistance when Monsieur d'Aubagne went in to get the *rosbif*. It was Monsieur d'Aubagne who found the Englishman there."

"He then turned them over to you?"

"Only after taking them to the *corps de garde*, m'sieu'. He spoke to the English captain and then had them thrown in the cells. He directed me to guard them until – ah—"

"Until the next morning. When they were to be shot."

De Guimond looked down, his heat-reddened face turning even darker. "I did not agree with that order, m'sieu'."

"You did not *agree*?" The *capitaine* sat up.

"They were prisoners of war, m'sieu'. Three were officers, and one the captain of a frigate. Not felons to be shot out of hand, like escaped *forçats* from the galleys!"

The *capitaine*'s dark, glittering eyes bored like a snake's into De Guimond's.

"Might this remarkable morality of yours have led you to sympathise with these English, *enseigne*?" he asked, smoothly.

"I – I'm not sure I understand, *capitaine*," said De Guimond, fear beginning to stir.

"Sympathy. For men treated dishonourably. Unlike gentlemen."

De Guimond cleared his throat nervously. "Somewhat, m'sieu'. Yes, in fact."

"And that led you to do what?"

The *enseigne* looked startled. "How do you mean, m'sieu'?"

"Did you, shall we say, compromise your duty in any way? Give some sort of aid to the English, for example?" The dark eyes were watchful of their prey.

"I am a loyal subject of my King, m'sieu'," said De Guimond.

"Of course, of course. You will therefore be as alarmed as I to learn that the English have escaped from their prison. And stolen a boat." The *capitaine* paused. "I was under the impression, as was Monsieur d'Aubagne, that you had posted sentries to watch them. Is this not so?" he purred.

"They have *escaped*?" De Guimond's expression was convincing. "I – of course, m'sieu'. Sentries at the cell door, and on the jetty! I was to see the *caporal* in half a glass from now to ensure that he had exchanged sentries on the hour as ordered; my boat is waiting. If they have escaped, I am at a loss to explain how, m'sieu'!"

"A most distressing situation, it appears," said the *capitaine*. "The sentries, however, were *withdrawn* sometime after midnight, *hein*? When I sent an officer over in a guardboat to verify the identity of the prisoners, they were gone. And the boat into the bargain."

"*Withdrawn*?" De Guimond opened his mouth and then shut it. "I have no excuse, m'sieu'. It was to be an arduous duty the next morning. Executions always are. I felt the men needed rest, and that the *corps de garde* would be secure enough." He looked down. "Clearly I was wrong, m'sieu'. And I should not have been misleading you, as I now was." Then he lifted his eyes. "But if they are not long gone, m'sieu', we can pursue them. With your permission, I can alert the guardboats immediately, and then send a rider to—"

The *capitaine* raised one slim hand. "Of course. You are quite right. Don't be too harsh on yourself, *enseigne*. I have had moments of sympathy for enemies that have clouded my own judgement in the past. And all may not be lost, *hein*?" He leaned forward. "Go at once and have the signal swivel gun on the quarterdeck fired. Ensure the master gunner knows you act on my order. That will alert the guardboats for anything suspicious, and we can get word to them by a picked boat's crew. That should be a good first step, *enseigne*, I'd think!"

De Guimond nodded, his face damp with sweat. "Should I not be off, then, m'sieu'? Unless you have—?"

The *capitaine* waved an elegant hand. "No! By all means, go. We shall speak later, but of course I understand your concerns for your men. A commendable quality in a junior officer."

De Guimond allowed himself a relieved smile. "Thank you, m'sieu'. I – forgot one other thing, however, m'sieu'. Monsieur d'Aubagne has learned from his cousin in the *amirauté*, who in turn has an uncle in Villefranche, that the ship we destroyed was exceptionally well-known. The *Diana* frigate. She is, or was, commanded by a *bostonnais*. An American."

The *capitaine*'s eyes widened, and then took on a frightening intensity, as if De Guimond had touched a hidden nerve. He began to massage one wrist slowly, and asked, in a voice of silk-clad steel, "And what was the name of the colonial? Did he say?"

De Guimond began to feel real fear at the disturbing expression on the *capitaine*'s face.

"Ye – yes, m'sieu'. He is a lieutenant, although the vessel deserved a *capitaine de frégate*, at least. I believe the name was Mainwaring, m'sieu'."

For a brief moment the *capitaine* was motionless in his chair, and De Guimond could not move, so powerful was the force of the malevolent energy that bore into him from the dark, glittering eyes. Then the *capitaine* relaxed, one hand waving languidly in the air.

"No matter," he said. "We must recapture the fellow and his people, however. So do be on your way, and alert the guardboats." There came a thin smile. "You needn't look so anxious, *enseigne*. You are clearly a valuable servant of His Majesty, and I wish you now to get on with your duty. You have nothing to fear, I assure you."

De Guimond stepped back a pace, still shaken by the abyss he had glimpsed in the dark eyes.

"Thank you, m'sieu'. *A vos ordres!*" he intoned, his voice shaking somewhat. He made a leg, inclined his head, and then left the cabin quickly.

The *capitaine* waited until the door had shut and the sounds of De Guimond's footfalls had died away before looking over steepled fingertips at the bulky form of the *sergent*.

"Well, Jacques?"

The *sergent* snickered. "He lied badly, m'sieu'. I know he ordered the cell door unlocked. The lad who did it came to me afterwards."

"Dear me. Such gentlemanly concern for the welfare of the enemy. Or for abstractions about honourable behaviour."

"M'sieu'?" queried the *sergent*.

"No matter," said the *capitaine*. "Speak to the *enseigne en seconde* at the jetty head. Tell him I want one of those damned useless cavalry *cornets* to gallop to le Mourillon and another to l'Eguillette. They're to alert the battery commanders that the boat – or maybe more, knowing this particular man – may try to slip through to sea before dawn. Tell them I have full *amirauté* authority, and they're to raise the boom immediately. Any vessel putting to sea before dawn is to be sunk by gunfire. You follow, Jacques? *Any* vessel!"

The *sergent* pulled himself to the Position of the Soldier and touched the front cock of his tricorne.

"*A vos ordres, m'sieu'!*"

"Good. Emond has been writing the order, even as we speak. Haven't you, Emond?" enquired the *capitaine* in a cold tone.

"Yes, m'sieu'!" said the little clerk, scribbling furiously. "Done in a moment."

"*Bon.*" The *capitaine* turned cold serpent's eyes on the *sergent*. "We must catch this particular colonial, Jacques. You might say he is one with whom I have had an acquaintance. Someone I never thought to see again, but whom Providence has once more brought near me, as if fated to do so, *hein?*"

The smooth tones were sending another ripple of discomfort up the *sergent*'s spine, and he licked his lips. "Of course, m'sieu'! I shall see to the passing of your orders immediately, m'sieu'." With a trembling hand he clutched at the paper the clerk held out.

"There is one other thing, Jacques." The *capitaine* smiled gently. "Please ensure that De Guimond does not see the light of day. His Majesty cannot be served by traitors."

The *sergent* paled. "But he – he is an *officer* of the *Compagnies Franches de la Marine*, m'sieu'! He – I cannot—"

The *capitaine* levelled a smiling look at him. "Jacques, Jacques! Whatever will I do with you? Do you not understand?" He glanced at the two sentries meaningfully. "It is very simple. Either De Guimond departs this world before dawn, or you shall. I really cannot make it any clearer than that. Or must I try?"

The *sergent*'s face became grey stone. "It is quite clear, m'sieu'. You may be sure your – your orders will be carried out."

The *capitaine* smiled. "I'm most pleased. Now, do be on your way. We wouldn't want this fellow to slip away from us, would we?"

"No, m'sieu'." The *sergent* touched his hat again and was gone.

As the *capitaine* looked at the back of the door a slow smile spread across his face.

Once more the wheel of Fate turns. And we come together. So much revenge is owed, Mainwaring. So much. But perhaps I shall succeed in killing you this time. This time!

And the Chevalier Rigaud de la Roche-Bourbon smiled at his clerk, who sank in his chair, feeling again the fear he always experienced.

4

When Edward Mainwaring burst out of the aft cabin companionway on to *San Pablo*'s weatherdeck, Howe and Pellowe had just arrived, each hefting a cutlass and with an expectant look on their faces. Both were breathing hard, their eyes fevered and intense in the pale light of the stern lantern.

"What's below aft, sir?" asked Howe.

"One man, probably the captain, dead of his own drink, it would appear. There's no other sign of life. What've you got for'rard, then?"

Howe considered. "There's four, perhaps five men in the fo'c'sle, sir. One of 'em's the musician. Likely they're the anchor watch."

Mainwaring stared. "That's *all*?"

"Aye, sir," nodded Pellowe. "You were right about the Dons. The ship's practically empty."

"Well, I'll be buggered," breathed Mainwaring. "Then it's virtually ours!"

"Sir?" stared Howe.

"Listen carefully, both of you," said Mainwaring, briskly. "We're taking this ship. And we're going to take her to sea, out of here!"

Howe and Pellowe exchanged a startled glance.

"With due respect, sir, how—?" began Howe.

"James, I know. But my mind is made up. With luck, we can manage this but we must move quickly!" He eyed both men. "Now, I need your full support. No wishing to be off in the boat, and that sort of thing."

"What's first, sir?" said Howe, without hesitation. Pellowe nodded.

"Good. James, we've got to secure those Dons first. Take Evans and Williams and break up their little concert. If they resist, don't play games. I want them sealed somewhere

82

below, or tied in the scuppers here on deck out of the way until we can put them over the side in the boat, once clear. But waste no time. Do it now, and send the other lads aft to me. Unless you want more help?"

"No, sir. The taffies will be all I'll need!" And Howe was off forward, his bare feet quiet on the planking.

Mainwaring turned to Pellowe. "Stephen, we're moored fore and aft, head to wind. The cable off the stern is led there" – he pointed – "to the timber bitts abaft the mainm'st, and runs off over the larboard quarter through the rail. Odd, but there it is. We've got to give ourselves sternway, cut away the anchor for'rard, and let her go astern until she fetches up against that after cable. It'll either lose its ground, or it'll hold, and we can use it like a spring to get us round. Take Winton and Shanahan, get below, find an axe somewhere—"

"Saw one by the fo'c'sle companionway, sir."

"Our luck holds, then. As soon as James has those Dons secured, get below and for'rard. Start on the cable and don't stop till you've cut through. Then get yourselves back on deck as quickly as you can. Clear, now?"

"Aye, aye, sir!" Turning on his heel, Pellowe saw the little clutch of Dianas trotting aft, and directed a finger at Winton and the Irishman. "You two, with me, for'rard! Quickly, now!"

The remaining men – Slade and Sawyer – arrived and were staring at Mainwaring, eyes wide in wonderment.

Mainwaring took Slade's arm in a rare breach of service etiquette, feeling the iron-hard muscle under the coarse ticking of the shirt.

"Slade, you'll be senior hand. Call Price up out of the boat to add some muscle. The three of you get for'rard and put your hands on the jib halyard and sheets. Mind the sail's not stopped or lashed. I want you to hoist it straightaway, but let the sheets fly. As soon as I give you the word, flat it right out to *larboard*, so she'll pay the ship's head round to starboard. We'll be going aft against the mooring, and trying to swing her head to seaward. Do ye follow, now?"

Slade's eyes widened in the darkness.

"Christ, sir!" said the little man. "Are we *takin'* th' ship?"

"That we are, if you move lively enough. And the wind's fair for the open sea. Now get for'rard on that headsail!"

"Aye, aye, sir!" The teeth of the two little men flashed in excited grins as they scampered forward, Slade barking over the side for Price to come aboard. Instantly the latter was wrestling himself up over the rail, his bare feet, ragged breeches, torn shirt and wild hair a far cry from the redcoated, stalwart figure in gaiters, stock and mitre of a few days before.

The sudden blast of a musket was followed by a muffled thump below decks, then another, and the raucous singing of the Spanish changed abruptly into a shriek, a curse — and then silence. A moment later, there was a clumping and banging progress up the forward companionway, half-hidden from where Mainwaring stood aft by the ship's longboat on its gallows amidships, and Evans emerged, pulling after him a scrawny and visibly terrified little Spaniard with a long, rat-tail queue and a torn red shirt, who, immediately upon arriving out on deck, fell to his knees beseeching the burly Welshman with upraised hands and a torrent of Spanish.

"Oh, stow it, for Christ's sake!" Mainwaring heard Evans growl. "There's no need to wail like a bloody washerwoman!"

Behind them, a second Spaniard, heavy-set, swarthy and stupefied by drink, was thrust out by Williams, to fall sprawling on the deck. Howe emerged last, his cutlass blade dark from point to guard with blood, black in the dim light, and came aft quickly to Mainwaring.

"Secured, sir," he said calmly. "Two dead with musket balls in 'em, and I had to run through a third who went at me with a handspike. These two are all that's left." He coughed lightly. "Sorry lot, if you ask me, sir."

"Well done, James. Tie 'em up and let them lie in the scuppers, out from underfoot. You're certain there's no one else below?"

"Just our lads. Met Stephen as I was coming up. Shanahan ran the whole length of the gun deck and found all the glims doused and seabags missing. The garlicky swine are all ashore, like you said, sir."

"Thank Christ for that!" Mainwaring paused, hearing the distant thump of axe blows. "That'd be Stephen cutting the cable off the bow, unless some Don is acting upset." He pointed forward. "Slade and Sawyer are with Price on the fo'c'sle, there. They're to hoist the jib and be ready to sheet in. That should get us round if we can use the after cable like a spring. Might rip out a stanchion or two. Now, for making *sail* out of here—"

"Mr Hooke, sir?"

"Indeed." Mainwaring was at the rail and peered over, seeing Hooke in patient dignity waiting in the longboat's sternsheets. "Mr Hooke?"

"Zur? Wot th' bloody 'ell's 'appenin', zur?"

"This ship is what's happening, Mr Hooke! Make the boat secure to the chain plate or the irons and clamber up here!"

Hooke spat, already rolling forward in the boat like some beached sea otter. "Aye, zur! I'll manage that topman's trick on th' wale, for'rard to th' battens, zur!"

"Quickly as you can, Mr Hooke." Mainwaring turned back to Howe.

"Jib going up its stay, sir," reported the latter. As he looked down the first lieutenant realised that his cutlass blade had dripped a small black pool of blood on the decking by his feet. With a shudder he tossed the weapon into the scuppers.

"Good," said Mainwaring. He cupped his hands, trying to keep his voice low and penetrating. "Mind those sheets run free, Slade! We can't let her draw off to larboard, or she'll foul on the after cable!"

"Aye, sir!" croaked the Cockney. His voice was muffled by the whisper of the breeze, light now but steady, and setting directly for the dark, distant mouth of the harbour.

Mainwaring peered ashore, looking along the line of anchored ships for any sign of reaction, the telltale moving lantern of a guardboat. Then as his eyes turned to the dark, humped shapes of the fortress batteries on either side of the harbour mouth, he felt a cold knot of fear grip his stomach. They seemed so far away, the channel between them, twinkling invitingly in the blue moonlight, so narrow. In the arc of fire from either battery, any escaping ship would be exposed to a terrible pounding. But it was through there that they had to go; there, that—

Inshore, a pink flash caught the corner of his eye and the thump of a gun reached his ears.

"Signal gun, sir!" said Howe at his side. "Swivel, or small truck gun, belike."

Mainwaring banged the rail with a fist. "Damn! That tears it. The bastards are on to us. James, get below as quickly as you can and see what the devil is keeping Stephen from—"

Suddenly the axe blows from below in the ship stopped. And then, from forward, a slithery spash sounded. A barely perceptible motion began in the mastheads against the stars.

"He's done it! Thank Christ!" Mainwaring stepped quickly to the rail. "Slade! Sheet in, there! Flat it hard out to larboard!"

As Hooke came puffing up the quarterdeck ladder, Pellowe and his grinning mates burst out of the forward companionway, sweaty and triumphant. There was a squeal of a block on the single purchase of the jib sheet as it was hauled taut, the sail forming a pale, tall triangle on the *San Pablo*'s larboard bow.

"Mr Pellowe! Come aft, quickly! Bring Evans and Williams!" called Mainwaring. He spun to Hooke. "Is she coming around?"

The sailing master had recovered his breath. "Aye, zur, that she is! An' I can see wot yer about!" He squinted aloft. "Comin' round smooth as silk. Making sternway a touch. Should fetch up agin th'after cable directly, zur."

Mainwaring cupped his hands again. "Shanahan! Take down that lantern, for'rard! Williams? Get that stern lantern doused, and lively! No sense in announcing our departure by making it easy to see us, although the Dons know what we're up to, I'd warrant!"

Hooke was watching the shoreline swing. "Ye did it right well, zur!" he said, his voice full of admiration.

"A youngster in a dinghy has done as much, Isaiah. What kind of sail can we get on her, once round?"

"Wiv so few 'ands, zur, it'd be best t' set canvas on th' forem'st. The course'd be too 'eavy, an' wouldn't catch the lighter airs, 'igher up." Hooke spat thoughtfully over the side. "Let fall the foretops'l while th'yard lies at the cap, an' then 'oist, zur. An' ye c'd keep 'er afore the wind wiv th' sprits'l, zur!"

"The jib?"

"She'll still draw some. Sheet 'er slack, an' leave 'er."

"Cap'n, sir!" Winton's voice was sounding from ahead. "Lights on the shore, movin' fast, sir!"

Mainwaring squinted inshore. A half-dozen small pinpricks of light were moving rapidly along the edge of the dark mass of the shoreline, out towards the humped shadowy form of the battery at le Mourillon. Lights that bobbed up and down rhythmically.

"Horsemen," said Mainwaring. "On the gallop to sound the alarm!"

He touched the muscular shoulder of the Welshman, Evans, as the latter reached the quarterdeck, and pointed with his other hand at the great mainmast timber-bitts.

"Take the turns off that stern line, Evans. All but a turn, so she'll hold. When the strain comes on her, remember the Dons rove it out through the rail, and it'll likely give. Don't stand in the damned bight!" He coughed. "But cast off the last turn and let it go over the side the moment I call for it! Clear?"

"Aye, sir!" The man dived down the ladder and was at the bitts, casting off the great coils with strong, sure motions.

"That'll leave us only the bower anchor, sir?" said Howe.

"Freedom's worth an anchor or two, James." Mainwaring replied. "Steady, now, Evans! Strain coming on the line!"

With a straining, popping sound, the cable suddenly drew bar-taut, the railing stanchion of beautifully turned wood creaking and cracking under the enormous pressure.

"'Er 'ead's almost round, zur!" cried Hooke. But Mainwaring was already watching forward. In a moment, the long, swinging finger of the jib-boom would be on the gap between le Mourillon and l'Eguillette.

87

"Williams! On the wheel, here, and smartly! Meet her, and steer on the gap! Off turns and slip, Evans! Ease the jib sheet, there! Let her draw, now!"

Evans' arms flashed in the dim light as he cast off the turns of the heavy cable and let it go, the dark, snaky shape slithering out over the side and splashing into the sea.

"Damned good thing that was light cable and not true hawser stuff, sir!" breathed Howe.

"Aye. Luck's still with us, James!" Mainwaring swung to the wheel. "Steerageway, Williams?"

"Aye, sir! She's barely a-creep, but she's respondin', sir! Steerin' for the gap, sir!"

Mainwaring glanced at the dark, sleeping fleet, the line of anchor lights, and the bobbing line of horsemen's lanterns nearing the dark battery walls.

"Your foretops'l, Mr Hooke!" he cried. "I'll trouble you to set it!"

"Aye, zur!" boomed Hooke. "Evans, get for'rard, 'ere! An' Mr Howe, an' Mr Pellowe, zurs. All 'ands is needed—"

"Yours to command, Mr Hooke!" grinned Howe, and in the next minute he was running forward, Pellowe at his heels.

"Aloft wiv ye, all!" roared Hooke. "Slade! Sawyer! Belay that sheet an' lay aloft! Lively, lively, all!"

There was a rush by the small knot of men for the foremast shrouds, even by the willing Price, until Hooke halted him with one huge paw and pointed at the foremast fiferail.

"Yew scull about there, Price, me son, till we puts 'ands on th' topyard lifts an' 'alyards! Aloft is seaman's work, and ye be a bullock, no offence."

Within moments the scrambling, monkeying men were indistinct shapes out along the footropes of the topsail yard, which had been left by the Spanish lowered almost to the cap. Working with quick, feverish motions, the men cast off the gaskets that held the roll of heavy canvas in its harbour furl.

"Ready to let fall, sir!" came the cry.

"Winton and Slade! Pick a lad each an' come below, 'ere, to th' brace an' sheet pins!" Hooke waited until the four men were safely off the yard and monkeying their way down. "Let fall, there!" he shouted.

With a whump the great sail fell open, a huge grey quadrilateral, beginning to lift and curl immediately to the night breeze, ballooning out ahead of the top and the main course yard.

"On deck, now, all of ye!" railed Hooke. "Lifts an' 'alyards, now! Lively, ye web-footed ducks! Move yer-selves!" The men slithered down the ratlines and shrouds in careless abandon and dived at the pinrail, casting off the turns for the yard's lifts and halyards.

"You'll need all hands, Mr Hooke!" said Mainwaring. "Steer small for the gut, now, Williams! Nothing to either side!"

"Aye, sir! Nothing to either side, sir. Oh, Lord, she's ready to sail, sir, can't I feel it!"

Mainwaring sprinted forward and was with the others, jammed around the foremast foot, each reaching for a grip on the lines. Overhead, the great sail ballooned and collapsed in heavy thumping that shook the deck.

"Think we can do it, Mr Hooke?" asked Mainwaring, through his teeth.

" 'Ave to, zur!" grinned the bearish master. "There be none other t' do it!" He shifted his tobacco plug to his other cheek, stepped in and took an iron grip on the tarry line. "Check away those braces an' sheets as we 'oist, now, Winton. Damn' good thing the buggerin' Dons overhaul'd the buntlines!" he growled. Then he looked at Mainwaring, saw a nod, and spat on his hands.

"Now, lads. Crack yer backs! Pull like the doors o' hell are gapin' at ye! One t' six, *heave*! Oh, *heave*!"

Gasping and cursing, the men hauled down on the lifts and halyards of the yard, feeling the thumping of the sail through the rough, slivery line. At first, the yard seemed barely to move. Then the power of the pur-chases told, and with a creaking of the blocks the long yard and its sail rose in rhythmic ascends to the top of the foretopmast, each motion upward the result of a straining effort by the little knot of men at the foremast foot.

To Mainwaring, it felt as if he were pulling his arms from their sockets, and he wondered as he gasped and sweated with the other men if they would be able to do it at all, until abruptly Hooke rasped, "High enough! Turns, fer Christ's sake, on th' pins!" Then the burly master was detailing off hands to help Winton and Slade at the braces and sheets, and Mainwaring was running aft to the quarterdeck, his arms aching and limp, the breeze a cooling delight on his sweat-soaked back.

"Making way, sir!" beamed Williams. "Damned near a knot or two more!"

Mainwaring gained the quarterdeck and looked forward. San Pablo was footing along respectably under the single topsail, which was now hauled in to a still, arched shape against the starlit sky, the jib rippling and lolling before it. On the fo'c'sle, Hooke was visible, giving his orders for the setting of the square spritsail below the jib-boom. That would add a pinch of speed, and keep San Pablo's head to leeward. If only they could set more canvas—

Pellowe appeared up the ladder from the waist, his shirt ripped open to the waist, and his blond locks blowing in the freshening breeze. "We're lucky the moon's still behind those clouds, sir. Those moving lights ashore, sir. D'ye think they've seen us?"

Mainwaring nodded. "I'm virtually certain they have, Stephen. Those were horsemen, making for the battery, there. But they may be too late to rouse the gunners. Luck may still be with us." He smiled. "Thank you for your effort on the cutting of the cable. It was well done."

Pellowe beamed. "Thank you, sir!"

Hooke appeared up the ladder from the waist, touching at a forelock. "Sprits'l set an' drawin', zur. Adds a half-knot. Wiv yer permission, zur, I'd loike t' set the maintops'l."

Mainwaring pursed his lips. "That's a damned large bit o' canvas, Isaiah."

"Aye, zur. But the Dons left th' yard 'oisted snug up, zur, wiv the sail furled as fer sea. It'd be nought but lettin' fall, an' bracin' an' sheetin' 'ome, zur."

90

Mainwaring nodded. With the maintopsail set as well, *San Pablo* would move indeed. And it was still a long way to the safety of the open sea.

"Very well. Set it, and as quickly as you can!"

"Aye, aye, zur!"

"Mr Pellowe?" said Mainwaring, as Hooke made off forward.

"Sir?"

"Find Mr Howe, for'rard. Tell him I want the Spanish prisoners put over the side in the longboat and let go. No sense in making them suffer any more than they have already. And they'll be in the way."

"Aye, sir," said the youth, and was off forward.

Mainwaring turned to Williams, who was gripping the great wheel carefully, his eyes on the leech of the foretopsail.

"How does she respond, Williams?"

"Beautiful she is, sir. Like a feather. The Dons build good ships, sir. Beggin' yer pardon, sir."

"Aye." Mainwaring reflected on how true that seemed to be. British vessels were almost invariably heavier built, with competent enough workmanship but little grace or spirit. One wag had remarked, in an oft-repeated phrase, that British vessels seemed to have been built by the mile and cut off as required. *Diana* had been a beautiful ship, but the grace and proportional beauty of *San Pablo* spoke of a quite extraordinary inspiration. The graceful sheer of the hull, the elegance of the joinery and carving, were all a delight to observe, as if the ship were more the product of cabinetmakers than rough and ready shipwrights. And the ship sailed effortlessly, and now as the maintopsail fell open with a rushing thump, and was sheeted home, he felt the graceful vessel lift to the breeze with a lightness and quickness that even his *Diana* would not have shown. Already they must be making three to four knots, and if the wind held in this quarter, they would be through the gap and into the open gulf before—

From the dark hump of land that marked the point of le Mourillon and its ramparted battery on the northern jaw of the harbour mouth – now no more than a quarter of a

91

mile distant — a ripple of startlingly brilliant pink flashes erupted followed in the next half-second by the ragged, deep-throated blast of heavy rampart guns. A sound like ripping linen filled the air and four enormous, glittering geysers, gunmetal grey in the half-light, shot up in a close-bracketing fall of shot not ten yards from *San Pablo*'s reaching jib-boom.

"God *damn* them!" spat Mainwaring. "So much for getting out of here quietly!" He leaped to the waistdeck rail. "Mr Hooke! Braces and sheets, fore and main! Trim and brace up, wherever she bears!"

"Aye, aye, zur!" boomed Hooke, in the shadows. The men in the waist made for the pinrails at a run, Howe and Pellowe leading them.

Mainwaring swung on the helmsman. "Williams, wheel over, and put the helm to starboard, ten points! Let her swing to larboard, hard!"

"Aye, sir! Helm to starb'd, ten points, sir!" The great double wheel spun, the spoke capped with a brass cup flashing as it caught the faint starlight. *San Pablo* swung smoothly round until her long jib-boom bore directly on the dark mass of the battery from where the salvo had come. And from where more would surely come. Aloft, blocks squealed as Hooke and the others sweated at the braces and sheets to keep the topsails drawing full as the wind came on the quarter.

Another cluster of brilliant pink flashes erupted from le Mourillon's battery, and in the lurid light Mainwaring caught a frozen image of Price bundling the terror-stricken Spanish prisoners over the side into the longboat with none-too-gentle kicks and prodding from a musket butt. Again the sound of ripping cloth was in the air, and the astonishing geyser cluster leaped up in hissing majesty off *San Pablo*'s starboard bow, collapsing in a patter on the deck and a drifting cloud of mist.

"Jesus, sir!" burst out Williams. "Right where we'd—"

"Shut your bloody mouth and do your duty, man!" snapped Mainwaring. "Now! Helm hard to larboard!"

"Helm to larboard, sir!" cried Williams, angry with himself, spinning the great wheel with slaps of his hard hands on the spokes. *San Pablo* swung ponderously to starboard, heeling a little, the topsails rumpling briefly until Hooke's haulers did their work. Now the ship bore on the gap between le Mourillon and the silent companion battery at l'Eguillette.

Mainwaring stared at the looming hump of le Mourillon's battery, his heart pounding in his throat. *San Pablo* was hurrying along barely three hundred yards from the muzzles of those great guns somewhere in there in the shadows. And somewhere in those shadows, the gunners were feverishly reloading, running the guns out – was that a squeal of gun trucks he could hear? – priming their vents, the glowing portfires arcing down—

Turn again! cried his mind. *Now!*

"Helm to starboard! Hard over!" he barked. *San Pablo* swung, the blocks squealing anew, the sea hissing under her bows as the ship turned in towards the dark shadows wherein lay the hidden, murderous guns.

Again, Mainwaring's sixth sense had been right. The battery fired once more in a ragged thunderclap of a salvo, the pink light freezing Pellowe and the others in statuary poses in the midst of their frenzied hauling. And again the thunderous concussions punched at them, deafening now, as barely a boat's length abeam to starboard the deadly geysers leaped up, awesome towers of hissing spray rising in slim grace to topmast height. At the same instant a sharp snapping sounded aloft, and Mainwaring looked up to see the starboard foretopsail studdingsail boom canting up, as if triced up while the sail was being reefed; a shot fragment must have parted the heel lashing. *San Pablo* was otherwise still untouched, still sailing on towards the gulf beyond and her freedom.

Dear God, thought Mainwaring. *How long will this last*? He stared straight in front, trying to gauge the distances. The narrows between the two batteries was barely two hundred yards ahead. If he brought *San Pablo* round to a broad reach, diagonally across the gap, she would make a damned difficult target for le Mourillon's gunners, and the gunners that might be waiting in the Eguillette for the ship to reach point-blank range – he could think of no other reason why they had not fired – would be faced with a traversing target moving so quickly that it would be difficult to handspike around the guns quickly enough to bear.

"Helm to larboard, Williams! Steer for the point of land yonder, beyond the gap, to starboard! The point of St Mandrier!"

"Larb'd the helm, an' steer for the point o'land, aye, sir!" Williams responded crisply. The great wheel spun again, and again Hooke's bellows brought the yards squealing and rumbling round, the sails drawing taut. With the wind larger now on her quarter, both topsails filled cleanly, and San Pablo lay over a little with a creak, noticeably accelerating under Mainwaring's feet. The sea hissed under her bows and gurgled and rushed under her counter and round her rudder.

Now they were at the closest point to that damned shadowed battery that had been flinging death at them. If those guns were laid and trained well, within seconds San Pablo and all of them might die in a hail of iron shot.

The darkness was rent by the lightning flashes of the battery guns, blindingly close, pink tongues of flame licking out from the dark embrasures. At this point-blank distance the concussion was like a thunderclap, and Mainwaring waited for the horrid impact of the shot, for the hail of flying splinters and the iron or wood missile that would disembowel or maim him, or leave him a bloody ruin in the scuppers.

But instead, some twenty feet astern of the hurrying ship, the geysers lifted harmlessly in their glittering grandeur, a sudden wash of moonlight from the parting clouds giving them a silvery, ghostlike iridescence. Spray from the collapsing columns misted over San Pablo's quarterdeck, drenching Mainwaring and Williams where they stood, forming a bizarre blue-green rainbow for a moment as the cloud drifted across the moon's beam. Mainwaring cuffed with his shirt at his dripping face and craned forward to see where San Pablo now was. A thick, reeking cloud of gunsmoke from the battery's salvo suddenly enveloped the ship in a dark, stinking miasma to masthead height, and San Pablo shot through the narrows between the two batteries shrouded in the smoke of the guns that had been trying to kill her.

Mainwaring sprang to the other side of the quarter-deck, staring at the half-obscured bulk of the Eguillette battery. He could see the white French ensign drifting lazily in the moonlight from a single flagstaff. But the battery was still silent as it came abeam and now was drawing aft. Why on earth had it not fired? On this course, *San Pablo* would soon be clear of the arc of fire from both le Mourillon and l'Eguillette, and then only the small battery at Balaguier, a little further along from l'Eguillette, could stop them. The headland of St Mandrier peninsula, Cap Cépet itself, would be all that remained to rush past, and the ship would then be free in the Golfe de Giens.

But there was still one other unanswered factor, thought Mainwaring.

"The boom," he breathed. "The bloody boom!"

Howe was abruptly at his side. "The smoke's hidden us, sir. Perhaps that's why they're not firing again. But the boom—"

"Exactly, James. I think they intend us to spill our guts out over the boom again. But with this smoke I can't see the damned thing!"

"Just before the smoke cloud I could see clear out into the Gulf on the moonlight path, sir. It isn't raised, I'm sure of it."

"Then the bastards must be at the windlasses now, cranking the damned thing up. I'd like to think we'll get to sea before they lift it. But I can't recall where it lay, exactly. Can you?"

"No, sir. I don't."

Mainwaring spat forcefully over the rail into the sea. His stomach growled, and he remembered that none of them had had anything to eat or drink for quite some time. "Then we'll just have to hope our luck holds!" He turned to Williams. "Take her to larboard two points. Steer for the open sea!"

"Larboard, two points, aye aye, sir!" grinned Williams, his teeth white in the moonlight.

"Mr Hooke!" barked Mainwaring. "Can you set the forecourse?"

"Aye, zur. It'll be a touch slowly done, but—"

"Then do it! We need every knot we can give her! Lively, now!" Mainwaring turned back to Howe. "James, you've got the quarterdeck. I'm going aloft, up the fore. Steer exactly as I call down. Clear?"

"Aye, sir. What is it ye plan, sir?"

But Mainwaring was already off, sprinting along the deck, down the waistdeck ladder and forward to the foremast shrouds. He leaped lightly up on the rail, grasped the tarry shrouds above the lanyards, and swung up over the shearpole to the ratlines. Quickly he climbed upward, thrusting his feet into the narrowing space as he neared the top. Then he was at the futtock shrouds, scrabbling out around them in a sweaty-palmed terror until he seized the topmast shrouds leading up from the foretop. Struggling up them, his heart pounding, he came level with the topsail yard and swung over to it, gripping the jackstay atop the yard and setting his feet in the footrope.

Below him the ship was a dark, small shape, pushing a white bow wave ahead of her into the silvery, moonlit tranquillity of the Golfe de Giens, the dark shore to the left touched here and there with a twinkling point of yellow light in the shadows. *San Pablo* was footing on smoothly, and Mainwaring peered off into the distance ahead, not sure he would recognise what it was that he sought.

Then he saw it: a dark, snaking line in the water, ripples gleaming faintly in the moonlight as unseen hands ashore toiled on great windlasses to lift it.

The snare for the escaping rabbit, said his mind. It was perhaps three hundred yards ahead of *San Pablo*, and the huge logs that formed the key links of the barrier had not yet surfaced fully. But they would in a moment, and *San Pablo* would face the same hideous nightmare as had *Diana*. Mainwaring would have a choice: wreck this beautiful vessel in a snarl of rigging and collapsing masts, or heave to and await the mercies of the Spanish and French.

"*No!*" he found himself crying out, banging one fist on the yard. He cupped his hands to call below.

"Deck, there! Mr Howe!"

"Deck, aye?"

"Steady as you bear! But stand ready to alter course the instant I call!"

"Aye, aye, sir!"

Mainwaring swung back, his heart pounding. *San Pablo* forged on, the sea hissing under her bows. Where was the boom? Where were the gaps between the logs? A gap large enough to—

"Deck, there!" he cried out suddenly. "Take her to starboard, two points! Lively, now!"

Howe's answering cry was lost in the ship's creak and groan as it heeled slightly with the course change, turning with surprising agility and quickness. Mainwaring clutched at the jackstay as his perch swung, but his eyes were locked ahead, on the dark, tubular shapes lying awash in the water; shapes linked together closely.

Except for one point, in the middle of the long line, where a larger gap showed, perhaps the point where the chains were shackled or locked together. It might be cable, or even chain, but it was not a log. That was where he had to steer *San Pablo*. It was now only a hundred yards before the onrushing jib-boom end. If the chain or cable held—

She'll ride over. Or break through. She must. She must! cried Mainwaring's mind.

"Steady on this course!" he shouted. "Nothing to larboard or starboard!" Below and behind him, the great, powerful face of *San Pablo*'s main course fell open with a thump and bellied to the wind, the ship surging ahead under it with a burst of power as Hooke's curses and bellows brought it sheeted home.

Fifty yards. Then twenty. Then ten.

Mainwaring fixed a grip of steel on the jackyard, and closed his eyes in silent prayer.

Then *San Pablo* struck. Rising up as if in a sudden swell, she still forged ahead, the masts and yards shaking with the impact, groans and creakings echoing through the hull. But then the bows were crunching down, and a deep, sonorous note like the snapping of a bowstring sounded from somewhere deep below the ship's keel, and *San Pablo* was rushing on, the great logs drifting apart and away to either side as the ship swept out into the wide waters of the outer harbour and the moon-silvered Golfe de Giens.

From below, Mainwaring could hear the men cheering and hooting in joy and relief. For a moment he was unable to move, so strong was the deep emotion that the breaking of the boom had released. Then, with a strange lightheadedness making him feel very odd indeed, he began the long descent to the deck.

5

The great cabin of His Britannic Majesty's Ship *Namur*, ninety guns, was stifling hot. The windows of the broad arc of stern lights were jammed open but little if any breeze was coming through from the oily, sun-glistened surface of Villefranche harbour. The town, a pretty collection of whitewashed and red-tiled buildings, lay shimmering in the heat below Mont Boron, and amidst the litter of small craft that worked unhurriedly about the harbour, the mustard-coloured bulk of another British line-of-battle ship, *Royal Oak*, was visible, with seamen busy about her afterdeck rigging awnings of striped tentcloth.

The cabin was sparsely and simply furnished, surprisingly so in that it was the cabin of Vice-Admiral Thomas Mathews, the blustery and choleric little man whose task it was to ensure the execution of British naval policy in the Mediterranean. The trestle table which served as Mathews' desk was littered with papers, added to periodically by a harassed clerk who scuttled in from time to time to lay another folio before Mathews. Edward Mainwaring, still in his ragged shirt and duck trousers and as barefoot and rough-looking as a topman, sat in one of two hard, straight chairs before the table, while Mathews glowered at him from his armchair like some cornered hedgehog in full-bottomed wig, lace-frilled stock and scarlet suit. His round face was pink and running with sweat.

"Let me be quite clear as to what your report states, Mainwaring," he said, in an odd, high-pitched voice. "You say you took your ship, the *Diana* frigate, into the harbour of the French at Toulon, and engaged a Spanish vessel that put out to attack you."

"Yes, sir. I did not threaten her, or fire on her first, sir."

"A somewhat academic point, Mainwaring, given that you were virtually *in* the French anchorage, which is not something they could with any honour tolerate." Mathews coughed. "What in God's name possessed you to go in there in the first instance? You've lost me your ship, so I hear, and I cannot afford to lose so much as a ship's boat in our present situation. There'll be a Court, I hope you realise. Obligatory on the loss of one's ship."

Mainwaring nodded. "I – yes, sir. Of course. I was attempting to determine the strength of the French and Spanish squadrons, sir."

"What, by *attacking* them? Don't play me for a fool, Mainwaring."

"Not at all, sir. But if you'll read my report" – and Mainwaring was of the feeling that the little vice-admiral had not – "you'll see a complete list of the vessels we found there, sir. A list it would not have been possible to make from a position off the headlands. We counted fifteen French ships, of which twelve were line-of-battle ships, sir, that is, with sixty guns or more. And the Spaniards had at least seventeen ships, of which twelve at least could lie in the line. And there were at least twenty fifth-rates: sloops-o'-war, and the like."

Mathews' small, pale eyes locked on the American. "My word. Are you serious, Mainwaring?"

"Yes, sir. I made as careful a count as I could, and had my officers do the same independently, sir."

Mathews wilted visibly in his chair. He pulled a vast hand-kerchief from one cuff and mopped his brow. "Oh, dear. This is a dreadful development. Oh, dear," he breathed.

"I'm sorry, sir?"

"Mainwaring, you've not brought the sort of news I wished to hear, although with some reluctance I suppose I should commend you for doing so. I've just spent the morning with our consul at Turin as well as M'sieu' de Corbeau, the Sardinian commandant at Nice and M'sieu' de Vettes, his counterpart here at Villefranche. They have been beseeching me to put into effect My Lord Newcastle's latest intelligence to me – we are at liberty now to engage the French freely, 'neutrality' nonsense or not, in case you were unaware – by gathering my ships off Toulon, and having at 'em." He shook his head. "By what you report, the preponderance of power is clearly with them. I should put into effect the Fighting Instructions, only to be defeated piecemeal. I've only twenty-one ships capable of lying in the line, and damned little chance of more. Engagements off Toulon are out of the question."

Mainwaring found himself wondering what it was about himself that led senior officers to unburden themselves to him. He put it down to the confusion caused by his classless American accent – whether wealthy or poor, all men in the Americas sounded alike – and his complete lack of 'interest' in the form of patrons. He cast the matter from his mind, and concentrated on what Mathews was saying.

"Our squadron at Naples cannot be recalled for quite some time yet, and I must continue in this damnably slow process of helping our gallant Sardinian allies fortify Villefranche. By the time I *can* put out after the enemy, I will likely lose. It's bloody disturbing, I can assure you, Mainwaring."

"I understand, sir."

"And it isn't helped by the loss of your ship, you know. I've not got fifth-rates and sloops to scatter about like seeds in the wind."

"Quite, sir. But I was able to take a vessel of equivalent strength, sir."

Mathews sat up, the little eyes widening. "You did *what*?"

"With respect, it's there in my report, sir," said Mainwaring. "With the officers and men who survived the destruction of *Diana* I was able to escape from prison and find a longboat. While putting out to sea, we determined to try to take the Spanish vessel we originally fought. By luck we managed it, sir. She's anchored there, inshore of *Royal Oak*."

"And you did this with how many men?"

"Ten seamen, sir. And one marine."

"Eleven men. Good Lord." Mathews wielded the huge handkerchief once more. "I'll read your report carefully. You've had extraordinary good fortune, Mainwaring. If *San Pablo* is even slightly suitable, I shall buy her into the Navy, to replace your unfortunate *Diana*. She'll have to be surveyed, of course. I'm not sure about the question

101

of prize money." He paused. "You're dressed like a raga-muffin, Mainwaring. Where the deuce are your clothes?"

"Lost with the ship, or in the escape, sir."

"Your men?"

"Your captain kindly let them draw from the slops, sir, so they'll be all right. But my sailing master, my two lieutenants, and myself—"

"Yes, yes. Can't have one of my officers looking like a grubby fo'c'sle hand. I'll advance you sufficient to ensure you and your officers dress properly, Mainwaring. As to what to *do* with you, that is another matter. *San Pablo*, of course, is out of the question, even if I buy her in—"

Mainwaring's face was impassive. It was to be expected that Mathews would have his favourites to whom command of prizes would go.

"—but I cannot afford to keep you idle, even without having had your Court sit." The pale eyes eyed the folios before him. "I've a fireship. Small thing, eighty tons and ship-rigged. Using her as a tender to *Namur* till I can find something to burn. Her commander got into some kind of disgraceful scrape in a brothel ashore and took someone's knife in his guts. The ship's yours if you want it. And I'll draft your officers and men into it, along with a few more, to give you a ship's company. Well?"

Mainwaring's heart sank. A fireship: old, rotten or condemned vessel, too decrepit to sail well or keep for useful purposes; meant to be thrown away by their crews in self-destruction. A far cry from *Diana*, or his long-lost graceful schooner, *Athena*, not to mention *San Pablo*.

"I'd be honoured, sir, of course," he said, as graciously as he could manage.

"Splendid. She's the *Trusty*, and she's lying in near the west side of the sea wall. You may have seen her when you put in. I'll have the necessary orders drafted, and you can read yourself in as soon as you get ashore to a tailor and take on a more gentlemanly appearance. Send your people into her immediately, and see my purser about victualling. I'll carry you as a tender vessel for the present until your ship's accounts can be brought into order."

"Thank you, sir," said Mainwaring.

"I'm not insensible to how you must be feeling, Mainwaring. But I need that ship manned."

"I appreciate your concern, sir."

"Then perhaps you will also appreciate that at the moment I have not the slightest idea how to deal with this vast force you say is lying inside Toulon. I'm pretty sure they're bound to sail soon, either to support the French garrison at Villefranche, or to ship more damned Spanish troops to that wretched Montémar fellow in Italy. And there's precious little I can do about it all!'

"With respect, sir, there is something you can do," Mainwaring found himself saying.

"Eh? Explain."

"May I suggest, sir, that the very strength of the French and Spanish, packed together in Toulon with batteries guarding them, is also their weakness. They're not spread out at sea, difficult to find. They're all in one spot, sir. And I wager they have no real or accurate picture of how strong you actually are, sir."

"Go on." The little eyes were intent.

"You need time, sir. Time to assemble the squadron, for the ships off Naples to return, for the work ashore to be done here. You could get that time if you could manage to keep the French and the Dons bottled up inside Toulon, sir. Keep 'em there, till you're ready for 'em."

"And how might I affect that with a handful of ships?"

"Work on their *fear*, sir. Make 'em afraid of you, unsure of how strong you are, whether or not you've got a whole damned battle fleet sitting out just over the horizon, waiting for them to try to escape. But make them think you're a wolf at the door waiting for them to make a false move, and damned anxious and ready for them to come out — by using a smaller force that can create the *illusion* that you're there."

"I couldn't spare a force of large ships to do that, Mainwaring. It wouldn't be—"

"With respect, sir," interrupted Mainwaring, "you wouldn't need a large force. Appoint a competent officer with a good record of initiative and give him a little flotilla of lesser ships: fireships, tenders, cutters, virtually anything.

Give him orders to make such an aggressive nuisance of himself off Toulon that he hinders or delays the efforts of the French and Spanish to get to sea, and convinces 'em that he's the outlying arm of a much larger force waiting offshore! At the very least, he can send a fast vessel to warn you if the combined squadron does sail."

Mathews sat back in his chair and regarded Mainwaring through narrowed eyes. "I believe I see the role you wish for yourself in all of this," he remarked. "Still, you're a bold enough fellow, Mainwaring, and you may have something there." He fished a heavy watch out of a waistcoat pocket. "Get yourself into your ship, and dress properly. And for God's sake see a barber. I'll trouble you to return aboard tomorrow night at the beginning of the first watch. We'll have a conference of captains to look into this."

"Thank you, sir." Mainwaring stood up to leave.

"One more thing, Mainwaring," said Mathews.

"Sir?"

"For God's sake, whatever I agree to let you do, don't cost me any more damned ships. I can't afford 'em!"

Mainwaring grinned. "I'll try not to, sir," he said, and closed the cabin door gently behind him as he left. He was still grinning to himself as he passed the cold stare of the marine sentry, who clearly wondered how a tarry lower-deck man should have access to the vice-admiral's cabin. And he was still grinning as he went off to find Howe, Hooke and the others somewhere in the bowels of *Namur*.

Fourteen hours later, the great cabin of *Namur* was several degrees cooler, with the sun low in the west behind Mont Boron and a fresh breeze filtering in through the stern lights. But it was considerably more crowded. A trestle table had been set up, flanked by half a dozen of the uncomfortable ladderback chairs Mathews favoured, and at its head the vice-admiral sat, eyeing the gentlemen assembled around the table with an expression that oddly mingled truculence and suspicion.

At his right hand sat Wilson, captain of *Royal Oak*, and at his left, Deane of *Namur*. Both men were of remarkably similar appearance, as if the captaincy of a line-of-battle vessel called for an angular, thin-featured face and a piercing look, and a sombre manner of dress on a thin, narrow-shouldered figure. The first lieutenants of both ships flanked their captains: Howard of *Royal Oak*, a burly, likeable Scot, and Edwards of *Namur*, a taciturn, watchful man in impeccable lace and wig, with a livid duelling scar cutting through the smallpox marks on his cheek. The two remaining chairs were taken up by the commander of a xebec-rigged tender vessel, the *Barb*, a piratical-looking fellow with grey hair queued back into a waist-length rattail, a velvet patch over one eye, and a crippled arm which he kept thrust into the open front of his waistcoat – and Mainwaring, who had learned that the xebec commander was another Scot named McCallum, with a quick smile and ready wit for all his corsair appearance.

Mainwaring was the last to file into the cabin and sit, and he pulled his chair close as quickly as he could, conscious of the others' eyes on him. Thanks to Mathews' generosity, he was once more dressed like a gentleman in a well-tailored suit of light blue wool lined with linen, white hose, new French shoes – which hurt his feet – a finely-laced and ruffled linen shirt and white stock, and an unlaced tricorne which he balanced on his knee. He had refused the tailor's insistence that he purchase a full-bottomed *perruque*, and wore his own sun-dusted brown hair queued simply back. As he settled himself, he saw McCallum nod and give him what he thought was a friendly wink with his one pale blue eye.

"Gentlemen," began Mathews, nodding to his clerk at a small side table, "your presence is necessary in order to secure your views on a proposal Lieutenant Mainwaring here, late of the *Diana* frigate, has made to me."

"The chap who brought in that Spanish fifth-rate?" asked Howard. "Splendid. Damned nice thing, that, Mainwaring."

"Quite," came in Mathews, in a tone of annoyance. "We are all appreciative of Lieutenant Mainwaring's remarkable luck in bringing out the *San Pablo*. He has, however, lost his own vessel, although that is not the point of this meeting. He has made a proposal to place a small flotilla of odd craft off Toulon in an attempt to bottle the

French and Spanish in there until we are in a position to challenge them."

"If you'll permit me, sir," said Captain Deane. "Mainwaring, are your figures on the ships at anchor in Toulon correct? It seems a vastly larger fleet than we had intelligence of heretofore."

"They are correct, sir. My count was corroborated by my two officers' observations."

"Disturbing news, then, I must say," went on Deane, turning his heronlike gaze on Mathews. "Deuced difficult to handle that sort of throng even with all our ships assembled, sir."

Mathews nodded irritably, mopping at his brow with a large handkerchief. "Yes, yes. But sooner or later we shall have to chance that particular event. For at least a fortnight we cannot even conceive of such a challenge, and I must have Lestock's views on that matter. Mainwaring has a relevant idea to all this, which is why you're here, as I've said." He waved the handkerchief at Mainwaring. "Go on, Mainwaring. The details, if you please."

"The principle is simple, sir. To delay a successful escape of the Spanish and French squadrons, I propose that we may be able to turn their known reticence to engage us to our advantage."

Wilson, of *Royal Oak*, eyed him coldly. "We haven't a ship to spare, Lieutenant. It isn't clear how anyone might bottle up this force, or otherwise intimidate it, in the face of that most singular fact."

Mainwaring nodded. "With respect, sir, the key is not to have ships but to *appear* to have them."

"I'm not sure I follow," sniffed Wilson.

"The Dons and the French spend so much of their time dodging us, sir, that they are now reluctant to engage us readily. They have gradually come to think in terms of avoidance rather than confrontation, excused by thoughts of keeping the fleet intact, and so on. Should they sail to engage us, they would be anxious, I believe, to have time at sea to work up their ships and crews, and generally steady their nerves. But if we are hovering about their harbour mouth clearly intending to storm in on them the instant they hoist the first topsail yard, they'll be reluctant to sail, sir."

"Do you claim to know Spanish or French character that well, then?" demanded Edwards.

"Not entirely, Mr Edwards," Mainwaring replied. "But enough to know that they fight us defensively, when they do, and largely wish to avoid fighting us at all. But we are all aware of this. It is a weakness, a fear of us, that we can and must exploit."

Edwards' cool gaze was steady. "What sort of action do you have in mind?" There was a hint of approbation in his tone.

Mainwaring caught a reassuring nod from McCallum and took a deep breath. "Quite simply, we detach virtually any small craft we can to serve in a special-purpose flotilla, which we then station as close aboard the harbour of Toulon as possible. It should act as if it is the harbinger of your main force, Admiral, lying just over the horizon and anxious for a fleet action. And while continually acting as if an extension of the offshore force, the flotilla should attempt to increase the anxiety of the enemy by active harassment as they lie at anchor. Cutting-out parties, fireships, landings ashore if possible, the lot."

Deane snorted. "For God's sake, what sense would there be in putting a rag-tag mob of ship's boats in against a fortified seaport covered by batteries, packed with line-o'-battle ships, and inhabited by a strong garrison? You'd be brushed off like flies."

"It's not a matter of sense, sir," said Mainwaring. "It's a matter of fear."

"Sorry? Of what?"

"Fear, sir. Uncertainty. Unknown factors. An enemy acting as if he clearly has the upper hand, as if he is operating in advance of a vast force in full command of the sea outside the harbour mouth. And if we add to that fear with some well-directed destruction . . . " Mainwaring paused, turning his eyes to Mathews, "it could buy the time needed until our actual force *can* be gathered together."

Wilson sat back, his eyebrows high. "Well, damn me if I know what to say. Bloody audacious enough. But—"

"More akin to suicide, I would think," said Deane. "A damned silly idea, to my mind."

McCallum sat forward, his single eye alight with energy.

"With respect, sir, Mainwaring's right. It's no but action, and bold action at that, that'll keep the buggers in their hideyhole. And, Christ save me, I'd like to be part of such action. We've had too much damned skulking about, and not enough fighting, tae my mind!"

There was a chorus of comment. "See here, my man—" began Deane.

"Order, gentlemen, if you please!" Mathews banged a fist on the table. He coughed. "One might discuss this idea of Mainwaring's a good deal more, but other matters press. I have made a decision which I hope I shall have no occasion to regret." He shuffled some of the papers before him and eyed the scribbling clerk. "There will be a small flotilla detached to work inshore at Toulon, with orders to impede the sailings of the combined squadrons as best seems practical." He eyed McCallum. "They shall be supported by *Barb*, as a storeship, and will include your fireship *Trusty*, Mainwaring. For the rest, I believe we can only spare the pinnaces from *Royal Oak* and *Namur*. You will provide these craft, gentlemen, armed with swivels, stands of arms, and manned with volunteers."

"Surely, sir, that's not necess—" began Wilson.

"Obedience to an order, Captain Wilson, continues to be a necessity as I am sure I need not point out to you," said Mathews, his small eyes suddenly bright with anger. "There is in addition a prize, an Algerian *tartane*, which is expected in from Naples in several days. I will spare her as well to the task." He paused. "The question of command remains to be settled."

Howard, *Royal Oak*'s first lieutenant, sat forward. "I've nae doubt, sir, that ye c'd find a competent officer in the wardrooms o' either of our two ships. But why not give the task to Mainwaring himself, sir? Any sea officer that could winkle a ship out o' that place in one piece clearly knows what he's about. And it is his idea, in the bargain, sir."

Mathews frowned. "What do the rest of you think? Captain Wilson?"

"It's a damned silly idea, the whole thing, to my mind. But if any time can be bought for us, all to the good. If Mainwaring wants a French ball in his guts while trying, I'd give him the chance, sir."

"Captain Deane?"

"I'm somewhat of a fatalist, sir. I expect the Frogs to be out within the week, if our overland intelligences are correct, and that there'll be damned little we can do about it. A futile gesture like this can neither help nor hurt, except for the loss of my pinnace and a few hands. Let the colonial try, if he wishes."

Mainwaring's face flamed, but he bit his tongue.

"Very well," said Mathews. He sat back in his chair. "I'm inclined to agree, Mainwaring. But do you honestly think you can buy a fortnight's worth of time through this deception?"

A fortnight! Mainwaring tried to keep the despair from his face. He had imagined a lightning series of raids, successful for perhaps a week at the very most until the French and Spanish perceived what was going on. But a fortnight meant attempting a virtual blockade.

"You'd have to do what you claim," went on Mathews, "until I have assembled our squadrons. A frigate would arrive off Toulon to tell you that we were ready for the enemy to come out. I shall have to call away the frigates now watching in order to assemble our ships. And if the enemy get past you and move out while *that* is the case – I'm sure I need not finish, what?"

Mainwaring nodded. He heard himself say, "You'll have your fortnight, sir."

Mathews' expression was cold. "I hope you realise the extraordinary latitude I am granting you, Mainwaring. And quite without immediate justification. You've still to be brought before a Court over the loss of your ship, but I have no time for that now. You had better achieve what you set out to do," he said.

The small eyes that glittered at Mainwaring and the cold faces around the table were devoid of encouragement. At that moment Mainwaring felt in all its force the isolation that his American birth and his lack of 'interest' imposed

on him in the midst of these members of his supposed pro-
fessional fraternity. He had willingly put a noose around
his own throat, and Mathews would draw it tight without a
second thought if need be. Only in the face of the one-eyed
xebec captain, McCallum, did he see any emotion other
than a cold indifference.

"I hope I shall, sir," he said simply.

"Very well," went on Mathews, in a businesslike tone.
"You'll victual and store against my account. The Clerk
of the Cheque at Gibraltar will be apprised. Mind that
you'll need to succour the pinnaces as well. And see that
you've sufficient powder and shot for your damned guns.
I'll ask you, Captain Howard, to ensure the water hoy is sent
alongside *Trusty* and *Barb* in the forenoon watch tomorrow.
Have the pinnaces alongside *Trusty* by noon, mind."

Mathews plied his handkerchief once more. "You've
read yourself in, Mainwaring?" he went on. "Of course
you have. Then we can expect you to sail before nightfall
tomorrow, what?"

Again Mainwaring had to prevent the dismay from crossing his features. *By nightfall tomorrow!* *Trusty* was a shambles
of half-stowed gear and stores, with James Howe working
with Hooke and Pellowe to make some sense of the chaos.
They had gained six new men in *Trusty*, willing enough but
still leaving the fireship desperately short-handed. Pellowe
was acting as temporary purser, and had a list of missing
requirements as long as his arm, ranging from candles
for the glims to cutlasses and half-pikes. The fireship, a
handy-sized little ship-rigged vessel, was not unappealing,
in spite of her rough carpentry and joinerwork, and her
reversed gunport lids. But to put to sea in twenty-four
hours would mean little or no sleep or rest for all aboard.

"I can't speak for *Barb*, sir," began Mainwaring.

"But I may," broke in McCallum, heartily. "An' she's
ready tae put to sea the moment Lieutenant Mainwaring
signifies we should, sir!"

Mainwaring glanced at him gratefully, and then looked
back at Mathews. "It'll take a bit of work, sir. But we can
sail by nightfall tomorrow if we can lighter over the ship's
stores you've offered. And the pinnaces—"

"You'll have 'em, manned and ready, by noon," snapped Deane.

"Then, yes, sir. If the wind is fair, we shall sail by nightfall tomorrow as you request."

Mathews' expression was unfathomable. He nodded.

"Very well. You and McCallum had best get to your ships. There is other business this meeting must deal with."

When Mainwaring and McCallum had shut the cabin door behind them, Mathews looked round the table, his small eyes bright with an odd amusement.

"Well, gentlemen? What do you think?"

Deane snorted. "I think you will have little need to convene a Court to try Lieutenant Mainwaring on the loss of his ship. I'll give him three days off Toulon before he puts his vessel up on a ledge or the French swat him like a fly."

"Captain Wilson?"

"Quite, sir. He's an undisciplined Provincial who will undoubtedly act as rashly as he did when he lost his ship. I should think you will prove the winner in whatever he does, sir."

"Eh? How so?" asked Mathews.

Wilson smiled in a tolerant amusement. "Well, sir, should he in fact manage to hoodwink the Dons and the French into staying in the harbour for another fortnight, then we will be able to concentrate as many of our ships as possible against them. That is a consideration of some importance. But should he fail, we will be no worse off than we were before Mainwaring hatched this scheme. You will be able to report to Their Lordships that you attempted a commendable act of initiative – which they will no doubt applaud – and at the same time have the question of Mainwaring's Court and the disposal of his prize, the *San Pablo*, resolved. He will either be dead, a prisoner, or subject to reprimand so severe that very little will redeem him. And that will mean forfeiture of his, and his men's, share of the *San Pablo* prize, I should think, which will enhance your – and our – share."

"Aye," said Mathews. "And if in fact he *does* succeed?"

"It's quite simple, sir," said Wilson. "Commend him; inform him he'll be given a lieutenancy in a line-o'-battle

111

ship at the first opportunity, but have him stand his Court. The Court can award the *San Pablo* prize elsewhere as part of the decision on Mainwaring over the loss of his ship."

"And we lose nothing," said Mathews.

"Exactly, sir," said Deane.

Mathews' round features broke slowly into a smile.

"Well, then," he said quietly, "may Fortune do what she will with our fishpot colonial!"

The Chevalier Rigaud de la Roche-Bourbon fixed a cold, dark gaze of fury at the figure of the *Troupes de la Marine sergent* who stood trembling before his desk in the great cabin of the line-of-battle ship *Normandie*. The man was fidgeting with his tricorne, running his fingers along the cheap gilt lace that edged the hat, and avoiding those furious eyes.

"What do you mean, *escaped*?" hissed Roche-Bourbon. "You were sent, Jacques, to ensure his end. Do I now find myself required to end your miserable life in his place? *Hein*?"

"M'sieu' – please – he seemed to be aware of what we were about as we followed him. He ordered the signal gun fired, to alert the guard boats, and I sent off the cavalrymen to le Mourillon by giving your orders to the lieutenant of the troop. But then De Guimond took a fresh horse and galloped the other way, before we could stop him, around the harbour towards la Seyne and towards l'Eguillette battery, m'sieu'. We – I had placed my men on the road to le Mourillon, and by the time we found out he had—"

"You fool, Jacques!" raged Roche-Bourbon, through tight lips. "You mindless fool! I have had to watch a Spanish vessel stolen from under our very noses, which is creating vast anger and displeasure with both the commandant and the *amirauté*. And I have had to watch as the battery in le Mourillon demonstrated an unbelievable incompetence by allowing the same ship to escape. The one consolation I warmed myself with was the thought that you were disposing of that turncoat marine officer. But you failed in that."

The *sergent* was sweating profusely. "By your leave, m'sieu'. I – we did everything you might have wished, and more. The officer of the *Ronde* was told, and he alerted the town major, and the watch. The officer commanding the guardboats had a runner sent to him to explain the true meaning of the signal gun. The troopers who rode to le Mourillon were told to pass the order to raise the boom, and to destroy or halt the ship by gunfire. All these were passed as your orders, m'sieu', as I was sure you wished. I cannot think—"

"You are quite right, you fool, that you cannot think," cut in Roche-Bourbon savagely, "if it has not occurred to you that the battery at l'Eguillette, which surely would have sunk the *San Pablo* at such point-blank range, *did not fire!*" He pointed a long finger at the *sergent*. "Your escaped *enseigne* clearly reached there, and if they did not fire, I ascribe it to him!"

Roche-Bourbon rose and paced slowly behind the desk, like a great velvet-clad cat. His gaze had left Jacques and the latter relaxed slightly, wondering if his life might yet be spared.

"The battery," Roche-Bourbon was murmuring. "And all those damned fisherfolk along that shore, who rescued and actually cared for the wretched English. The longboat the English so conveniently 'stole' from that shore as well." The glittering eyes fell again on the *sergent*. "I smell traitors, Jacques. It is a particularly bad smell. We must do something about it, *hein*?"

"*D'une certitude, m'sieu'!*" agreed Jacques. "But what, may I ask, m'sieu'?"

"Death is the great cleanser, Jacques," purred Roche-Bourbon. "It leaves no loose ends thereafter." His fingers tapped lightly on the steel of a small Miquelet pistol that lay before him.

"To begin with, you will carry my compliments to Monsieur de Chazy, and inform him that I will need a particular company of the *Troupes* called out. It is not to be a company of the guard, nor your own; and none of De Guimond's company, even a fusilier, must know of this!"

"But, m'sieu'—"

"Silence! The town major owes me a debt, and he will give you his own major's company, as evil a lot as I've ever seen. Admirable for my purposes. Monsieur de Chazy is to call out the company but not their officers. You'll see that their stand of arms is correct and march them immediately to the fork in the road leading round the harbour to la Seyne. Halt them in the courtyard of Charron's *taverne*. I'll join you there." He smirked. "They're a vicious lot of ex-galley slaves, *forçats* to a man. Turn your back on 'em and they'll cut your guts out, Jacques. Is that clear?"

Jacques was deeply afraid of Roche-Bourbon. But Jacques was also a rough and brutal product of the lash and the drill cane, who had achieved the gold cuff lace of the *sergent* by being able to match the animal viciousness of the barrack room in a half-hundred savage little alleyway fights and *taverne* brawls. His ability to handle a company of brutes equalled the indifference with which he inflicted pain or death whenever he was ordered.

"*A vos ordres, m'sieu'*", he said. "What then, after we meet?" A grin of expectation was beginning to spread across his heavy features.

Roche-Bourbon raised an eyebrow. "Your interest is piqued, is it, Jacques?" he purred. "Very likely we shall gather up every living wretch along that shoreline, and entertain them in l'Eguillette. And should we find De Guimond there, he will join us in our little assembly." He smiled coldly. "I must know who saw to the succour and release of the English swine, Jacques, and your company of dogs will enjoy forcing it out of them, no doubt."

Jacques' leer broadened. "*Oui, m'sieu'*," he breathed.

The misty dawn light was beginning to reveal the ghostly shapes of the small hulls that were reaching off to the southwestward, across the light nor'westerly blowing down off the *massif* behind Cap Blanc. Standing out to clear the Ile de Porquerolles through the Grande Passe, Edward Mainwaring's small flotilla – the word brought a smile to his face – was footing along reasonably well before the mist-laden wind, the light now making the gently arched sails glow milk-white as the white tendrils swirled around them.

114

Mainwaring stood in the comfort of his tattered duck trousers, loosened shirt and old tricorne on the windward side of *Trusty*'s small quarterdeck. His feet were thrust bare into his salt-rimed buckle shoes and he had ripped his shirt open to the waist in thankful relief after throwing off the stifling prison of the blue wool suit as soon as they had sailed two days before. Most of his contemporaries, he mused, thought little of going through the day's routine dressed as elegantly as possible, in order to accentuate the social as well as disciplinary differences between gentlemen and those who served before the mast. Mainwaring was aware that this was a newly developing tendency in the Royal Navy, whose officers – 'sea officers', to use the correct term – had once prided themselves on a rough and uncultured manner that gave away very little to the most hardened inhabitant of the fo'c'sle or gun deck. As an American, a somewhat less critical eye was turned on him with regard to gentlemanly elegance or social pretension, due largely to the assumption that a Provincial was incapable of the former and unqualified for the latter. For Mainwaring, the question of dress was a minor one. Untroubled by a desire to rise in a society in which he recognised his undeclared exclusion, he geared his mode of dress to what was functional and comfortable. And at the moment, the cool, easy practicality of duck trousers and a loose shirt were uniform enough.

With McCallum's odd-looking *Barb* leading the way, a single hooded lantern set at her transom rail – the Scot had sailed this coast for twenty years, and knew every rock by memory – *Trusty* and the two fragile-looking pinnaces had worked their way out of Villefranche harbour and stood off across the steady land breeze on the long sou'westward reach towards Toulon. During the first night the pinnaces had hung off *Trusty*'s quarter, their twin lugsails faint, pale shapes in the starlit night, as *Barb* had led them on past the headlands: Cap d'Antibes, after the Baie des Anges; then the low, flat darkness of the Iles des Lérins; rocky Cap du Dramont on the high shoreline of the *massif* of l'Esterel; then the long fetch across the Golfe de Fréjus towards Cap de St Tropez, and beyond that in quick succession Cap

Camaral and Cap Lardier. When daylight had come, with the wind still miraculously steady out of the nor'west, the xebec had pitched on ahead, the squaresail on the foremast looking strange and ungainly in front of the great, winging lateens on the main and mizzen. The men in the pinnaces, which were nothing more than very large ship's boats, had looked cramped and worn. Mainwaring had brought them aboard *Trusty*, leaving the pinnaces to trail on tows with their lugsails brailed and one man alone at each helm to keep the boats towing properly. With McCallum reefing in his mizzen and foresail, Mainwaring had managed to keep *Trusty* in pace with the high-tailed xebec. On the second night, McCallum had sent a boat across to say that the current in the approaches to the Iles d'Hyères was treacherous, and advising that they heave to for the night. Mainwaring had agreed, and *Barb*'s windward ability had kept her the mark towards which Mainwaring had steered *Trusty* under light sail through the night. With the dawn light, the two ships had shaken out sail, having lost little more than a half-league, and with *Barb* again the leader, they had stood on towards their goal. Once clear of the Hyères, they would round Cap d'Arme, and there to the northwestward would lie Cap de Carqueiranne once more, and the waters of the Golfe de Giens, where *San Pablo* had carried them to freedom – and where *Diana* had died.

There was a slap of feet on the short waistdeck ladder, and Isaiah Hooke, in a loose red shirt and tar-smeared petticoat breeches, padded over to join Mainwaring. The sailing master's peppershot blond hair was looking greyer in the morning light, but his eyes were bright, and he had about him the ursine half-swagger that meant all was reasonably well in his world.

Hooke looked up at the tattered white Bourbon ensign that curled over *Trusty*'s quarterdeck, a duplicate of the one fluttering above *Barb*'s ornate stern.

"Them Froggy rags've done it, zur," he grinned. "All yesterday, an' likely will today. It were a smart move o' yours, zur."

Mainwaring smiled, his eyes flickering forward under the ducked-up mainsail foot to the brightening shape of

Barb. He turned to the helmsman at *Trusty*'s small wheel.

"Full and bye, now, Winton. But mind ye keep astern of her. She's the one that knows these waters."

Winton nodded. "Full and bye, sir. An' I'll hang on 'er like a terrier to a rat, sir."

"Well put," laughed Mainwaring. He turned to Hooke. "Yes, Isaiah, I thought the false colours would do it, although I had a bad moment when that English forty-four altered course to close with us off Cap de St Tropez. Did you recognise her?"

"It might've been *Harwich*, zur, by the cut of 'er. Not sure. Thank Christ she fell off after a bit. Must've thought we were a touch too close inshore for 'er, zur."

"Aye." Mainwaring could see Stephen Pellowe sitting cross-legged on the gratings with Evans and Williams, wiping down the locks and barrels of half a dozen muskets. "Where's Mr Howe? I take it he's got Mr Pellowe on to those small arms."

"Aye, zur, 'e did," said Hooke. "Mr 'Owe's in the magazine, zur. Showin' Shanahan 'is new duties as gunner's mate, zur." He spat accurately over the leeward rail into the coal-black, mist-drifted water. "Not that there's much to be a mate to, zur, beggin' yer pardon."

"Oh? How so?"

"Oi 'eard Mr Pellowe sayin' t' Mr 'Owe, zur, that more'n 'alf th' stands uv arms what were sent aboard from *Namur* ain't worth tuppence, zur. Locks missin' or stocks cracked, an' most nothin' that c'd be fired wivout blowin' yer own 'ead off, zur."

Mainwaring's eyes took on a cold glint. "What about the cutlasses and the pistols?"

"Cutlasses are fine, zur, 'ceptin' fer a touch o' rust. But the pistols be a lot o' gash, zur. Ain't hardly a pair that'll snap."

Anger and frustration rose within Mainwaring and he turned to bang one fist down hard on the rail. *Damn the bastards*, raged his mind. *Damn Mathews for his narrow, short-sighted stupidity!*

He turned back. "How many workable small arms does that leave us, then?"

"Don't rightly know, zur. Likely them six Mr Pellowe an' the lads are workin' on be all, zur. Besides the cutlasses."

Mainwaring sighed. "All right. We'll bloody well simply have to make the best of it." He looked over the transom rail at the shapes of the pinnaces, tugging obediently along on their lines in *Trusty*'s wake. "Where are the pinnace crews?"

"Slade 'ad 'em below, zur, gettin' some biscuit an' whatnot into 'em. An' I'll change the lads at their 'elms soon. They were all purely famished, zur. Their ships sent 'em off wivvout a biscuit bag, jes' some fruit an' a jug o' water." He spat again over the rail, this time with some violence. "They're good lads, mostly. Landsmen an' volunteers. 'Ave t' put their 'ands on th' right pin, but they appears willin' enough, zur."

"How many of them are there?"

"Fourteen, zur. Six a boat, an' a cox'n. T'ain't 'ardly a pinnace's crew, t' my mind, zur."

"Nor mine, but it's what we might have expected, I can see," Mainwaring said grimly. "Are the boats armed?"

Hooke gestured with his thumb. "Them one-pounder swivels in th' strongback set in th' towin' bollard port, for'rard in each boat, zur. The lads say they've about ten rounds fer each gun. A clutch o' cutlasses in each boat, an' that's all, zur."

"Good Christ!" breathed Mainwaring. "What have I got us all into?"

"Zur?"

"Nothing, Isaiah." Mainwaring looked forward; the mist was lifting and the growing light revealed the ship in clearer detail. With her yards braced sharply up, *Trusty* lay gently over to the easy breeze and pitched in a slight, slow motion through the sea that hissed rhythmically at her bows and under her counter.

"I had another quick wink at the chart while you were for'rard," Mainwaring went on. "McCallum, there, should have us clear out to seaward of the Hyères in another hour or so, if this wind holds. And I think the current's fetching fair for us, about a knot or two. When we harden up for the tack into the Golfe de Giens, you'd better call away

118

the pinnace crews and have 'em stand ready to sheer away from us and *Barb*. If the French come out after us, at least they can work into the shallows and perhaps escape. And if not—" He paused, lost in sombre thought.

Hooke knew the mood, and waited for a moment. "Wot is it ye *do* intend for us, once into th' bay, zur?" he asked, presently.

Mainwaring's tone was steady and businesslike. "We'll sail a pattern at first; a few boards across the Golfe, from Cap Sicié on the west, eastward across to those damned rocks we nearly put *San Pablo* up on."

"Them's w'd be the – the—" and here Hooke struggled with the pronunciation, "the Fourniques, zur."

Mainwaring grinned. "Your French is getting better, Isaiah. We'll hold that pattern, like a picket, with *Barb* further inshore and ourselves on the Cap Sicié line. The pinnaces can run between us with a few meaningless messages. I've already prepared Mr Howe and Mr Pellowe, but we've got to make sure our one-eyed Scot over there knows what we intend. The moment you get a crew away in the first pinnace, I'll give you a packet for the coxswain to carry across to *Barb*. He knows to heave to and wait for us to come up if we fire a gun." He paused. "There's one other thing, Isaiah."

"Zur?"

Mainwaring's grin widened. He poked a thumb upward at the Bourbon ensign.

"Directly we clear the Hyères and harden up for the Golfe, take down that bedsheet and put up our true colours. And the jack at the foremast head. We should let the bastards know we're here, after all."

Hooke beamed. "Aye, zur! That I will!"

6

Mainwaring had gone down the waistdeck ladder, sinking into the cool dark of the after companionway. He continued aft along the narrow passageway to his cabin, his mind still grappling with the reality of what the weapons report actually meant. He pushed open the door, threw his hat on the narrow settee under the stern lights, and looked morosely at the chart that lay, weighted with a cutlass, on the small table that served as his desk.

The indifference of Mathews to what Mainwaring was undertaking could not have been made more plain. And that indifference was likely shared by the other captains. Mathews' forces were clearly stretched to the limit and he desperately needed time to assemble them if the vessels lurking in Toulon were to be dealt with. A sudden sailing of the enormous French and Spanish squadrons before the English were ready would quite simply lose the Mediterranean for the Royal Navy. Nothing could be clearer, yet Mathews had chosen to do the least possible for Mainwaring's little force, almost as if to guarantee failure.

A cold fury gripped Mainwaring as he thought of the half-starved pinnace crews, the perplexed look on Hooke's face as he described the pitiful arms situation. He remembered the efforts of that blustery and emotional little vice-admiral, Edward Vernon, to look after his crews and ships as a first priority. Clearly Mathews was not cut from the same cloth. But why? Was it lack of vision, or simply indifference? Or was it an unspoken contempt for a colony-born junior officer translated into a shoddy unwillingness to see him properly supported?

Damn them! thought Mainwaring, staring at the chart. *They're putting the fishpot colonial in his place. And risking so damned much as a result. So much!*

He focused a fierce gaze on the chart. Atop it he had put the little sheet of diagrams from the *San Pablo*, showing the vessels anchored and moored within Toulon. Again the knot gripped his stomach as he studied the figures. That overwhelming force *had* to be kept bottled up until Mathews languidly collected his ships, whether or not Mathews possessed the intelligence to see what was actually at stake. England could not lose a vital advantage because the man she had entrusted to guard that advantage was acting perilously like a fool.

His eyes narrowed. Essentially, the Cap Cépet-Cap de Carqueiranne line formed a demarcation beyond which *Trusty* and *Barb* and the pinnaces would under normal circumstances risk abrupt destruction. He could not repeat the wasteful sacrifice of *Diana* unless a clear result made such a sacrifice thinkable. But would simply hovering off the headlands as the simulated picket for a fictitious offshore squadron be sufficient to keep the French and Spanish lying to their hawsers? Doubt began to creep into his mind.

His eyes found the narrow throat of the inner harbour, the Petite Rade; the gap between le Mourillon and l'Eguillette where the boom stretched, and where *San Pablo* had burst through by blind luck.

A narrow throat, he thought. *To keep an enemy out. Or keep one in*. His mind began to race, a daring plan beginning to form, its elements crystallising in his thoughts and dropping into place one by one, until he could see the final result almost with the clarity of a Watteau sketch. The risks it implied appalled him; but in the same moment he felt rising in him a reckless, fierce conviction that had a kind of odd joy in it. His mind whirling with detail, he snatched up his battered tricorne and ducked out of the cabin doorway.

As he went up the companionway he felt *Trusty* cant beneath him, feet thumping on the deck as men moved about, rumpling canvas a deep sound behind Hooke's barked orders. Mainwaring emerged into the glare of light to find that they were standing in now towards the Grande Rade, Cap Cépet lying large on the larboard bow.

Ahead, *Barb*'s great lateen shook as its foot was rhythmically hauled in by a knot of seamen visible at the mainsheet falls, the graceful xebec dancing along under its streaming pennant and blood-red ensign, leaving a frothy wake in which *Trusty* followed.

Hooke knuckled his brow to him as he gained the quarterdeck.

"Ship's 'ead bearin' on th' outer 'arbour, now, zur. An' th' wind's come round to th' sou'west, zur. Makes it a reach in."

"Very good." Mainwaring moved to the binnacle box and crouched, taking quick bearings on Carqueiranne's headland to starboard and Cépet to larboard.

"We're about a league and a half off," he said, after some thought. "But I've a few different things in mind, Mr Hooke. And our Scottish friend over there must be told." He squinted to seaward, then along the shoreline. "Any strange sail in sight?"

"Nought, zur. I've doubled th' lookouts, an' there be nought but fishermen out. No sail, and no Frenchies, sartin, zur."

"I see. If Shanahan's up to it, pass the word to Mr Howe that I need that gun fired to have *Barb* bring to. I'll be below writing my orders for McCallum. And call away the jolly boat to take 'em."

"Aye, aye, zur," said Hooke. Then he jerked a thumb aloft. "Them colours look better, aye, zur?"

Mainwaring looked up. From *Trusty*'s fore truck the Union flag fluttered out in pretty colour, and from the main truck, a lancelike red pennant with the cross of St George at the hoist curled and floated out. And at the crown-capped ensign staff, the brilliant splash of a huge Red Ensign streamed out to leeward.

"Aye, Mr Hooke!" grinned Mainwaring. "And there's none better!"

It took all of Mainwaring's concentration to compress his thoughts into coherent orders for McCallum, and he hoped the energetic Scot would grasp the role he had to play quickly and in the full understanding of what Mainwaring intended. He was sprinkling sand over the last sentence when the thump of the gun sounded and he heard the squealing block and stamping, shuffling feet that meant the little jolly boat, or yawl, was being swung out on the mainyard tackles. A small cockleshell of a craft, barely fifteen feet long and boasting four oars, it was handy for use in situations where the larger ship's boats would be too cumbersome.

Dropping a dollop of hot wax on to the folded paper, he sealed it with a quick press of the spare waistcoat button he kept in lieu of a seal, snuffed out the candle, and went on deck. Within minutes the jolly boat was bouncing over the dark waves towards the hove-to *Barb*. Pellowe was at the tiller, bareheaded, his blond locks gleaming in the sun, and four hands tugging industriously at the oars.

For a moment Mainwaring watched the little boat dance away and then turned as James Howe and Isaiah Hooke arrived together on the quarterdeck, their expressions questioning.

"James, Isaiah," Mainwaring said quietly. "I want you both to listen carefully. It is most important that you know what it is we shall be about."

The two men exchanged a glance. "Change of plan, sir?" asked Howe.

"Not in the eventual aim, James, but in tactics. Are we right in assuming we've only a few useful weapons?"

Howe's face was grim. "Four workable firelocks, sir. No more than thirty rounds of ball cartridge for each. Enough cutlasses for all, if that's a comfort."

"The swivels?"

"I think Mr Hooke told you, sir. Serviceable, but with no more'n ten rounds per gun. Tools and priming horns are correct enough."

"What of *Barb*?"

"McCallum told me he's got four truck guns, all three-pounders. And a few light arms, mostly fowlers. A pistol or two as well," Howe replied.

"Good God." Mainwaring was furious with himself suddenly, knowing he should have badgered Mathews for some rectification to the little flotilla's miserable arms inventory, knowing he should have asked for real guns in *Trusty* instead of sailing her now towards action with gunports that would gape empty when opened. But then the mood of the meeting on *Namur* came back to him. They were lucky to have any arms at all, he reflected.

His mind began working again, shifting the elements of the plan. He looked up, squinting at *Barb* where she lay pitching slowly to the swells, her huge lateen rippling as *Trusty*'s boat went alongside. The oar blades flashed as they were tossed, gleaming wetly.

"It'll all have to do," he said after a moment. "We've done more with less in the past. Mr Hooke, you'll call away the pinnace crews as soon as we've finished talking. Divide the serviceable arms between 'em. Ensure each man has a cutlass, at least. And put every round of musket-ball cartridge into the boats." He paused. "Mind a biscuit bag and a hogshead o' small beer is put in each as well." His eyes turned to Howe. "James, you'll command the second pinnace, I'll take the first. We'll add a few of our own lads to flesh out the crews." Mainwaring flicked mentally through the list of *Trusty*'s ship's company. "You take the two Welshmen, Evans and Williams. I'll have Sawyer and Slade."

Hooke's expression slowly turned to one of astonishment.

"Lor' lummee, zur, not bloody *boats* again!"

"Yes, boats again. But why such concern?"

Hooke reddened, aware of his outburst. "Beggin' yer pardon, zur. Took me aback, is all, zur. Wot was it ye plan fer me, zur, an' th' lads?"

Mainwaring's tone was brisk. "You'll command *Trusty*, Isaiah. You're to hold the patrol line between Cépet and Carqueiranne as best you can, weather willing. Beat out if the wind turns foul or any threatening vessel appears to seaward and you think you'd be trapped. But stand ready to come in when the signal is given."

"*Come in*? How d'ye mean, zur?"

"I'll need you one of two ways, if I call. The first would be to stand in and take off the pinnace crews, and get away to seaward. The second would be to bring her in and fire her, make her strike where I direct and then get out to sea in your boats."

124

Hooke stared at the American. "Christ on a crutch! 'Ow'll yew get word t' me, zur?"

"*Barb* has two yawl boats. One of 'em will pull out to you with orders." He paused. "If I can't get a boat to you, watch for a red Ensign hoisted somewhere ashore there, on the Eguillette or the Mourillon battery. If you see *that*, old friend, come in like the furies of hell are after you, if the wind allows. But only then. Mind you don't leave your patrol until then, even if you see *Barb* stand in, as likely ye will."

"Why is that, sir?"asked Howe, who had been watchful and silent until now. His eyes under the shadow of his cocked hat had grown brighter at the mention of the two batteries.

"She's a bit better manned than we are, James. I've ordered McCallum to put together a third boat's land party of his best lads. He's to watch for fires on the shore: two will mean he's to send them to the Eguillette; three, to the Mourillon. That'll tell him which of the two you and I have managed to reach and need assistance in attacking."

"*Attacking*?" Howe gaped for a moment. "Ah – seriously, sir?"

"Very much so, James. Isaiah, you've got to keep *Trusty* out of harm's way while you play your role, pretending you've got the whole bloody Navy sitting over the horizon. And when I call you in, bear in mind that there'll be little I can tell you. The call will simply mean to bring her in and raise a deuce of a row."

"Go at the Dons alight, y'mean, zur?" said Hooke.

"It'll have to be as you see fit. But you'll be the prize-fighter's knockout punch, Isaiah. If James and I can't knock the Dons and the French back from scratch, then the last blow goes to you."

Hooke's small bright eyes gleamed. "Ye c'n count on *Trusty*, zur. An' she's readier t' burn than a pine knot, she is."

"Good. Let Jewett exercise and watch-keep, if need be. I think he could manage it."

"Aye, zur. But how are ye—?"

Mainwaring glanced at the hove-to *Barb*. The little jolly boat was leaving the side, the oar blades glinting as she danced back towards *Trusty* over the swells.

"This is not an attempt at imaginative suicide, Mr Hooke. The Dons and the French must be kept locked up in their bottle, and if the boom and batteries arrangement they've contrived can keep ships out, it seems likely that they can keep ships *in*." His eyes narrowed. "James, we'll row in as dusk is falling, staying close to those bluffs to the left of the harbour opening, on the St Mandrier peninsula. Once darkness falls, we make for whichever of the fortified batteries seems appropriate. They're the anchor points for that damned boom."

"What then, sir?" Howe enquired.

"Simple enough. We take the place and keep the French bottled up for as long as we can, with McCallum's help and with Mr Hooke here to put in the final punch if we need it."

Howe blinked. "With, er, twelve men, sir? They'll have the gunners and likely an infantry garrison of sorts. That same lot of weedy ruffians that took us on the beach. And then there's the ship's companies at anchor, and the main dockyard garrison of *Troupes de la Marine*. Heavy odds, sir."

"Initiative may supplement numbers, James. Try to think we've got the buggers outnumbered," said Mainwaring drily. He glanced at *Barb* again, seeing the vessel turning slowly as its broad square foresail was braced up. A flash of red suddenly showed above its transom rail as McCallum set in place his own British ensign, and a coiling red pennant rose like a floating snake to the peak of the enormous lateen yard.

Mainwaring squinted at the sun. "Almost the change for the forenoon watch, gentlemen. We'll play the picket vessel until evening. James, I'd ask that you begin preparing the pinnaces and their crews. We'll slip in the First Dog, all else being equal. Questions, either of you?"

Howe and Hooke looked at each other, exchanging slow, reckless grins.

"No, sir," said Howe.

"Then carry on, please," said Mainwaring, and went forward down the waistdeck ladder.

Hooke looked at Howe and spat over the rail accurately.

"Wot d'ye think, zur?" he asked after a moment.

Howe frowned. "His orders are clear enough, Mr Hooke."

"Terrible long odds, zur. Two boats' crews agin a whoreson garrison battery?"

Howe found himself grinning at the grizzled sailing master.

"You know as well as I do that he's not one to hang back, Mr Hooke. And he has this uncanny knack of knowing the right thing to do." He paused. "I'd rather take a chance at sticking it to the Dons and the Frogs in some spectacular way than sit out here and wait for that fellow Mathews to show at his leisure."

Hooke nodded. "That's 'ow th' lads feel, zur. It got all through th' messdecks, 'ow th' admiral like as dismissed our Ned wiv barely a thought o' supportin' 'im, zur. 'Ee's worth more'n that."

Howe smiled slowly, looking forward at the straight figure standing at the foremast foot talking to Jewett, the boatswain.

"Aye," he agreed quietly. "And if he wants me to pull a boat into hell with him, Mr Hooke, I doubt if I could say no. Even if it wasn't an order."

"Me neither, zur," rumbled Hooke.

"I'd best see to our boats," murmured Howe, and made off, his expression thoughtful.

Hooke turned to the helm, where Winton gripped the tall double wheel with a firm hand.

"Look sharp, Winnie. We'll brace round an' git under way soon as the cap'n gives th' word."

"Aye, aye, Mr Hooke," said Winton. He grinned. "We be fixin' t' attack them shore batteries, ain't we, sir?"

Hooke's teeth flashed. "Aye, Winnie. Aye, by God, we are!"

Some hours later, *Trusty* was hove to again, but now less than half a league off the bluff mass of Cap Cépet. It was at the end of the day, and the deep peach tone of the sunlight had turned the surface of the sea to copper, lighting the gathered canvas of *Trusty*'s sails and the faces of the men grouped at her rail with the same golden wash.

Edward Mainwaring, his stomach fluttering somewhat unpleasantly, was looking aloft to where doubled lookouts were scanning for sign of the sudden appearance of a hostile vessel from seaward, or putting out from the shore. Then he eyed the assembled party of men who stood watching him intently, swaying unconsciously as *Trusty* pitched slowly beneath them. Evans and Williams; Slade and Sawyer; Howe; these men he knew. The others were from the pinnace crews, and although they had seemed competent enough, and almost pitifully grateful for the treatment they had received from Mainwaring, they were an unknown quantity. There had been no choice in the matter; he could not have stripped *Trusty* of reliable men like Jewett or Winton, for Hooke needed every good man possible to manage the fireship, and even so would have the very barest of skeleton crews. Now the men were watchfully waiting for him to speak before they swung over the side into the two pinnaces, hooked on alongside one abaft the other, their double lugsails brailed up snug against their yards, rumpling gently in their tethers with the breeze.

"Are we ready, Mr Howe?" asked Mainwaring.

"Aye, aye, sir. Each boat has ten rounds for its swivel, sir. There's two muskets in each, and cutlasses for all hands. And we've struck spare sweeps into 'em as well."

"Victuals?"

"Breadbags and a cask of small beer to each boat, sir."

Mainwaring nodded. He patted the pockets of his stained linen coat, feeling for his small telescope and the penned sketch of the ships at anchor in Toulon. Howe had been thorough, as usual, it appeared.

Mainwaring stepped before the men and doffed his battered tricorne, wiping his brow with the sleeve of his coat before setting the hat back on at a determined angle.

"Pay attention this way, lads," he said. "We're putting in to Toulon harbour with these boats. Our task is to find some way to keep the Dons and the French allies penned up in there for as long as we can. The only reason they're not here blowing us out of the water is their fear that we've a fleet at sea waiting for 'em to try. In truth, the admiral *is* attempting to gather our ships together, and our job is to give him enough time so that when the enemy's squadron gets out, our ships are waiting for them. You've already been told the size of the combined squadrons in there. Fail, and it'd mean disaster for England: we'd be driven piecemeal out of the Mediterranean, and Christ knows where it would stop. Minorca, Gibraltar – all of it would be threatened." He paused. "What we're about to do will be dangerous. If we don't die with a French ball in our guts we could spend the rest of our lives pulling an oar in one of their damned penal galleys. But we're going to try to take one of the harbour-mouth batteries. *Barb* will send some more hands to back us up, when we need 'em. And *Trusty* will stand ready to do her task when we need her." He looked round the watchful faces. "I need every man to give his best in this: nothing else will do. Any man who wants to step out of it, and stay in *Trusty*, can do so now. Nothing less will be thought of him for it. Well?"

A dark, thin man with tiny braids beside his ears and a gunpowder tattoo of a death's head on one cheek stepped forward, knuckle to his brow.

"Beggin yer 'onour's pardon, zur," he began.

"Yes? You're Jackman, aren't you?"

" 'Zur. Fo'c'sleman, in *Royal Oak*, zur. Th'other lads o' th' pinnace crews axed me t' speak fer 'em, zur."

"Then do so." Mainwaring kept his expression neutral, but a cold knot rose in his gut. He had opened the door away from duty with the offer to leave any man behind who did not wish to go. Would these new men bolt through that doorway? He needed them now, and they knew it.

The man spread his bare feet and wiped his hands on his tar-smeared petticoat breeches.

"Me an' th' lads ain't met wiv such smart care since we wuz in *Burford* wiv Old Grog hisself, zur. Why, yew an' Mr 'Owe, an' th' master, ye be gennulmen, smart as paint, an' ye give Jack 'is rights, ye do, zur." Jackman sniffed. "We knows this 'ere lark be like t' put us in th' way uv a Froggy ball or two, zur. But there ain't a

129

man who'll not go wiv ye, zur, an' there's me divvy on it, zur."

Mainwaring nodded as the other men murmured agreement, the old Dianas among them grinning knowingly. He felt a surge of gratitude, mixed with the usual perplexity he experienced when the loyalty he seemed to arouse in such rough-hewn men – for reasons he never entirely comprehended – surfaced, always unexpectedly. His throat was tight as he replied.

"Thank you, Jackman. We'll try to give you a bellyful of fighting to make it worthwhile. And hopefully no French musket ball!"

A sudden roar of approval burst from the clutch of men, and they beamed at him, Jackman baring a gap-toothed piratical smile worthy of a merchantman's worst nightmares.

"Good on 'ee, zur!"

"Bugger th' Frogs, zur!"

Mainwaring grinned. "We'll do that right enough, given the chance! Mr Howe?"

"Sir?" Howe stepped forward. He had put off his coat and wore a seaman's check shirt and loose neck-scarf.

"Call away the boats' crews, if you please."

"Aye, aye, sir!" Howe turned to the waiting men. "Jackman, Traynor, Lount, MacNeil and Forrest. You're with Slade and Sawyer in the captain's boat, hooked on aft. Oldham, Martin and Adams. You're in mine, with Evans and Williams. Strike your gear into the boats and into 'em yourselves. Roundly, now!"

The men swung their legs over the rail and went down the battens into the boats, the first there catching the small seabags thrown down to them. Mainwaring watched for a moment and then turned to Hooke.

"Very little I can say to you, Isaiah. Just let *Trusty* play her part in the bluff. When I need you – and, God willing, the wind is fair – come in with every inch of canvas you've got, and ready to burn her if necessary."

"Aye, zur." Hooke cupped his hands, and his voice suddenly rose to a bellow. "Mind that weather fores'l tack, Mr Jewett! Keep 'er well aback!" Then, "Sorry, zur."

"No matter. You know what to do, in any event. But no foolish heroics, old friend. Tow your best boat astern, and get away in her. If some Frenchman comes hounding up after you looking for a fight, get away to seaward. If you're clear, we can get out to you somehow."

"Beggin' yer pardon, zur, but do ye have a clear plan, like as t' wot ye'll do i'there?"

Mainwaring smiled. "You're a perceptive old sea dog, Isaiah. In truth, I've no plan other than to let audacity, darkness and luck have their way. God grant they do."

"Aye, zur. Oi've no fear they won't, zur."

"I wish I had a guarantee of that. Keep well, now." Forcing his hat more firmly on to his head, Mainwaring went over the side, glad as he went down the splintery battens that he was in loose, calf-length duck trousers, shirt and docked linen coat. To struggle down in the full imprisonment of breeches, waistcoat, hose, dress pumps and woollen coat was almost always an invitation to disaster, the heels-up tumble into the sternsheets or worse, the hapless splash into the water alongside and the indignity of being hauled, dripping like a wet dog, into the boat by snickering hands.

Then his feet were on the gunwale, and he stepped inboard to the centre of a thwart, his weight low, stepping gingerly aft over the thwarts past the hunched, ready men and the lashed mass of the brailed-up main. A moment more and he was settling into the pinnace's cluttered sternsheets.

"Slade? Lay aft. You'll be coxswain. Jackman, you'll relieve him as necessary. Stand by the lines, there, fore and aft. Cast off the brails. Traynor? Butt-end that boathook against the ship's side, and bear us off, for'rard, there!"

Ahead of them, Howe's boat had already cast off its brails, the two tan-coloured lugsails rumpling and snapping as they felt the fitful wind round *Trusty*'s interposing bulk. Then the boat was thrust off with a heft of a boathook's butt, and it bobbed away slowly forward as the hunched figures in the little craft sorted out sheets, ready for the full press of the wind when they moved out of *Trusty*'s lee. In the next moment they were clear, the wind filling the broad sails with a whump, the men scrambling to get their weight on the weather side – but now all down on the floorboards as Service boatwork required, their heads looking in the boat like chess pieces in a box, ready to be taken out – and Howe beside the man deftly handling the tiller bar, barking orders as the pinnace lay over to the wind and accelerated smartly from under *Trusty*'s bows.

Mainwaring watched them go, the pinnace glowing in the amber light, the contrast sudden and stark with the black, shadowed wall of *Trusty*'s side, the brilliant light on the canvas giving it a look of still, curved bronze. Now it was his boat's turn. The foresheet was being hauled in by Lount, the Martha's Vineyard man Sawyer 'swigging' off and hauling taut on the halyard near him. Further aft, Jackman deftly cleared away the mainsheet, Mainwaring noticing that the man had a long rattail queue to match those before his ears, the back one reaching almost to the small of his back down his check shirt. Mainwaring saw now that at the ends of the two small braids before Jackman's ears, two tiny bells glistened and tinkled.

Then his own pinnace was footing out under the over-hang of *Trusty*'s bowsprit and jib-boom, Slade gripping the tiller, and Mainwaring was barking "Down, lads, on the floorboards to windward!" as the craft took the sudden rush of the wind, heeled over with a creaking and popping of sheets and shrouds, and moved away in a rush from the ship, punching steadily through the coppery wavelets. Ahead, the shoreline glowed orange and purple, and Mainwaring was struck by how stark and clear-cut things became in the evening light: the brightened surfaces shone as if firelit, and small panes of glass far inshore beamed painfully bright miniature suns back over the dark water. It was a beautiful and sad time, and Mainwaring always felt a queer mixture of the heat on his face from the low, reddened sun and the chill of the coming night. It was, he remembered, a light he had known on clear September days, beating in against cloudless westerlies past Cape Ann towards Marblehead Neck and Nahant, along the North Shore of Massachusetts, inbound towards Boston with a cargo of fish and rum from Louisbourg. It filled him with a pang of longing for home, for the snug coves and fire-warmed, tidy frame houses nestled among the evergreens, the open hearts and minds so different from the cold, socially exclusive world that had confronted him in the Navy, and to which Edward Vernon had been a rare exception.

It filled him, too, with a deeper longing for Anne Brixham: for her wide, sunlit smile; the laughter and love in her dark, blue-green eyes; the toss of her dark curls against her cheek; the wanton eagerness of her in his arms. She was somewhere, a universe away in the powdered and patched artificiality of London, with her father as he turned his plantation wealth into a kind of purchased social standing. And he could not remember when he had felt so apart from her, or had needed her so much.

Jackman thumped down on the floorboards at Mainwaring's feet, his hands locked like claws on the mainsheet, looking up at the leech of the sail. Then, unexpectedly, he grinned at Mainwaring, propping big, black-soled feet against the leeward gunwale.

"No disrespect, zur. But 'tis a fair wind that gives us a seaman fer t' be an awficer, an' not them lace-edge ponces like in *Royal Oak*, zur."

Mainwaring pursed his lips, bracing his own feet as the pinnace heeled to a gust, boiling along with a roar. "Kind of you to say, Jackman," he said, aware that the informality he had permitted in *Trusty* had likely given the man the thought that he could approach the captain of his ship in such a direct way. "You may be less enthusiastic when we get ashore."

"Not me, zur. Nor the lads. Ye'll steer us true."

Mainwaring caught the looks on the faces of the others. It was clear that there was agreement with what Jackman was saying. To Mainwaring, it brought mixed feelings: a lift, to know that the new men would be willing fighters rather than sullen and reluctant participants; and a pang of responsibility for them. He knew how impossible were the odds facing them.

Lount had finished coiling down the foresheet after giving it a few last tugs, and the pinnace was moving now at close to the best speed it would ever achieve, Mainwaring thought.

"Full and bye, Slade," he said. "Steer after Mr Howe's boat there."

"Aye, aye, zur," replied the wiry little man. "Full an' bye 'tis, sir. Christ, she's a sweet 'un, ain't she, zur?"

"Aye, she is. Now mind you don't sail her under."

"No fear, zur!" grinned Slade, displaying yellowed teeth.

Mainwaring cupped his hands. "MacNeil? You're larboard lookout, for anything from dead ahead to dead astern. Traynor, you're the same to starboard. Sing out if you see so much as a nightsoil pot. Clear?"

"Aye, aye, sir!" came a chorus from forward, both men wedging themselves into places at the foot of the foremast. With the bundle of long sweeps lashed together amidships in a fore-and-aft line atop the thwarts, there was very little room to do anything but hunch down on a seabag in the narrow gap between the thwarts, so that only the heads of the men protruded above the gunwale. Now Forrest, a thickset and powerfully-muscled youth with dark Latin features, and Lount, who was blond and thin like Slade, wrestled themselves around to be able to see aft.

"Sawyer, you and Forrest see to that gun," ordered Mainwaring, pointing to the ugly little one-pound swivel that sat in its strongback post which was set in an opening in the thwart just before the foremast. Held in a yoke-and-pin carriage, the miniature ship's gun could be swung from side to side by the curved iron bar that projected behind it, like a tail. "The tools and box for its rounds were struck in there, for'rard of the strongback. See that it's in order: tools, cartridges, priming wire, priming horn, the lot. Then when you've done that, make sure that both muskets are workable. Keep one for'rard and send one aft here, with a cartridge box. And see each man gets a cutlass."

"Aye, sir!" chirped Sawyer. With a grin at the burly Forrest, who began to struggle out of his burrow, he moved to cast off the lashings on the little gun. It was a vicious-looking object, but suddenly it appeared to Mainwaring to be a ludicrously pathetic weapon with which to engage

134

an anchoured squadron of line-of-battle ships and two fortified batteries.

Dear God, what am I leading them into? Mainwaring's mind said, and for a moment his plan, which had filled him with such excitement and determination, seemed suicidal and childish.

He squinted aft. *Trusty*, so oddly still in the manner of ships seen from small boats that leapt and moved like living creatures, was off the wind, drawing in stately dignity away to the westward and Cap Cépet, glowing in the light like a copper vessel against the dark sea and cobalt sky. Ahead, steering in for the hostile shore, Howe's boat bobbed and curtseyed, so brave and tiny against the looming panorama of the purple-shadowed shore. Hopeless or not, the plan Mainwaring had concocted was under way. He could see *Barb*, exotically Moorish with her huge winging lateen, standing off in the other direction towards Carqueiranne, heeled before the wind, the long pennant and rippling ensign so pretty and delicate that it gave him an odd pang in his chest to see them. *Barb*, too, was turned fire-orange by the exquisite light, and it occurred to Mainwaring that if he had set all these men – and himself – on a course which led to destruction and perhaps death, then the setting for the sacrifice was beautiful.

"Bread, zur?" Jackman was holding out two chunks of heavy, hard-crusted biscuit, and Mainwaring remembered that he had not ordered the hands to their midday meal. He took one of the biscuits and gave the other to Slade.

"Thank you, Jackman. And my apologies to you all. Get some biscuit and beer into each one of you. But a firkin of the latter; no more." Absently he began to tap the biscuit on the wood of the sternsheets until he saw Slade grinning at him.

"No weevils in that, zur. Fresh-baked in Villefranche, 'twas."

Mainwaring grunted. "Still the same damned ship's biscuit," he said, worrying the thing with his teeth. "Christ knows how salt pork and this get us as far as they do."

"Sheer bloody-mindedness, zur," offered Jackman. "Yer true-born Jack, why, 'e wouldn't know what t'do wiv good tucker if 'e 'ad it, zur. Make 'im soft an' womanly, 'twould."

"If you say so, Jackman. But it's still like chewing damned round shot." Mainwaring gnawed at the rock-like biscuit and peered at the shoreline towards which they were sailing. For all that Toulon was the principal harbour of the French Navy in the Mediterranean — and now a key element in the efforts of the Spanish to mount some support for their military in Italy — the waters around it were uncannily empty. The Golfe de Giens, and even more the confined waters of the Grande Rade, were astonishingly vacant, save for a few small lateen-rigged chaloupes, likely fishermen, who were visible as white specks just off Cap Brun. *Trusty* and *Barb* were the only vessels of consequence in view. Perhaps the very reaction Mainwaring had counted on was taking place: seeing the two small warships as picket vessels for an imagined main body of English warships over the horizon, the French and Spanish — merchant-men or naval vessels — were staying at their moorings until it became clear what the English were about.

We are such unpredictable buggers, thought Mainwaring, smiling to himself.

Mainwaring squinted at the bluffs of St Mandrier, looming now above the peach-tinted sails of Howe's boat, perhaps a quarter-league ahead. What watchful eyes were there, ready to send swift couriers galloping round the bay to the inner harbour and the garrison commandant? He reached into the tail pocket of his old linen coat and took out a small leatherbound telescope. Standing with his feet braced wide on the floorboards, he pulled it open and raised it. With the boat's motion it took a moment before he adjusted the flattened image. Briefly he was looking at Howe's boat, seeing Howe squinting back at them as Mainwaring stood. Then his view swept up the Cap Cépet bluffs. Atop the cliff stood a stone lighthouse, the oil-lit lamp feebly visible through the multi-paned glass of the tower's top. But at the foot of the bluffs, the shoreline was empty of buildings and of human figures. Now he could see an indenta-tion or pause in the line of low surf; a place no more than ten yards wide, where the white breakers did not flash. And as the pinnace moved under him, Mainwaring saw the relief of the bluff walls suddenly become clear.

"A cove," he breathed. "Small and shallow, likely. But a cove. How bloody timely!"

He sat down, putting away the little glass. "Steer a point to starboard of that lighthouse on the bluff, Slade. There's a cove below."

"Shelter, zur?" asked Slade.

"Aye," said Mainwaring. "We'll shelter there until night falls. When darkness comes, we'll make our move." He raised his voice. "Sawyer? Mr Howe's watching us. Hold up a sweep for him to see. It's a signal for him to wait and let us come up."

"Aye, aye, sir!" Sawyer wrestled one of the long sweeps into a 'tossed' position, and within minutes Howe's boat had brailed up its sails against their yards and lay waiting in the dark swells for Mainwaring's to approach.

"Deuced empty sea, sir, what?" Howe called as the two craft closed. "Where are the Frogs?"

"They're waiting, James, I assure you!" Mainwaring called back. He pointed inland as his pinnace surged past. "Follow us in. There's a cove where we'll keep out of the way until night falls."

"Aye, aye, sir!" Howe's sails shook open, and his boat was dancing along in Mainwaring's wake.

"Sir?" It was Traynor, ahead in the boat. "Smoke, sir, behind th' 'eadland, there, sir!" The man was pointing with one grimy paw.

Mainwaring narrowed his eyes. The peninsula which jutted out from the shoreline to end at Cap Cépet effectively formed the larger, western arm of the inner and outer harbours. He knew it was called the Presqu'ile de St Mandrier; and as he looked up at the bluffs and the grey stone lighthouse, he could see, off to the left from further inland, a thick pillar of smoke, tinted orange by the setting sun, rising into view and being pushed off to the east by the wind.

"Wot th' deuce be that, zur?" murmured Slade. "Ship afire in th' anchorage, beloike?"

137

Mainwaring shook his head. "Haven't the slightest notion, Slade. But whatever it is, we can hope it helps to direct attention away from us." He fell silent for a moment. The column of smoke was rising, it appeared now, from near where the Eguillette and Balaguier batteries were located. Had some disaster involving a magazine taken place? There had been no report, no muffled blast.

It was also where the line of fishermen's cottages and boatsheds stood; the homes of the kind, helpful people who had done what they could for the survivors of *Diana*'s destruction. The home, too, of the work-aged, gentle woman who had soothed him with her body.

A premonitory shiver ran up Mainwaring's spine as he concentrated his gaze on the little cove towards which they sped.

Dear God, his mind said. *They had so little. Let it not be them.*

"Steady as you go, now, Slade," he said quietly.

The Chevalier Rigaud de la Roche-Bourbon reined in his beautiful white gelding at the dusty corner of the harbourside cart track where it branched to go round the shore to la Seyne or from the shore across to Six-Fours. In the purple, hazy light of the evening he could see along the la Seyne shore the line of little houses that were the dwellings of the traitorous *pêcheurs* who had aided the surviving English. He was a quarter-league or so away, but by standing in his stirrups he could see the flash of white gaiters on the grey-and-blue-clad tiny figures swarming around the little homes; the tiny figures which he knew were that particularly capable company of the *Troupes de la Marine*. They had been waiting, two hours earlier, at the crossroads as Roche-Bourbon had ordered; Jacques had not failed in his duty. And there, Roche-Bourbon had smiled with inner satisfaction at the hard, cruel faces of the musketmen. They would be the kind of scourge he needed.

Now the houses were beginning to leap with fire, and he could hear faintly the hoarse shouts and curses of the soldiery as doors were beaten in and torches thrown into the interiors. Already, the first red-tiled, whitewashed little structure was lost in a column of flame and smoke, and Roche-Bourbon could see the small figures of the fisherman and his family as they were thrust ahead of levelled bayonets in the direction of the Eguillette battery. The cries and screams of the women carried on the air like a shrill counterpoint to the whoosh and crackle of the fire. He saw the husband turn, confronting the soldiery with upraised arms, saw the pink flash of the musket and the fall of the little figure, his family sinking to their knees round him as the faint bark of the musket reached Roche-Bourbon's ears.

"How poignant a scene," he murmured.

A wretched little column of men, women and children was being pushed away from the burning buildings, forced along the shore towards the grey ramparts of the battery. That, too, was according to Jacques' instructions. Roche-Bourbon hoped that Villard, the dull officer of *canonniers-bombardiers* who commanded the battery, had received Roche-Bourbon's letter, ordering him to seize and detain the *enseigne* Saint-Luc De Guimond, and to open his gates for the arrival of the traitorous fishermen. The prospect of questioning the wretches was enjoyable to dwell upon. As was this sight of licking flames leaping up from virtually every small building along the la Seyne shore, producing a peach-tinted column of smoke that boiled hugely up into the evening sky and then drifted off to the east.

Roche-Bourbon's eyes narrowed. A rider was moving along the la Seyne roadway towards him, galloping past the shambling wretches being brutalised by the soldiers. The flash of colour identified the rider as a *cornet* of cavalry; one of the despatch riders relied on to transmit orders round the vast, sprawling dockyard and its defensive system. Within minutes he was galloping closer, and Roche-Bourbon spurred ahead to meet him.

"M'sieu'! M'sieu'!" the *cornet* called, reining in his lathered horse in a dusty jangle of tack. "The English! They are sending in some boats!"

"What do you mean, *boats*?"

"The *enseigne* of the guard at the lighthouse sent word, m'sieu'. There are two small English vessels in the offing, and by their behaviour they appear to be part of a larger force!"

Roche-Bourbon pursed his lips. Only the day before, in the offices of the *amirauté*, he had heard intelligences that the English ships were scattered like sands before the wind, and that the time was ripe for the combined squadrons to sail and reclaim mastery of the Mediterranean. Lead elements of the fleet, a clutch of frigates, were in fact due to put to sea that very night.

"Indeed," he said coolly. "And what of these boats?"

The *cornet* fought with his mount as it danced and chewed the bit.

"Two, m'sieu'! Small boats, only half a dozen men in each. They were dropped off Cépet and appear to be making for the headland, m'sieu'."

Roche-Bourbon sighed. He would not believe for a moment that the English were at sea in force off Toulon; not from what he had heard. And he would let nothing stand in the way of the necessary – and enjoyable – process of questioning the fishermen. There was also the problem of Saint-Luc De Guimond to resolve. Two small boatloads of suicidal English could have no effect on the massed warships of the squadrons, but they might be attempting some kind of annoying devilment that would require opposition. They might, for example, be attempting to disrupt the operation of the lighthouse, and that would cause some difficulties for the ships expected to sail later in the night.

"Very well. What is the *enseigne* doing?"

"He's got six men at the lighthouse, and says that he'll barricade himself inside until help comes, if that's what they're after, m'sieu'."

"Sensible of him," said Roche-Bourbon. "That should hold off any silly attempt to put out the light. The tower is more like a fortress than anything around here. Ride at once to the *corps de garde* on the Baie de Sanary road. Tell the officer there he's to signal the guardboat – mind he knows it's the launch with the four-pounder gun and twenty men – to pull out round St Mandrier and see what

140

the English are up to. Tell him as well he is to send that half-company of dragoons to gallop to the lighthouse directly and see if your *enseigne* is in trouble. Do you understand all that?"

"Yes, m'sieu'."

"Then be off with you," said Roche-Bourbon.

The *cornet* slapped a gloved hand to his tricorne in salute and spurred his trembling mount into a gallop along the harbour road.

Roche-Bourbon smiled to himself. Those measures should, he thought, provide the rash Englishmen in their little boats with a disagreeable surprise.

He eyed the tall column of smoke, darker-tinted now as the sun began to slip behind the horizon, and the pathetic figures who were being pushed towards the grey mass of the Eguillette battery by Jacques' men.

And now for more agreeable work, he thought, kicking the white gelding into a trot.

7

"Brail up, fore and main! Lively, now!" Mainwaring called. Hands seized the brail lines, and the fore and mainsails crumpled up. Barely fifty yards off the narrow, cliff-sided cove, the pinnace lost way and lay rocking in the dark swells.

"Cast off those oar lashings, there. We'll need only two. Jackman, put one out to starboard. Lount, you've a sturdy look; put the other out to larboard."

"Aye, zur!" growled Jackman. With a deft slash of his knife he cut the tarred marline that had bound the long oars together, and with much grunting and banging – and jocular curses and encouragement from the other men in the boat until Mainwaring cut them short – the two men wrestled a long oar each from under the snarl of sheets and gear, thumping them into place in their thole pins.

"Handsomely now will do it, lads," said Mainwaring. "No need to break a blade. Give way together.' Slade, steer us for the cove opening. Mind those damned rocks to starboard, there."

"Aye, zur," said Slade. "Damned narrow cove, zur, ain't it?"

"It is. And a good place to sit out of the way of the French until dark. Steady, there, Lount. Take your stroke from Jackman." Mainwaring glanced over his shoulder, seeing that Howe's boat had brailed up its own canvas and was stroking in after them.

Mainwaring peered ahead. The grey-white rock bluffs rose sheer from the water, it seemed; there was not even the hint of a beach or shelf. High above, at the edge of the drop, stood the lighthouse tower, cut from the same stone, the roofing on the glassed light chamber the same red tile as the houses of Toulon. As the boat edged in towards the cleft, the slap and wash of the dark swells against the rock face on either side of its mouth became louder. It was fortunate that no appreciable swell was running, as—

"Sir!" came a voice from one of the men in the bows. "By the lighthouse, sir! Musketmen!'

Mainwaring snapped his head up. In the narrow musket-slit windows of the tower's first level, figures appeared; figures that extended out glistening musket barrels. In a moment Mainwaring's boat would be in under the curve of the bluff, safe from musket shot. But not so Howe.

"Pull, lads! Pull! Get us in!" Mainwaring barked, and the two men at the oars pulled with furious vigour. Within seconds they were gliding in through the narrow cleft into the sheer-sided, echoing little cove that seemed like nothing so much as a cave open to the sky.

There was a distant popping sound and Mainwaring realised the musketmen in the lighthouse had fired. He spun on his seat to see the spatter of several miniature geysers from the flying lead shot bracket Howe's boat, as his men pulled with equal fury for the inlet. In the next instant, they too were in, gliding up alongside Mainwaring's boat, the oarsmen gasping over their looms.

"Hold water, Jackman!" ordered Mainwaring. "Sawyer? Get our anchor line over the side, if you can clear that foul I see there."

"All done, sir. Drop the hook, sir?"

"Yes. Jackman, Lount, get your oars shipped inboard." Mainwaring glanced over at Howe. "Close call, Mr Howe. Glad you weren't hit."

Howe grinned. "No more than we are, sir!" From forward in his boat, one of the burly Welshmen, Evans, put their anchor over the side, carefully paying out the line as the cast-iron hook sank into the clear, dark water.

"What's the depth, Sawyer?" asked Mainwaring.

"Damn' near forty feet, sir. Wouldn't a-thought it."

"Nor I. Leave the rode fairly short." Mainwaring looked at Howe, the boats now riding a few feet apart. "Well, James, it appears someone knows we're here. Lighthouse keepers don't usually deliver volleys of musketry."

Howe nodded. "I think it was inevitable, sir. Every eye on the coast likely saw us coming in. Any change of plan, sir?"

"Essentially, no. We'll wait until dark – unless those gentlemen above find a means to get at us – and then row in round the headland. Hopefully the buggers won't notice us in the dusk. Thin enough, I know." He looked at the waiting, listening faces in both boats. "You'd best get into some biscuit, all of you. And we'll broach the small beer in moderation, Mr Howe."

"Aye, aye, sir!" said Howe, as his men exchanged grins. "Lookouts, sir?"

"Indeed. Set your lads to watch for the first half-glass. We'll take the next, and then it should be dark enough. Keep someone's eyes overhead all the while, as well; I wouldn't put it past the Frogs to roll rocks down on our heads, if they realise we're in here and not continuing along inshore."

"Sir," said Howe.

Mainwaring scanned the bluffs overhead. He was distinctly uncomfortable sitting in the little inlet, for all that the virtually unscalable bluffs were hiding them from direct view – and presumably direct attack – from the French above. But sooner or later the enemy *would* respond more directly. Picket vessels in the offing were one thing; boatloads of English up to no good on the shoreline were another. Mainwaring knew he had only a small window of time before the French would be upon them, one way or another. He looked at the dark shadows rising slowly up the walls of the bluffs. There was perhaps forty-five minutes of real light left, and there would be a period of half-light after that. Would the darkness come in time to let them slip away before the French found them? He looked up again, musing that a few exploratory grenades in the hands of grenadiers would wreak havoc in the two pinnaces. It would not take much imagination on the part of the French to—

"Sir!" It was Williams, the other Welshman in Howe's boat. "Listen, sir! Oarlocks, look you!"

The men in both boats froze into sudden stillness. Even over the rustle of the wind and the slap-lap of the waves against the inlet-mouth rocks, the sound was clear: the distant creak-thump, creak-thump of heavy sweeps in oarlocks.

"Christ, zur. Sounds like a bleedin' galley!" breathed Slade.

"Keep silent!" hissed Mainwaring. The sound grew, echoing off the bluffs above them. There was little doubt what it was: a large, heavily-manned rowing craft, the steady rhythm marking it almost certainly as naval. It had the sound of an armed longboat, probably a guardboat or ship's boat. Hunting, and very likely hunting for them.

It was time to act.

"Mr Howe!" called Mainwaring in a low, penetrating voice. "Clear away your swivel and muskets! Prime and load. Put one hand ready to break out the anchor, one on the gun, the rest with oars in their locks, ready to pull like the devil! Quickly, now!"

Their eyes wild in sudden excitement as Howe repeated Mainwaring's orders, Howe's men threw aside their half-gnawed biscuit and began frantic preparations. But Mainwaring had already turned to his own boat, his voice low and strong in controlled urgency.

"Listen carefully, lads. Mark what I say, for your lives. Sawyer, prime and load the swivel, double shot it, and ready your match. MacNeil, prime and load the muskets, an' lay 'em on to either side of the swivel. Forrest, heave us short on the hook, and break it out the instant I tell you. The rest of you, for everyone except Sawyer, get an oar in each lock. Now, *out oars!*"

Working in quick, tight-lipped silence, the men prepared the pinnace, their faces suddenly pale and set as they wrestled the oars into their thole pins as quietly as possible while Sawyer and MacNeil worked at their weapons in efficient frenzy with cartridge and ramrod. Mainwaring glanced towards the inlet mouth, hearing the other craft's noise louder now, voices audible over the rumble of the oars. In the next instant both pinnaces were ready, the men at the oars with their blades held clear of the water, waiting to dip and pull; the anchors hove short, the men gripping their lines with their eyes on Mainwaring, ready to tug them free; the brails tightened to keep the sails gathered safely out of the way; and behind the two murderous little swivels, Sawyer and, in Howe's boat, Williams hunched with

145

smouldering portfire in hand, both men having managed somehow in the quick chaos to light the impregnated match with their flint strikers kept in the gunboxes.

Mainwaring cupped his hands to direct his low voice to Howe's ears. "Keep your bows on the opening, James," he whispered harshly. "Now, lads; break out both anchors and get 'em inboard! Give way, Mr Howe! Handsomely, now! No noise!"

With the oar blades of both boats dipping slowly, the two craft edged towards the inlet mouth, where still nothing was visible. Mainwaring's heart was thumping in his very throat, it seemed, but he kept his expression deliberately impassive, aware of the taut, worried faces of the men turned towards him as they rowed.

"Stroke . . . stroke. Gently, now, Lount . . . stroke. Take your rhythm from Jackman . . . stroke . . . "

The boats moved out, side by side. The inlet mouth still gaped empty but the creak-thump of the heavy sweeps continued. And the voices, clearly now, shouting questions in French. To whom? Lookouts above on the bluffs? Other boats behind? The thought of a flotilla of heavily-armed guardboats sent a chill through Mainwaring. The two English craft would be virtually blown out of the water by the storm of shot. What a fool he had been to—

"*There*, sir!" burst out Howe in the other boat.

As Mainwaring stared, the prow of a heavy naval long-boat inched into view, bows burdened with an enormous-looking truck gun on a rail platform, men in a mix of seamen's dress and the grey and blue of the *Troupes de la Marine* packed in it. The two English boats were no more than twenty feet from the inlet mouth; the French longboat was no more than twenty feet beyond it, in full broadside view. It was virtually point-blank range.

"Now, lads!" barked Mainwaring. "*Fire!*"

The portfires arced down as one, and both swivel guns fired within a split-second of each other, the reports deafening in the enclosed inlet, the sharp bangs painful and unexpectedly stunning. Two clouds of smoke, almost the height of the pinnaces' masts, pushed out ahead of the guns, blotting out the view of the longboat until the wind began to shed the clouds away.

"*Pull for 'em lads!*" roared Mainwaring. "*Pull*, you—!"

With a cry, Jackman and the others threw themselves against the oars, the water alongside churning suddenly to froth, the pinnace leaping ahead into the smoke. More sharp flashes and bangs sounded as the gunners took up the muskets and fired, Sawyer pitching his back to MacNeil for reloading and then moving with catlike speed to sponge and reload the swivel as the boat rushed in.

"Stroke! Stroke!" Mainwaring's voice was hoarse with strain, sounding over the rhythmic splash of the oars, the grunts of his men, and the cries and screams now audible through the smoke ahead.

Suddenly the boat burst out of the smoke, and the longboat was before them, a huge craft, lapstreaked white hull slewing round in the water as sweeps trailed in disarray, the gunwales crowded with fierce-featured men struggling to bring muskets to bear, their shouts and curses mingling with the horrid screams of wounded men who threshed about amidst their fellows in dreadful closeness. Then the two swivels fired again, almost as one, the reports ear-splitting, the smoke billowing out to turn the longboat into a dark, nightmarish shape echoing with shrieks and cries. A quick, uneven series of pink flashes dazzled Mainwaring, blasts sounding in the same half-second, and he realised that some Frenchmen had fired their muskets as balls hummed by him – again, that curious, low bumblebee hum – a hand-sized fragment of the gunwale just ahead of Mainwaring's hand leaping suddenly into the air and whirring past his face.

In the next instant, they were at the longboat, the cloaking, reeking cloud of gunsmoke turning all into a confused jumble of black, struggling forms and shadows. The pinnaces struck the longboat's side and slewed round alongside it, grinding together as Mainwaring felt a blow on his shoulder and was propelled in a fall across both gunwales into an indescribable mêlée of cursing, struggling men and the thump and clink of deadly encounter. Somehow he was on his knees on a clear length

147

of thwart in the French longboat, a slick patch of dark scarlet spreading over it. A musket blast tore at his head, the flash seemingly in front of his eyes, and then he was clutching behind him, miraculously feeling under his hands the heavy cutlass he had put on the thwart beside him — was he still in his *own* boat? — and then a grey-coated figure rose up amidst the struggling mass no more than two feet from him, bayonet-tipped musket drawn far back for the killing lunge at Mainwaring, the dark eyes wild in a sallow, thin-cheeked face. With a strange growl in his throat Mainwaring felt his own body surge forward and he stood, his arm bringing the cutlass down in a savage overhand cut, and he fell on to both knees, feeling as he did so the cutlass striking home with a blow that sent pain shooting through his wrist. His opponent screamed, the musket falling across Mainwaring's back, the cutlass twisting in Mainwaring's grip as the man fell away. Mainwaring felt the cutlass torn from his hand, and then someone held the shoulder of his coat and was pulling him to his feet, and the French musket with its bayonet was in his hands. A French seaman was coming at him across two thwarts, teeth bared and a strange, scimitar-looking blade arrowing for Mainwaring's throat. He put up the musket to the guard position, and then the body of a heavy Frenchman, shrieking as he clawed at a horrid cut across his face, cannoned into Mainwaring, sending him sprawling headlong into the sternsheets of the longboat atop two gore-spattered bodies of French seamen. With the musket still in his hands, he wrestled himself to his knees in time to see a slim French officer sitting behind the tiller coolly level a small Miquelet-lock pistol at Mainwaring's head and pull the trigger. The pan flashed, but only the pan. Off balance, Mainwaring lunged with all his strength with the musket. It arrowed the bayonet into the officer's chest with a sharp impact that shook loose Mainwaring's grip on the weapon. As Mainwaring fell in shin-banging awkwardness at the Frenchman's feet, the latter opened wide, astonished eyes, his mouth making fishlike gulping movements until a pulse of blood emerged from one corner and he fell over the side, his eyes still wide in astonishment as he slithered over the gunwale.

Mainwaring struggled to get to his feet and turn, only to lose his balance and sit down heavily on the bodies of the two dead seamen. But he could see: the smoke was gone, now, drifting to leeward. And the fight was over. The boats drifted, all three locked together. Several bodies floated in the water about them. The boats themselves were full of bodies, some still, some struggling to rise, jammed together in every conceivable contortion and angle. But now, here and there, some of Howe's men and his own were rising to their feet, bloody cutlasses in hand, faces blackened or blood-streaked, eyes staring round them and their chests heaving as they gasped for breath. No French were standing, and for a moment Mainwaring thought they had all been killed until he saw several men hunched round the bow gun, hatless and dishevelled, their hands raised in surrender.

Mainwaring got to his feet, his throat suddenly dry and burning. His hand hurt from the wrench of the cutlass being torn from it.

"Mr Howe?" he croaked. "James? Where are you?"

"Here, sir." Howe was in his boat, in the act of tossing the corpse of a shirtless French seaman over the side. "Are you all right, sir?"

"Yes. See what's happened to your lads," said Mainwaring. "Traynor? Can you use that arm? Help me get these chaps off poor MacNeil."

It took fifteen ghastly minutes to put right the chaos of the fight; ghastly because of the tight, awkward proximity of the bodies and carnage the savage struggle had produced. It was a grim enough toll. Of a crew of some twenty, only four of the Frenchmen were alive, and one of those was so seriously wounded in the chest that he would likely die within minutes. The men of the two pinnaces had fallen on the French with such ferocity that it astonished Mainwaring; at least three of the French corpses were headless, and the others bore bone-deep cuts from the cutlasses that spoke of blows given with savage force. One by one, the bodies were pitched over the

149

side until the drifting boats were surrounded by floating corpses. Mainwaring felt ill and was trembling uncontrollably. He tried to hide that from the men, and to avoid looking too closely at the staring, sightless faces that drifted past him.

"Sir?" It was Howe, on his hands and knees in his pinnace, his face showing like a blood-streaked puppet's over the gunwale. "We've lost two planks in the boat, sir. She'll go down awash in a few minutes." Mainwaring suddenly became aware of several men bailing frantically with anything to hand, and that Howe sloshed about when he moved.

"Damn. Very well. You'll have to leave it, James. Is the French boat intact?"

"Aye, sir!" It was the Welshman, Evans, standing in the boat's sternsheets. "Few splinters off the gunn'ls an' thwarts, see, sir."

"Casualties, Mr Howe?"

"Williams took a bayonet thrust in one arm. And MacNeil, there, got knocked silly by a ball. Lost his bonnet, but all he'll have is a headache, by the look of him. Any on that side, sir?"

Mainwaring looked at the slumped, exhausted men that had ended the fight in his pinnace. "Not a mark on this lot." He coughed, his throat dry. "We'll not be so lucky again, James."

"Zur?" It was Slade, kneeling in the bows of the boat, forward of the swivel strongback. "We ain't so lucky, beggin' yer pardon, zur."

"How so?"

"The stem, zur. Shot clean through. First push on 'er, even a breakin' wave, an' she'll give way."

Mainwaring glanced at the bluffs, and saw that the clutch of boats were still obscured, still out of sight under the cliff wall, to anyone watching above. They would not have seen what happened.

"Quickly, lads!" barked Mainwaring, purpose flaring in his mind. "Strike your gear into the French boat! Muskets and cutlasses as well! Mr Howe?"

"Sir?"

150

"Out of that boat, you and the men with you, before it gives way under you! We're taking the French boat. But you'll need something else!" He pointed to the floating corpses.

"Not sure I follow, sir," said Howe.

"Get as many of the lads into French uniform as can wear 'em, James. Strip 'em off the prisoners, and these dead wretches if you have to!" He spun on the men nearest him. "Slade, Sawyer! Lount, you as well. You're about the right size to get into French uniforms. Wet or bloody, do it! Quickly, now!"

Howe was tugging a grey coat from the arms of a body slumped in the after part of his pinnace, his face a tight-lipped mixture of determination and revulsion. "Going to masquerade as the French, sir?" he asked, through clenched teeth.

"Aye, James! But move smartly if you want to live! After that fusillade, any watchers up there will be looking for evidence that their boat won. We mustn't disappoint them!"

It was a sombre and distasteful business, stripping the limp bodies in the longboat – or pulling back in one of the floating dead alongside – and clambering awkwardly into the cluttered, crowded longboat was made the more difficult by the smears of blood on gunwales and thwarts; but with Mainwaring and Howe urging them on, the men found enough coats and tricornes to masquerade as the mix of seamen and marines that had formed the French crew. A quick sluicing down of the bloody stains reduced the horror of the boat's interior somewhat, and with an extraordinary amount of banging and cursing the stores and gear from the awash pinnaces were transferred into the longboat.

Mainwaring looked grimly around. They were all in the French boat now, he himself with Slade and Howe in the sternsheets, the white Bourbon ensign rippling on its crown-headed staff above him. Aside from a few heavy gouges and splinterings, the longboat was in good condition. Of the two pinnnaces, one was now fully sunk to its gunwales and drifted forlornly alongside, the limp forms of the French dead scattered about and rocking on the swells. The surviving French prisoners were pushed roughly into the other pinnace, and were told through gestures to keep down out of sight and bail for their lives.

Mainwaring shuddered. Again he felt a wave of disgust, ill and sick with it all. But they had to carry on.

"Out sweeps, lads," he croaked. "Two to a sweep. Roundly, there, now!"

With enormous effort, the longboat's sweeps had been untangled and set back into their thole pins. Now they were thrust out, ready to dip, the blades hovering above the swells, the men's eyes on Mainwaring.

He looked up. They were just visible now to the lighthouse, and his heart leaped suddenly in his throat. In a long row of blue and silver, the figures of heavily-armed dragoons, dismounted and ready to volley, lined the crest. They were still within dangerous musket range.

"Steady, now, all of you!" said Mainwaring in a low, penetrating voice. "Remember, you've just won a fight against English interlopers. Haul cheerfully, now. Give way, *together*! Call the stroke, Slade!"

The men bent forward, the great sweeps dipped, and the heavy boat began to turn back towards the harbour as Mainwaring nodded to Howe to put the long tiller over.

Mainwaring looked up at the line of dragoons, seeing the tack of their waiting horses glinting in the dying light of the sun. Abruptly he stood, pulled off his tricorne and waved it back and forth over his head.

For a moment the line was motionless, and in a brief spasm of panic Mainwaring expected a ripple of pink flashes and a hail of musket balls to cut him down where he stood. Then the line wavered and shook as the dragoons raised their flintlock carbines over their heads, doffing their tricornes, and sent a ragged cheer echoing down the steep bluffs.

"Thank Christ!" breathed Mainwaring through his teeth as the men before him grinned at one another over the looms of the sweeps. Mainwaring looked ahead to where the high bluffs curved round to larboard, the waters of the Grande Rade opening before them as the longboat moved in.

Now, the narrow opening of the boom-defended gap between l'Eguillette and le Mourillon was visible: through it *Diana* had sailed to die; and out of it he had brought *San Pablo*, to live.

"There's your course, James," said Mainwaring evenly. "Steer for the gap. Keep the stroke handsome, Slade. Handsomely!"

He glanced over his shoulders at the slowly retreating lighthouse. The dragoons had remounted, and were galloping in tiny, silent pairs back away from the bluffs. By a fortunate turn of events, Mainwaring and his men had managed to escape from the first deadly pincer of the French defences. But their ruse would not last long; the failure of the longboat to report would arouse suspicion, followed by quick action. Mainwaring would have to strike swiftly before the vast resources of the garrison and the anchored squadrons came to bear on them.

"Stroke . . . stroke . . . use yer backs, lads . . . stroke . . . " Slade's voice was steady. Mainwaring made a mental note that the wiry little Cockney deserved confirmation in his acting rating as boatswain's mate.

Mainwaring saw the eyes of the men on his, concern mixed with trust visible in some faces. He kept his expression calm and his voice steady as he looked back at them.

"You've done well, lads. Luck is still on our side. We'll share a tot after this is done on how we put the fear of Englishmen into this particular clutch of Dons and their Froggy allies. Aye, lads?"

"Aye, zur! That we will, zur!" came the growl from several throats.

With the heavy sweeps thrashing out a slow rhythm, the longboat moved slowly through the deepening purple dusk towards the gap. The twin grey humps of the fortified batteries seemed huge now in the last of the failing light, and Mainwaring stared at their walls in inner despair.

My God, what have I done to us all? he thought. But he was careful to keep his face a mask of calm concentration, for all that his stomach was gripped in a knot of fear.

* * *

John McCallum stumped up and down the deck of *Barb* in an increasingly foul mood of anxiety while his first mate, a slim Cornishman named Trethewy, peered inshore with the help of an enormous brass-bound telescope.

"Can ye tell what the devil is going on?" McCallum snorted. "Och, if only I had my eyes the way they once were!"

"I think I've got it now, sir. That gunfire was Lieutenant Mainwaring and his boats attacking a French guardboat, sir. But I think they've taken it and – yes, sir! They're using it to stand in further, sir! They've abandoned the pinnaces!"

"They've *what*?"

"Aye, sir! And it looked like some of 'em have put on French uniform, sir!"

"Are ye sure they weren't taken by the French?" asked McCallum, his one eye clouded with concern.

"No, sir. I can make out Lieutenant Mainwaring in the sternsheets, and his first lieutenant, James Howe, beside him." Trethewy lowered the glass. "There were a good hundred French horsemen on the bluffs above 'em, sir, but they seem to have ridden off."

"Eh? Ridden off? How in hell—?" McCallum stopped, and moved to the shoreward rail. He banged a heavy fist down on the painted wood. "French uniforms? By Christ, I know what he's up to!"

"Sir?"

"They're masqueradin' as the French! He's pulling in an' hopin' tae fool the Frogs into thinkin' that he's the guardboat pullin' back in!" McCallum shook his head in admiration. "No lack of courage, b'God. No lack!"

Trethewy slid the long glass closed. "D'ye think he'll do it, sir?"

McCallum snorted. "That all depends on what it is we – or he – intends to do, Mr Trethewy. He was to signal us by burning off a flare o' cartridge powder when t' send in our own boat o' lads to help him. An' I can see ye've got Fulham and his cutthroats ready in the waist, there. Well, ye'd best tell them t' stand down a wee, for I've no idea what that young hellion's up to. In French rig, he could be headin' for the guts o' th' harbour, and Christ knows

154

what we could do for him then!" He spat vigorously into the sea. "Mind ye keep a double watch on the shore, Mr Trethewy. All through the night. An' give a glass to each of them. They're to watch for that flare and call me the same tick o' the clock they see it!"

"Aye, aye, sir," said Trethewy. "Fall off, sir?"

"Aye," grumbled McCallum. "Beat back an' forth twixt the headlands, and wave flags out at *Trusty* there from time to time. That young lad Pellowe will enjoy himself wavin' back." He looked up at the darkening sky. "Nightfall comes quickly. Ye'll heave to, Mr Trethewy, when ye canna see the masthead pennant. With this wind and the offshore set o' the current, she'll be safe enough. But keep the watch on deck an' the doubled lads aloft, mind!"

"Aye, aye, sir," said Trethewy, as the burly Scot turned and clumped down the waistdeck ladder. Then Trethewy opened the long glass again and fixed it on the rapidly-darkening shore. He could just make out, now, the blob of the longboat's hull against the dark mass of the shoreline that rose to Mount Faron, looming black against the dusk.

"And good luck to *you*, Lieutenant Mainwaring," said Trethewy, under his breath. "I think ye'll be needing it!"

The darkness had fallen, a purple mantle over the sea and the land, and Mainwaring brought the longboat round the headland and in towards the inner gap. The shore twinkled now with dim, warm pinpoints of lantern light, small spots and diadems of life against the blackness, sending waving rivulets across the water to the longboat. Here and there in the broad inner harbour, moving lights attested to small boats under way. Fishing boats, Mainwaring thought. Or were they other guardboats looking for their own?

"Way enough," said Mainwaring. "Rest on your oars."

With a sigh the men hauled the heavy sweeps in over both gunwales and slumped over them.

"Slade, go for'rard. I'll take the helm. See if you and Sawyer can find what it takes to get that bow gun working."

"Aye, zur!" The small man stepped nimbly over James Howe's form and made off forward over the thwarts, between the shoulders of the slumped, resting men.

155

Mainwaring gripped the tiller and looked at Howe, whose pale face was clearly etched with concern in the half-light.

"How do the hands seem, James?" asked Mainwaring quietly.

"Still willing, but tired and uncertain, sir. They've been at the sweeps for over an hour, and aren't sure where we are or what you've planned, sir. Might help them to know."

"I appreciate that, James. And in a moment I'll tell them. We're damned lucky to have got in this far. No doubt the guardboat was meant to show some kind of lantern. We'll not keep up this masquerade much longer."

"What *do* ye intend to do, sir?"

"Initially, to let the lads rest a bit more. Those damned sweeps are like trees. Then—" He pointed inshore.

"Not sure I follow, sir."

"Sorry, James. Look ahead there, just fine on the larboard bow. Can you see that pair of lanterns, reddish-coloured, one above the other?"

Howe peered. "Aye, sir," he said, after a moment. "They're faint, but—" Then he paused. "I remember them, sir! The night we brought *San Pablo* out, those lights were burning on the battery to starboard! The one that didn't fire at us!"

"Exactly. It's the Eguillette battery, James. I've been steering for it since before dark. D'ye recall where we were kept prisoner, in the guardhouse?"

"Aye, sir, I do. Where that Frenchman released us."

"Yes. That was about two hundred yards inshore along from the battery walls. Now, I recall no entry port on the side we saw, do you?"

Howe thought. "No, sir. Just recall grey stone ramparts, about twenty feet high, with guns in embrasures facing on to the harbour and the gap. And a flagstaff."

"That's my memory as well. The entry port is likely on the landward side, round from where we could see. But did you notice the jetty, just at the battery itself? Not the one where we found the boat."

"No, sir. Was there one?"

"There was," said Mainwaring. "And that's where we're going, James." He paused. "I mean to take that battery."

Howe gaped at him. And then, unexpectedly, grinned. "No half measures, sir?"

"No half measures, James." Mainwaring reached beneath the thwart and pulled out a heavy little cask. "This is likely good French brandy, or I'm a newt. Broach it and give the lads a good tot, James. The darkness will cloak us well enough for a while. Let us drift. Then we'll tell the lads, when the brandy's revived 'em."

"Aye, aye, sir!" said Howe, and cupped his hands to call Slade aft again.

Twenty minutes later, Edward Mainwaring stood in the sternsheets of the big longboat, feeling the tot of brandy he had drunk in one gulp from Slade's battered tin cup glowing like a charcoal fire in his stomach. Beside him, Howe was thumping the bung into the little cask, and the Dianas — Mainwaring still thought of the men in those terms — were wiping their mouths with the backs of their hands, tucking away leathern and tin cups into their seabags and grinning at one another and at Mainwaring with considerably more spirit and readiness.

Mainwaring looked quickly round. The boat was drifting half-way from the St Mandrier peninsula to the opening of the Petite Rade, just off the mouth of a secondary cove called the Baie du Lazaret. The two dull lights of the Eguillette could still be seen ahead, the lanterns of the anchored squadrons within the inner harbour just visible over the dark, unlit mass of the other battery, le Mourillon. Why, thought Mainwaring, was there no lantern on le Mourillon? To prevent the giving of a navigational marker to any vessel attempting just such a penetration as they were undertaking?

"Pay attention this way, lads," said Mainwaring, and the low whispering in the boat faded away. "Ye'll want to know what we intend to do. I guarantee ye'll have a bellyful of fighting from it!" He pointed forward. "D'ye see those lights in red, one above the other? They mark one of the batteries that guard the inner-harbour mouth. I've no idea how many men are operating it, or how many guns there be on its walls. But my intention is to take it!" He paused, hearing the sharp intake of breath. "And I need to know if ye'll stand with me. It'll be a hard fight, and perhaps a bloody one. But will ye do it?"

There was a moment of silence as the men exchanged glances. In the darkness Mainwaring could not make out their expressions. Was he asking too much of them?

The voices burst out as one. "Aye, sir! We're wiv ye, zur!"

Mainwaring nodded, relief and a kind of pride surging in him. "Well said! Well said, all of you. But it'll be our cutlasses against their muskets, lads. Ye'll need to close with 'em—"

"Zur?" It was Slade, forward by the bow gun again. "Beggin' yer pardon, zur. But me'n Sawyer jes' got these two gun chests open, zur, an' they be a-chock wiv French muskets an' cartridge boxes in one ov 'em, zur! 'Nough fer most o' th' lads, near like, zur!"

"Good Christ!" murmured Mainwaring. "And what of the other gun chest?"

"Tools fer th' bow gun, zur. An' a bucket wiv twelve cartridge fer it, all bound up wiv th' shot."

"Stroke of luck, sir," said Howe, beside Mainwaring.

"More than you know, James," said Mainwaring wonderingly. Again, a kind of inexplicable good fortune had taken place, as seemed so often to happen when Mainwaring most needed it. But he shook the thought away. To dwell on the luck would be to end it.

"Slade, you and Sawyer issue out those muskets. See if they've all got good flints, mind. And pass a cartridge box to each man who gets a musket. Keep 'em by you in the boat, lads, ready to hand when you need 'em. And each of you, keep your cutlass to hand as well. Once you're in close quarters a blade will serve you better than a musket ball!" He spat over the side. "Have I forgotten anything, Mr Howe?"

"No, sir. Now we just do it, sir."

"Quite right," grinned Mainwaring. He was glad of the reckless spirit he could sense in the first lieutenant. They would all need some of that spirit if they were to live through the next hours. But it startled Mainwaring that in place of his earlier fear he now felt only a burning resolve to inflict as much damage for as long as possible until the immense resources of the French overcame them. Whether that meant a virtual sentence of death he would leave to Providence to decide. It occurred to him that other than the love of Anne Brixham, there was little in life in which he had a stake; the Royal Navy, with the exception of Edward Vernon, was led by men such as Mathews and his officers who made it seem an institution largely indifferent to a man of Mainwaring's colonial background; his lack of standing was clear in the increasingly evident social ranking that was more and more the norm in the Navy's wardrooms. Where had gone that jocular, rough service in which a lieutenant's qualifications were a good 'jaw' of tobacco, a rattan, and a string of oaths? It was, instead, the trust and loyalty of the men – like Slade and Sawyer, grinning at one another in the bows of the boat as they hefted muskets while almost certain death waited for them ashore – that in the end held him to his sense of duty. There was a larger issue of an unspoken loyalty to a Crown and a nation that still stood for the concepts and principles that Mainwaring held dear, although in the venal atmosphere of the times it was difficult to keep sight of that commitment. He saw no conflict or inconsistency as yet with the principles of an Englishman's freedom and the place of Crown and Parliament as guarantors of that freedom, and the vast, forested seashore of the New World from which he sprang, with all its insistence on individual merit and self-reliance. Loyalty to those principles was an engine that drove Mainwaring far more than he would have been prepared to admit.

"Well, then," said Mainwaring. He licked his lips, and settled his tricorne more firmly on his head. "We've about a twenty-minute pull into the shore. Pray God we're not challenged. *Out sweeps! Give way together!*"

With a will the Dianas thrust the heavy sweeps out over the side, and to Mainwaring's count, began the laborious pull for the dark shore. But all eyes, shining with excited readiness, were on his own as he stood on the sternsheets,

159

the tiller bar in the small of his back, steering for the red lanterns that glimmered in the distance.

The men soon settled into a rhythm, set by the redoubtable Jackman and Lount at the stroke sweep; Mainwaring stopped counting and scanned the dark waters for any hint of threatening movement as the creak-thump sounded in regular rhythm. There was none.

As if he read his thoughts, Howe murmured beside him, "There really is a chance we've fooled them, sir. After the fight they may have reported the guardboat pulling victoriously back in. The boat may have had a circuit that lasts several hours, which is why they haven't sent someone after us, sir."

"You may be right, James. But there was an inner-harbour guardboat moving about when we boarded *San Pablo*. It showed a light, I'm damned certain of it. Can you remember what it was?"

"Sorry, sir."

"All right. Likely better off mucking about like this in the dark, in any event." Mainwaring peered into the night to larboard, intensely conscious of the dip and splash of the sweeps and the gurgle of water round the rudder. There was something large looming on the shoreline against the stars. That was likely the small Balaguier battery. It was dark, and he watched it silently as the longboat slipped past until it lay on the quarter. A minute or two more . . .

"There it is, sir!" hissed Howe.

Abruptly, the horizon line ahead of them was broken by another huge mass, far larger than the little Balaguier battery: high, crenellated walls, with overhung *guérites*, the odd, miniature towerlike stone sentry housings, at the corners. And high atop, a flagstaff carried – surprisingly, for it was night – an idling white Bourbon ensign. There were the two red lights, visible now as red-tinted lanterns slung on a line over the walls. A few other lanterns winked like distant candles along the ramparts.

Mainwaring cupped his hands. "For'rard, there! Slade! Can ye see the jetty at the foot of the place?" he called, in a hoarse whisper.

The Cockney was almost invisible in the gloom ahead in the boat, but his whisper came floating back.

"Aye, zur! A touch t' starb'd! Well! She's dead ahead, zur! Thirty yards, no more!"

"Way enough!" hissed Mainwaring. "Ship your sweeps, lads, but quietly!"

With enormous care, the men raised the dripping sweeps clear of the water and lifted them inboard on the thwarts with only the barest of muffled thumps to mar the silence. The boat drifted in, Mainwaring steering now on the bearing of the light he had taken when Slade's whisper had come. Mainwaring's heart was beating so hard within his chest that he was sure Howe and the others could hear it. Christ in heaven, would they never be there?

"Jetty, sir!" came a low call from forward. "Larboard side!"

"Fend off, there!" croaked Mainwaring. "Sawyer, the bow line, and Lount, the stern! *Roundly*, lads!"

A splintery jetty materialised out of the dark, the boat thumping in beside it. No sentry paced it, and no challenge or high-held lantern met their arrival. Sawyer and Lount went over the side like monkeys, their bare feet silent on the planking of the jetty. With deft, sure hands, the men passed the longboat's lines through ringbolts fitted to the jetty planking.

"Out of the boat, quickly, lads! Take your weapons. And not a sound!" Gathering up his cutlass, Mainwaring stepped carefully from the sternsheets on to the broad planking of the jetty. He crammed his tricorne down firmly on his head, looked up at the dark mass of the fortification, and then moved to the close knot of dark figures, the muskets picking up gleams of light from the lanterns, the men's eyes white as he moved to them.

"Pay attention, now, lads. Any of you still in French uniform? Strip it off, then. We'll fight as we really are!" Mainwaring sensed Howe at his shoulder. "Mr Howe, see each man has brought a cartridge box for his musket, and has his cutlass in the back of his belt."

"Done that, sir," said Howe quietly. "Slade says the flints are all proper as well. You're the only one without one, sir."

"Very well. Sawyer—?" began Mainwaring.

"All ready with'un fer ye, sir." The Vineyarder materialised out of the dark.

Mainwaring pushed back his linen coat, thrusting his cutlass into the broad belt that held up his duck trousers. He took the black leather pouch on its buff belt and slung it over his left shoulder so that it hung behind his right hip. A quick lift of the flap showed a full load of thirty paper cartridges in their wooden block.

"How thorough of the bloody French!" he murmured.

The musket was the familiar light, three-banded French infantry musket Mainwaring had seen and fired before. A rapid check of the flint in its jaw, of the frizzen spring, and a gentle touch of the ramrod down the barrel verified the weapon was in working order.

"All of you armed?" asked Mainwaring quietly. "Very well. Half cock, prime and load. And for God's sake don't make a sound, any of you! Slade, keep watch inshore, there!"

Virtually all of the men, including the new men who had come with the pinnaces, were evidently at ease with small arms, for they readied the weapons with gratifying speed, tearing open paper cartridges with their teeth, priming the pans, then casting the muskets about and emptying the remaining powder down the barrel. With deft strokes of the ramrods they rammed the paper and ball down atop the powder. Within a few minutes the last ramrod had clinked back into its housing under the musket barrel, and the men stood with the weapons in the vertical 'Recover' position, as they had been taught to do, their eyes again on Mainwaring, their breath coming quickly in their excitement.

"We'll divide into two parties," said Mainwaring. "Mr Howe, you'll take your boat's crew as one, and I shall take mine as the other. We'll move off in Indian file, but keep your party back ten paces from mine. If we're ambushed, you can recover and escape. Move to the end of the jetty now. Follow me!"

Silently, the few men with shoes walking on the outside edges of their soles to emulate the silence of the barefoot ones, the little party moved swiftly along the rough planking until they found themselves on a narrow, rocky beach, barely ten feet from the cliff-like dark wall of the fortification that rose into the night sky above them.

"All here? Good. Now listen carefully," said Mainwaring. He found he was trembling, for all that the night was warm. "We'll go off to the left. I'll lead. Mr Howe, you'll come last, at the rear. Take command immediately if anything happens to me. Who is your lead man?"

"Evans, sir."

"Very well. Evans, see you keep that ten-pace gap between us. Clear?"

"Sir!" nodded the muscular Welshman.

"Right, then. Not a word, now, all of you. Follow me!"

His heart pounding in his throat, Mainwaring lifted his own long musket again to the 'Recover' position: vertically by the left side of his chest, left arm holding the weapon in place, the right hand gripping the small of the butt, with the thumb hooked over the cock and its flint, ready to draw it back fully for firing. His eyes were opened wide, and he opened his mouth slightly for better hearing. Feeling his way over the stones, he headed off into the murk along the face of the stone wall, the men scuffling and crunching along behind him. He could see nothing ahead of him but the wall's face vanishing into shadow, and tiny pinpoints of light in the far distance. But what lay thirty or fifty feet ahead he could not say. Somehow, if they edged far enough around the mass of the building, they would come upon a—

Abruptly, a vertical rectangle of light opened in the dark wall, so close and so startling that it was only with the greatest difficulty that Mainwaring kept himself from crying out. The heavy ironbound door crashed against the stone as it was flung back, and the burly figure of a *Troupes de la Marine* sentry, lantern held high and musket slung on one shoulder, stepped out of the sally port.

"*Qui vive?*" enquired the man, peering towards the clutch of dark figures he could see beyond the lamplight. "*C'est toi, Etienne? Qu'est-ce que—?*" As the man turned further, the glare of the lantern fell full on Mainwaring, and the French marine's eyes widened in astonishment. His mouth gaped, and he sucked in a deep breath to bellow a warning.

But Mainwaring had sprung forward, and with savage force brought the butt of his musket down on the bridge of the man's nose with a horrid crunching sound. Blood spurted in dark jets over the man's mouth, and he sat down heavily with a grunt, the lantern clattering to the stones. Another blow from Mainwaring's musket butt struck the man on the temple, and he pitched on to his side into the shadows beside the open sally port.

"This way!" barked Mainwaring, and he ducked into the opening. The passageway was low and vaulted, reeking of mould and decay, and was lit every so often with guttering candle lanterns. Spiderwebs laced down everywhere, and underfoot was a rough, uneven *pavé* of broad stones. Mainwaring rushed along as fast as he could move, the cartridge box slapping at his hip, his own breathing loud in his ears. Behind him, the Dianas stumbled and clinked, bare feet slapping on the stones, a curse here and there telling of a stubbed toe or an elbow struck against the narrow passageway walls. Mainwaring lunged round a final corner and fetched up hard against another heavy ironbound low door. Panting and blowing, the Dianas crowded in behind him, their faces gaunt, strained masks in the odd yellow light.

" 'Tain't locked, be it, zur?" puffed Jackman, his torn shirt wet with sweat under his cartridge-box belt.

"No. Just an interior bolt." With his right hand holding the musket ready, Mainwaring eased back the bolt with his left and looked back at the bunched men.

"No telling what we'll find on the other side. Be ready for anything. Remember our job is to stop ships getting out, any way we can!" He spat on the dusty floor. "That's in case I take a French ball in my guts. Ready?"

The men nodded, eyes wild.

"Then, *come on!*" Mainwaring bellowed, and kicked open the door.

With Mainwaring in the lead, the Dianas burst into a scene that momentarily dazzled their eyes. The Eguillette battery was in effect a fort, with a central *terreplein* or courtyard, and walls which provided ramparts on which gun barbettes and infantry firing steps were built. The *terreplein* was ringed with lanterns set in cast-iron brackets on the inner walls, and casting a strange, orange glow over the hard flagstones of the courtyard. This was the site for the drilling of troops, whether of infantry or the *canonniers-bombardiers* of the gun batteries. It was indeed being used for infantry drill at that moment, but of a somewhat different sort.

"Dear God!" burst out Mainwaring.

To the left of where the Englishmen had emerged, along the landside curtain wall of the fortification, a series of rough, wooden frames stood vertically, like fishermen's drying racks turned on their sides. Some twenty yards away, a half-company of *Troupes de la Marine*, with dark, leering faces, were in the process of priming and loading their muskets as they lined up on a three-rank firing position supervised by a sergeant leaning on a halberd while a clutch of officers stood languidly to one side.

But it was the scene at the racks that had caused Mainwaring's involuntary cry. Tied against them were twenty-five to thirty civilians, men, women, children, bent old people. All – even the children – bore terrible signs of beating and torture: bloody faces, torn clothing, the dresses of several of the women ripped from their bosoms so that they sobbed in shame as well as fear and pain. The children cried and trembled, clinging to their parents, their eyes on the line of men who had visited cruelty and horror upon them, and were about to do more.

Mainwaring's lungs filled for an order. But it was too late, and unnecessary. As a red rage closed over him, he heard the roar that burst from the throats of the Englishmen around him, and recognised his own voice answering in like kind. Unbidden, the British muskets came level with lightning speed, and they fired a thunderous volley, worthy of a grenadier company of the Guards, almost point-blank into the line of grey-clad soldiery.

All was suddenly smoke and screaming, and Mainwaring's musket was clattering down at his feet, and he was holding the long cutlass, hearing the other blades woosh past him as they were drawn, hearing the deep, baying roar that formed on the lips of the Dianas. And it was on his own, and with them he was leaping forward, sprinting in a wild fury to get at the smoke-shrouded knot of men in grey.

"At 'em!" he heard himself cry. "*Diana! Diana!*"

They were on the French in an instant. But even with dead and writhing wounded all about them, the surviving men of the *Troupes* were hardened regulars, and reacted with the experience and skill of regulars. As Mainwaring rushed in, the man he had targeted spun on his heel, levelled his musket at Mainwaring, and fired. The weapon's blast stunned Mainwaring's ears, blocking out the shrieks and curses of the fighting; a pink flash dazzled him, and he felt a sharp tug at the cloth of his shoulder. But his fighting rage had control of him, and heedless of risk he moved at the man without breaking stride. The Frenchman's dark eyes widened as he saw Mainwaring emerge from the smoke, cutlass brandished high. With the butt plate of his musket, the Frenchman swung a blow that would have shattered the American's jaw had it struck. But Mainwaring angled his head away, felt the steel scrape his cheekbone. Then he cut down with all his strength with the cutlass, a whistling blow that struck the man at the base of the neck with a sickening thud, the blade sinking out of sight into the flesh and grey cloth as a jet of dark blood spurted on either side of it. With a cry, Mainwaring wrenched the blade free, and the man sprawled awkwardly at his feet, legs twitching. Wild to strike again, Mainwaring leaped over the man, the clashing, shouting tumult of the struggle now loud in his ears. He was conscious of Howe bellowing beside him, hacking at a man who parried his blows with his musket, and then Mainwaring had a brief, split-second image of Jackman falling to the ground, his hands locked round the throat of a Frenchman whose eyes were bulging from their sockets, teeth bared in a horrid rictus. In the next instant some inner instinct caused him to throw up his cutlass to the guard position, and his wrist was lanced with pain as the blade of another weapon, a French infantry hanger, struck it. The man was short, but stocky; his hat gone, his black hair out of its queue and falling round a dark,

166

hook-nosed face: a sergeant of *Troupes de la Marine*. He swore viciously – at least, Mainwaring presumed they were oaths – and cut vigorously at Mainwaring's head. Again, a bone-jangling parry, and then the man lunged for the kill in Mainwaring's chest. But as the blade arrowed forward, Mainwaring twisted aside, and then cut downward. The man's hand and cutlass leaped from the wrist as, screaming, he stared at the pulsing stump, and then a backhand cut across the throat pushed the wretch backward, a shriek dying on his lips as a bloody froth welled from them.

Mainwaring wrestled himself free of a body which had fallen across his feet, and staggered back, gasping for air, his throat burning as if on fire. He swung round, seeing grey shapes strewn obscenely in a welter, struggling bodies still everywhere. Off to one side, the clutch of French officers was struggling to escape through the main gate, which was ajar.

"James!" Mainwaring cried, unaware if Howe could hear him. "The gate! Secure it!" His voice cracked. "The guns, the rest of you! The ramparts! Get to the guns!" He swung round drunkenly, seeing the narrow stone staircase, the ramparts high above, the guns in their embrasures underlit by the orange, smoky glow from the *terreplein*.

And red-clad figures of gunners, spiking tools in their hands, running along the walls towards the guns that faced the sea.

Mainwaring collided into a knot of Dianas, and he seized their shoulders, pointing upwards with his bloody cutlass blade. "You lads, with me!" The men heard, and stumbled after him as he made for the stairs. In the next instant he was forcing himself up them as fast as he could climb. A blast sounded from somewhere above, loud and ear-piercing, even as the pink flame flashed his hat spinning from his head into the smoke of the *terreplein*. Out of the corner of his eye he caught sight of several Dianas at the gate, throwing a great bar across it, and of more Dianas racing up the other rampart stairway on the far side of the square.

Then he was up on the rampart surface, running along the long firing step towards the nearest gun barbette. On it was a long twelve-pounder, a huge thing, dull black piece on an ochre carriage, shadowed now in the unearthly light from below. And hunched over the vent, trying in feverish haste to fit in the spike that would render the gun useless, a thin, wild-eyed gunner.

With a bound, Mainwaring was there, a blow of his musket hilt sending the man sprawling with a cry to the edge of the rampart. He cowered there, hands raised in supplication, face twisted in fear. But Mainwaring ignored him. He tore the spike from the gun's vent and was on towards the next gun. Two men were there, bigger, again in the scarlet small-clothes and white gaiters of the *canonniers-bombardiers*, and they turned as they saw Mainwaring's rush. The nearest man snatched up a sergeant's halberd that had been leaning against the gun and threw it at Mainwaring, overhand, like a hunter's javelin. With a flash of steel in the lantern light, the long weapon passed over Mainwaring's shoulder, a horrid impact and a choked scream from behind telling that it had struck home in one of the Dianas at Mainwaring's heels. Mainwaring cut down at the man's head with his cutlass, but the man dodged aside with quick agility as the blow was struck. The blade rang against the black barrel of the gun, and Mainwaring gasped as the cutlass flew from his numbed grip, the pain in his arm suddenly paralysing. In almost the same instant the gunner's companion struck Mainwaring on the side of the head with the rammer, a blow that put the American down hard on the planking of the barbette, stars flickering before his eyes. But even as he fell, Mainwaring heard the man's snarl change abruptly to a shriek as the cutlass blade of a Diana buried itself in his stomach. Bodies pushed past Mainwaring where he knelt, and he saw as if in a dream the three gunners who were hammering furiously at the last of the line of guns go down under a wave of Dianas, the flashing cutlass blades choking off the brief shrieks as the French died.

Mainwaring stood, feeling his hand throb, feeling the dizziness course through him. Suddenly he was looking at Jackman, who was staring at him and mouthing words, his face a mask of dark concern. But Mainwaring could hear nothing save the growing hum in his ears.

Then the grey edges of his vision closed in, and his last memory was of the blood-smeared planking of the barbette rushing up at an alarming speed to meet him.

8

Anne Brixham was grinning at him in a way that always disarmed him completely; her smile called forth by an inner spark of humour or delight at something he had done. He turned from unpacking the wicker basket to see her sitting on the blanket, hugging her knees and beaming at him with that wide grin. Her eyes danced with delight, and the dark curls shook with laughter, wisped round her head by the Trade wind that had the palms overhead bending and curving.

"What on earth are you laughing at?" Mainwaring demanded, settling back on his heels with an armful of wine bottles, bread, cheese and a crock of chutney. "Never seen a proper meal before?" He had thrown down his coat and hat, and was in the comparative comfort of his linen small-clothes.

"You," said Anne, wrinkling her nose. "You looked like a badger down a hole, rummaging in that thing. Wherever did you get it all?"

Mainwaring spread his treasures over the rough nankeen blanket that was laid out on the fine sand of a Jamaican beach. He poked a thumb in the direction of the small rowing boat that was pulled up out of the gentle surf a few feet away.

"You should be impressed. Not only did I relieve His Britannic Majesty's Navy of the jolly boat belonging to *Diana*, but I also contrived to have the captain's servant of the said vessel put together a suitable repast. How about tucking in?"

Anne laughed, her even teeth white against the sun-warmed brown of her complexion.

"First things first, Lieutenant Mainwaring. I've yet to be kissed today. And there's no good rowing me all the way round here if you're not prepared to attend to a lady's pleasure."

He grinned at her. "Name your pleasure. I hasten to obey."

Her bare feet flashed under the simple white gown as she suddenly sprang at him over the clutter of the food, and rolled tussling with him on to the warmth of the sand. Laughing and panting, they fought for the upper hand – Anne Brixham had grown to womanhood doing a man's work in her father's coastal sloop, and had the strength of a small man – until Mainwaring yielded to her ultimate weapon, a skilful tickling, and lay on his back gasping with laughter. She hitched up her gown over her knees and sat triumphantly astride him.

Mainwaring looked up at her, seeing how her breasts pushed against the linen as she laughed, and how her curls framed her face.

"Dear God, m'love. You're so damned beautiful!" he breathed.

She wriggled wickedly on him. "Lie to me some more."

"Disbelieving wench. Come here", he said, and pulled her down into a deep, passionate kiss.

The brandy, when it hit his throat, burned like hot coal, and he gagged in a fit of coughing.

"Easy, Jacko, look'ee. Don't drown 'im!" said a voice.

Mainwaring opened his eyes. He was sitting with his back propped against one of the rampart guns, and kneeling beside him were the two wiry messmates, Slade and Sawyer. A worried-looking Jackman, his grime-streaked face strangely lit by the lantern light, was standing at Mainwaring's feet. Jackman's cutlass blade was stained a dark brown, and as full consciousness returned to him, Mainwaring realised that the stain was dried blood.

" 'Nother swig, sir?" asked Sawyer.

"No, damn your eyes!" croaked Mainwaring, and the two little men exchanged relieved looks. "Enough! What in Christ's name—?"

"Yew took a fair coshin', sir," said Jackman. "Put yer lee rail under, it did."

Mainwaring rubbed his neck. He gathered his legs under

171

him and got unsteadily to his feet. "What's taken place? Where are the French?"

Jackman grinned at him, and spat into the dust to one side of the barbette. "Yew did it, sir. The gunners were tryin' to spike th' battery, but rushin' up 'ere at 'em stopped 'em cold, so to speak, sir." He pointed down at the lantern-lit *terreplein*. "Mr 'Owe's groupin' th' prisoners, sir. All the gunners, an' what's left o' that cutthroat soldiery."

Mainwaring moved unsteadily to the edge of the rampart and peered over. A patch of grey and red marked a knot of weaponless men being pushed together in one corner of the courtyard by several Dianas with cutlasses. In the middle of the yard a welter of bodies lay strewn grotesquely, dark pools and rivulets of blood adding to the gruesomeness of the scene.

"Dear Christ," breathed Mainwaring. He could see a few seamen's forms among the dead. "D'ye know who we've lost?" he asked quietly.

"Aye, sir," said Sawyer. "Lount and MacNeil, sir. And the taffy, Williams."

Mainwaring winced. The affable and humorous Williams had been with him since the days of the schooner *Athena* and the attack on Porto Bello. He had been a capable hand and valiant fighter, a favourite of the fo'c'sle. Mainwaring knew that the loss would be felt most by the other Welshman, Evans, for by language and sentiment, the men had been inseparable messmates.

"I see," said Mainwaring, after a moment. "Where – where's Mr Howe?"

Jackman pointed with the bloody cutlass. "There, sir, just abaft that rack. Seein' to th' freein' o' the prisoners now, sir."

Mainwaring turned, feeling his strength returning; feeling as well the awareness returning of what was likely marshalling against them beyond the walls.

"The guns. We've got to—"

Jackman interrupted, bobbing his head in salute. "Beggin' yer pardon, sir, but Oi was rated gunner's mate in th' old *Centurion*, sir."

"Splendid. You two know your guns as well. Look over

172

this battery as quickly as you can. Determine if they've been spiked, where the gun tools are, if any cartridge has been brought up, whether there's round shot in the garlands, the lot. Jackman, I'll want guns that bear on that damned channel between us and le Mourillon. Report to me on what you find."

"Aye, aye, sir!" said Jackman, and in a moment the three men had made off swiftly down the line of guns.

"Now for those poor wretches," said Mainwaring to himself, and went down the narrow stone stairs to the courtyard.

He arrived to find Evans, his face like a thundercloud, using his seaman's knife to cut away the cruel rope bindings by which the people had been trussed up for slaughter. These fishermen in rough woollen breeches and wooden *sabots* tearfully hugged their wives who were gathering to them terrified, sobbing children still hysterical from the brutality of the soldiery and the final, bloody storm of Mainwaring's attack. Tear-streaked, grateful faces surrounded Mainwaring and hands reached out to touch him or grasp his own in strong, wordless clasps. The tone of their voices gave clear meaning to their words.

Then Howe was before him, his face powder-blackened, holding a small, sniffling girl in his arms.

"You're all right, sir?"

"Yes, James. And thank God, so are you, apparently. But are *they* all right?"

Howe shook his head. "They've been beaten, sir. One of the men is dead from it. This poor child's mother – we found her body in that casemate. They'd raped her and slit her throat."

"Dear Christ!" breathed Mainwaring.

Howe's lips were white. "What kind of animals would order this, sir? Or carry it out? Surely the French—?"

Mainwaring touched the little girl's hair, and she shrank against Howe's shoulder, eyes wide.

"Only one Frenchman comes to my mind about this sort of thing, James." He looked quickly round. "Did we, in fact, take any of their officers?"

"No, sir. Evans saw three of 'em dart out through the far

173

sally port as soon as we entered. They made no effort to fight at all."

Mainwaring nodded. "I imagine torturing children and murdering women exhausts one," he said bitterly. That meant the loss of surprise would be complete. They might expect an attack as soon as the French could gather their forces, and with the immense resources they had at their disposal, it would come in overwhelming strength.

"James, you'd best let the freed men release the others," he said briskly. "See if one of these casemates is suitable, and have 'em gather in there. Then have Evans take some of the men and ensure every gate and port is securely barred and barricaded, the main archway gate in particular. But we'll need to keep the prisoners under guard – one of these fishermen could be persuaded to do it, I'd warrant – and you'd best see to that as well. But quickly; we must strike while we can!"

"Aye, aye, sir!" said Howe. He gave the child a light kiss on the cheek, put her gently into the arms of one of the women, and made off, bellowing for Evans to follow him.

It had taken only a few moments of quick gestures by Howe to make himself understood to the fishermen, who had snatched up the bayonet-tipped muskets of the soldiery and taken over control of the terrified prisoners with brusque harshness. They herded the shuffling and cowed prisoners through a low door at the far end of the yard and into one of the casemates that opened on to the courtyard, prodding the soldiery with evident grim relish as they thrust them in. Further along, Mainwaring could see the women and children sheltering inside a casemate, one of Howe's men carrying in to them a vast armful of bread loaves he had discovered.

"Sir?" A seaman appeared in front of Mainwaring, tugging at his forelock in salute, and Mainwaring recognised him through the grime and powder-blacking as Traynor. "Mr Howe asks if ye can come t' the far casemate right away, sir."

"Very well."

Mainwaring reached the low doorway to see that its ochre-coloured surface bore, in white lettering, the words

Officier de la Ronde. That, at least, he understood. It was the day room of the duty officer of the guard. He ducked and stepped in, and was met by an incredulous-looking Howe.

"It's a French officer, sir. But he's been flogged."

"*Flogged? An officer?*" Mainwaring moved into the shadows of the casemate. To one side stood a small desk, and at the rear of the low, lantern-lit chamber, a narrow bed. A woman was leaning over the figure of a man: a man, lying on his stomach, bare to the waist, his back a dark, horrid mass of welts and bloody cuts. The woman was rinsing a cloth in a wooden bucket, touching gently at the cuts.

"Dear God. Is he conscious, James?" said Mainwaring.

"Couldn't tell, sir."

Mainwaring knelt by the bed. The woman turned to look at him and gasped a little, a hand coming to her throat.

"*Mon Dieu. Le jeune matelot,*" she murmured.

Mainwaring stared at her, seeing the same warm eyes, the gentle face, the full body in its rough woollens, the careworn hands that had soothed him. Now a livid bruise was high on one cheek and a trickle of dried blood ran from the corner of her mouth.

"You!" Mainwaring whispered. He reached out a hand to her cheek, feeling the flash of fury within him at the bruise, the blood, the pain in her eyes. "Dear God, if I knew who ordered this, and could—!" he muttered.

"M'sieu', you – really should be aware of – all the upset you've caused." The figure on the bed had spoken in a tight whisper.

Mainwaring stared. "De Guimond!" he burst out. "How the devil did this happen to *you*? Why are you here?"

The Frenchman laughed lightly, then grimaced in the pain it produced.

"The help – you and your crew received from these good people – was not appreciated by certain senior officers, *hein*? They seemed to form the opinion that – I had helped you escape."

Mainwaring nodded grimly. "As well they might. You did, after all, ensure the guardhouse was merely unlocked—"

"Not precisely, *mon vieux*. When – you sailed so bravely out in that Spanish vessel, I – ensured this battery did

175

not fire on you. Falsified orders are — simple enough to fabricate."

Mainwaring looked at him in wonder. "Good Lord! Then it was because of you that we managed to escape in the *San Pablo*. May I ask why you did that?"

"The *amirauté* are — unaware of what the — commander of the dockyard *Troupes* is capable of doing. He has been denying rations, diverting stores to his own use, stealing — from the King's purse. Then finally, the dishonour — of the way he behaved towards you. I simply acted as — a gentleman should."

"You are indeed that," said Mainwaring quietly. "And you have sacrificed a career on a point of honour."

De Guimond smiled against his pillow. "No, m'sieu. *Because* of a point of honour. My own, which I wished to keep intact."

Mainwaring nodded, admiration growing within him. "You are a brave man." He looked at the fisherman's wife, who had resumed her gentle cleansing of De Guimond's horrid wounds. "But how did *this* come about?"

"The gentleman in question sent a company of some of the — foulest men imaginable through the fishermen's huts, forcing them all in here. I was taken by them as I rode from here to inform the *amirauté* of what I saw happening. The battery commander here was my friend, and he had learned of the orders. They — shot him."

Mainwaring was incredulous. "A King's artillery officer?" Simply shot out of hand?"

"Indeed. My punishment was to be — more inventive. They had me lashed like a felon before the company. Later I was to be shot, after they had done away with the poor wretches outside. The story was to be that a *rosbif* landing party was responsible for it all." His eyes found Mainwaring's. "This woman he was keeping. The gentleman in question has a remarkable reputation as a rapist as well as someone who enjoys inflicting pain. She was to provide him a last entertainment before being given to those — dogs outside."

Mainwaring's lips were a tight line. "Who are we dealing with, De Guimond? Who is this creature?"

"You would not know him. The Chevalier Rigaud de la Roche-Bourbon."

Mainwaring stared, thunderstruck. *Him. After so much time. So much remembered anger.* The image of Anne Brixham lashed to an overhead beam while Roche-Bourbon slowly readied a vicious little knife floated before Mainwaring's eyes, and he felt the killing fury rise in his throat. *Him!*

"On the contrary, De Guimond. I am very much aware of who he is," he said coldly.

"*Comment? Mais, c'est impossible*! How would you—?"

"Trust me, De Guimond, I know him. I also know what he is capable of doing." Mainwaring thought of the clutch of officers escaping as the Dianas had attacked. "He is gone, I think. Escaped. But he will be back in force very soon, I am sure." He paused. "De Guimond, you are my prisoner. But your word shall be sufficient for me. I shall require your parole that—"

"If you please, m'sieu'," De Guimond interrupted. "If you will allow me. I cannot speak to you as a prisoner. My career as a King's officer is – finished. Roche-Bourbon would see to that in any event. The *amirauté* would not take my word against his, and he will have reported that I betrayed my King by aiding you." He smiled sadly. "I cannot therefore accept what I have not the honour to deserve."

Mainwaring's mind raced. "De Guimond, listen to me. I am uncertain if we will leave this place alive. If we do, let me offer you something: stay with us; and fight with us. Come with us to England, should we escape. There is always a place in the world for a courageous man who places principle and honour above all else." He laughed lightly, without mirth. "In any event, should Roche-Bourbon take us, you and I are both dead men. What do you say?"

De Guimond thought for a moment, and Mainwaring shared a long look with the woman. Her eyes told him she sensed the importance of what was being said.

"Very well, *Capitaine*," said De Guimond, quietly. "I am your man. What do you wish me to do?"

"Good man!" said Mainwaring, taking De Guimond's hand in a firm grip. "Firstly, can you walk?"

De Guimond brought himself up slowly to a sitting position, grimaced, but then nodded. "Yes. I shall simply ignore the pain." He shook his head at the woman in answer to her concerned look, forcing a thin smile. "But perhaps I shall be wearing nothing but a shirt for a while."

"I admire your courage, De Guimond," said Mainwaring. "The fishermen. Would they help us?"

De Guimond snorted. "After the gentle treatment they've received at the hands of their countrymen? They have nothing left to lose. What do you want them to do?"

Mainwaring's eyes were hard points. "Lead them, De Guimond. Arm them with the stands of arms that company of marines carried, and see that they know their use. I counted almost a dozen men who looked capable enough. Form them into a militia company under your command, to guard the prisoners, see to their families, and help defend this place!" He paused. "Tell them that, on my word of honour, if we can escape from here, I will see to it that they are transported by a Royal Navy vessel to Villefranche or another Savoyard port where they will be safe and have a chance to start anew."

De Guimond stood and reached slowly for his shirt. He pulled it over his head, the bloody marks beginning to show through the cloth almost immediately.

"I think, m'sieu', they would accept those terms. But I must begin working with them." De Guimond was pale, but his jaw was set in determined lines. "May I ask your name again, m'sieu'? I have forgotten."

Mainwaring took his hand in a firm grip once more. "Lieutenant Edward Mainwaring. Your servant, De Guimond."

"*Et le vôtre, m'sieu'*. You will not find us lacking in courage."

Mainwaring met De Guimond's clear, steady gaze. "That is already evident, M'sieu' De Guimond. Be certain of that."

De Guimond nodded, smiling faintly. His eyes moved to the woman, and he raised her broad, coarse hand to his lips like a courtier and kissed it murmuring something. Then he was gone through the casemate door.

Mainwaring looked at the woman, seeing suddenly how

small she was. The dark eyes that turned to his had tears welling in them, and on impulse Mainwaring moved to her and folded her gently against him. Her arms went round him, and a sob of release broke from her, and then another. She wept against him, and Mainwaring realised that in a fashion he was repaying the debt of the solace she had given him.

Abruptly, the casemate door rang to the knock of a cutlass hilt and swung wide as James Howe stepped in, hatless and in shirt sleeves like a brigand.

"Oh – er – sorry, sir," he said. "If you've a moment, sir, I can report our situation."

"Very well, James. I'll come out." Mainwaring turned to the woman, who looked up at him with a touching expression in her eyes. With one hand she gently touched the welt on Mainwaring's cheek.

"*Je comprends. Le devoir d'un officier,*" she murmured. With a long look of warmth and gratitude, she backed away, and then moved on bare feet out of the door with a brief smile for Howe.

"Lovely woman, for a fishwife, sir," said Howe.

"Lovely woman *anywhere*, James. What's our situation?"

Howe ran his fingers through his hair as Mainwaring joined him outside the door.

"Secure for the moment, sir, but only for the moment. We took three casualties – Williams among them, God damn and blast it all to hell – and we've locked the Frogs into a casemate. They'll not get out. The fisherfolk bound their wounds."

"After the way they treated them? Extraordinary."

"Indeed, sir. The French officer who helped us – De Guimond, is it, sir? – told me that he's joined us. He's over there, showing the fishermen how to handle the firelocks. They're all capable watermen. Gives us another eight armed men, sir. And they seem eager to settle the score. Damned lucky thing."

"Good. The doors and gates?"

"Double barred and barricaded, sir. I've got sentries above 'em all on the ramparts, although that doesn't leave us gun crews."

"That's my next thought. What *about* the guns, to seaward?"

"Jackman checked 'em over, sir. There's six guns on each face of the wall, except on the fourth wall that faces inland, sir. That one", said Howe, pointing with his cutlass. "It's a curtain wall, with no gun platforms. Obviously they expect no landside attack."

"And the guns?"

"The French managed to spike two in the battery facing along the Seyne shore, sir. The six facing le Mourillon and the six facing the sea approaches are fireable, sir. They're twelve-pounders. The gun tools are all in those lockers on the barbettes."

"What of powder and shot?"

"I sent Evans hunting, sir. Had to get his mind off Williams. He had to break in with a musket butt, but he's found the magazine. Plenty of cartridge, wad, and slow-match. And the garlands are full of shot."

"Very good, James. How many gun crews can we muster?"

Howe thought. "If the fishermen can help with the sentry duty and musketry, we could manage two full crews, sir. But not all the lads have had gunnery training."

"No matter," said Mainwaring. "Tell 'em off on the side tackles and put the experienced men on the gun tools." He paused. "One other thing. We've got to secure our longboat out of harm's way. It may be the only way out of here when things get grim."

"Done, sir. I've had it warped round out of sight and the lines doubled up."

"Well done." Mainwaring looked over to where De Guimond, his shirt back streaked with blood, was patiently ordering a clutch of musket-armed fishermen through the movements for the priming and loading of a firelock.

"James, check on the condition of the women and children, will you? De Guimond will look after 'em as soon as he gets his little army mobilised. Then ask Jackman to meet you and me on the rampart, and you'd best ask along De Guimond as well."

Howe nodded. "Aye, aye, sir," he said, and was off.

Mainwaring strode to the rampart stairway, his coat-tails

flapping behind him. As he reached the steps, he noticed a hat lying at their foot and recognised it as his own. He picked it up, raising his eyebrows at the gaping hole in the front of the crown and an equal hole at the back.

What damned luck, he thought. He crammed the hat on his head and went up the stairs. In a moment he was joined where he stood on the barbette of one of the seaward guns by Howe, Jackman and the still-pale De Guimond.

Mainwaring nodded to them, after peering out over the walls. Across the now moonlit gap through which *San Pablo* had sailed to freedom, the dark mass of le Mourillon battery sat, showing but one faint light.

"Gentlemen," said Mainwaring, in greeting. "Jackman, you're rated gunner's mate, as of now. Do well in all this, and I'll see that you get your warrant."

Jackman's grin split his sooty face. "I'd be oblig'd, sir."

"It may be well earned, before we're through," said Mainwaring. He turned to De Guimond. "M'sieu', how soon do you think Roche-Bourbon will return to attack us?"

De Guimond considered. "There would have been a small corporal's guard in the *corps de garde* on the la Seyne road, near where you were held prisoner. He would go there for his horse and to send messengers. A troop of dragoons galloped by earlier—"

"We saw them."

"—But they galloped back towards Toulon as we were entering this place. They've likely gone to barracks or the *tavernes* at La Valette." He paused. "Your men have told me that you captured the guardboat. Normally it would not complete its outer harbour patrol until midnight. It all depends on how quickly he can raise the alarm, I should think."

Mainwaring looked at the long, twinkling line of lights from the anchored squadrons, across the same dark water from which they had escaped, seemingly ages ago. "Would he come by sea or by land?"

De Guimond shrugged. "By sea, he'd be little more than a target, *hein*? The weakness of this place is the landward side; the curtain wall. No moat, no bastions for covering fire, and a wooden entry *porte*. I'd wager he'd call out the dockyard *Troupes*, and field guns as well, and strike us from landward."

Mainwaring scratched his chin. "The boom. Where is it raised from?"

"Le Mourillon. The windlasses are there. It's merely shackled down here, to an iron ringbolt on the outside face of the wall facing le Mourillon."

"Damn," said Mainwaring, and spat. "So we've no chance to seal the harbour shut by simply raising the boom and keeping it up." He turned and looked out through the embrasure again. By craning round he could look out into the darkness of the outer harbour and the Golfe de Giens. Out there somewhere, eyes on *Barb* and *Trusty* were watching, waiting for a signal. Mainwaring felt, rather than deduced, that he had perhaps an hour or two at the most before Roche-Bourbon would be able to raise the alarm in the fortress or dockyard proper. Mainwaring had the capacity to man two guns, and enough rag-tag musketmen, by the look of the fortification, to hold off any serious assault for several hours, but no more. If he simply sat there in control of the Eguillette, the French would come to him and eventually overwhelm him. But if he were to *initiate* the action, there might be the possibility of provoking the French into—

"Sir?" It was Jackman. "Beggin' yer pardon, sir. But there's a ship coming out."

"Is there, by God?" Mainwaring spun to look towards the inner harbour. And there, the moonlight illuminating the ghostly pale rectangles of its sails, a vessel of perhaps frigate size was gliding out from the anchorage of massed ships on the night's land breeze, her bowsprit bearing on the gap between le Mourillon and l'Eguillette.

"What d'ye think, James?" asked Mainwaring.

"Putting out at night to avoid our picket vessels and the squadron they think is out there, I'd say, sir."

"Aye. And I think, in the event, providing us with our first opportunity!" said Mainwaring briskly. "Mr Howe, call away a crew for the gun there in the second embrasure. Jackman, you'd best get a good fifteen rounds monkeyed up from Evans' magazine. Lively, now, if you please!"

"Aye, aye, sir!" said Howe, and with Jackman at his heels was off down the rampart stairs.

"M'sieu' de Guimond. Can you see to your men, now, and do what you can to mount guard on the entry ports and the prisoners?"

"*A vos ordres, capitaine.* I can likely spare you a man so that you can use your Jackman. Foncé, one of the fishermen, was an old *canonnier-bombardier*. He can break out cartridge for you, and I'll have two others act as – how is it you say, in English – 'monkeys'?"

Mainwaring grinned. "As we say in English, thank you, De Guimond. Please, get about it as quickly as you can!"

De Guimond was off into the shadows down the stairwell, but Mainwaring had already spun on his heel and was peering at the French vessel. It had the look of a frigate, well enough, of about twenty guns or so: the English would have called it a sloop-o'-war. Floating out under topsails and headsails like a silent wraith, it was completely dark; not a single lantern glowed anywhere about the ship. There was a flash of phosphorescence under the ship's bows, bright even in the moonlight, and the beauty of the moment brought a bitter thought to Mainwaring's mind.

How appallingly wasteful war is, he reflected. In a moment, with luck, he would be attempting to destroy that ship; to reduce to useless wreckage the product of months of ship-wrights' effort, of carving, paintwork, joinery, ropework and fitting; to bring death to the skilled men who made the ship a living, beautiful creation that delighted his seaman's eye. If there was an obscenity in the world, it was this endless cycle of destruction and death.

"Damn the bloody war!" muttered Mainwaring to himself.

A slap of bare feet sounded on the stone stairs behind him and Jackman appeared, followed by a clutch of Dianas.

"The Froggy officer sent me up, sir. Said 'e 'ad no need o' me, sir, 'cause 'e 'ad 'is own gunner wiv 'im, sir."

"And right he is. Jackman, you'll be gun captain on that gun. Slade, you've handled a gun well. You're number two. Tell off the other lads to positions. D'ye have a priming horn, Jackman?"

The man hefted a heavy horn that had been slung round out of sight on his hip. "Aye, sir. 'Twere in the magazine, sir!"

"Good. Slade, you carry on telling off the lads while I'm busy with Jackman, here."

"Aye, sir!" chirped the Cockney, turning to the other men with a bright look in his eye. "Listen up, yew lot. Them's as listens is them's as wot don't get kilt. Billy, yew'll ram. Pincher, yew'll tyke th' starb'd 'andspike—"

"Jackman," said Mainwaring. "We need a signal. I want you to break open a cartridge and use it to fire two flares atop one of the embrasure merlons, on the seaward side. Like loose powder in a pan."

"For th' lads at sea, sir?"

"Exactly. *Barb* is watching for it, to know when to send in a boat of lads to help us – and where. Can you do it?"

"Fire it in a clock's tick, I will, sir. Fine as kine."

"Good. Tell me when you're ready."

Mainwaring turned to see Howe arrive with the remainder of the Dianas and move quickly to the second gun. Following Howe's party were two of the la Seyne fishermen, staggering under the weight of half-a-dozen leather cartridge buckets.

"As quick as you can, Mr Howe! Tell me when you can open fire!"

"Aye, aye, sir!"

Mainwaring turned to his own gun. Slade had the men standing, three to either side of the gun, and facing aft at Mainwaring, their eyes white with excitement as they waited for the orders. There was a grunt and a thump on the rough planking behind Mainwaring, and another fisherman put down a wooden bucket which was filled with water. Rough notches had been freshly hacked into the bucket's rim and in them half-a-dozen lengths of lit slow-match smouldered. A similar bucket had arrived at Howe's gun.

"Our Frenchman knows his work, sir!" called Howe.

"Indeed he does, James!" answered Mainwaring. A quick glance showed that Jackman was still busy setting his flare; Mainwaring would have to begin the gun-readying process himself. He looked towards the slowly approaching spectre of the ship, and at the gloom of the inner harbour. Somewhere in there the counterattack was building, he knew. And when it came, would it—

Get on with it! cried his mind.

"Take heed, there, lads!" Mainwaring called. "Some of you have served a gun before, a few not. You *must* learn it this once as we do it: there will be no second chance!" He paused. "Keep absolute silence and listen. When Jackman returns, he'll be your captain. Obey him as you would me, quickly and in silence!"

He squinted at the gun. It was in the run-back position on the barbette, the side and trail tackles seized with lashings.

"Cast loose the gun!" he barked.

At the order, the men dived at the collection of long gun tools that lay in a rack to one side of the gun. Slade and Sawyer busied themselves cutting away the lashings on the tackles and then shook out some slack in the three-fold purchases, clear for hauling.

"Level your gun!" cried Mainwaring. "That means the handspikes, lads. The thing by your left foot, man! Good! Slade, stand by the quoin block." With Slade muttering at them under his breath, the man named Pincher Martin and a man called Oldham picked up the two tapered beamlike tools and thrust them under the rear half of the gun, resting the spikes on the stepped-back edge of the gun-carriage cheek pieces. Slade sprang behind the gun, holding a triangular block of wood in his hand.

Mainwaring glanced at the ship, trying to estimate its distance away. "Raise!" he barked. "Lower . . . lower . . . *quoin*!" On this last word, Slade thrust the triangular block under the heavy rear of the gun, fixing its elevation, and the two men hefted out their tools.

"Take out your tompion!" Sawyer sprang to the front of the gun and pulled a red-painted wooden plug from the muzzle of the gun, setting it to one side.

"Now, lads, it becomes dangerous. The French have been inhospitable enough to have the guns unloaded. *Load with cartridge!*"

Sawyer opened one of the leather cartridge buckets and took out a cylindrical paper cartridge, about the size of a cabbage. Carefully, with both hands, he placed it in the muzzle of the gun, the seam in the paper facing down.

"Seam down, Sawyer?" asked Mainwaring.

"Aye, sir. Wad, sir?"

"Yes. But next time wait for the damned order. Slade, stand by the vent, and put on that leather thumb-sleeve hanging there. Mind you seal the vent properly."

"Aye, aye, sir." Slade slipped on the leather cover for one thumb and leapt to beside the gun's breech. He put his leatherclad thumb over the hole of the vent and applied pressure. Although the gun was being loaded cold, it was a technique meant to keep a current of air from rushing through the gun as a new cartridge was rammed home, thereby blowing a spark into life from a previous firing that might prematurely ignite the cartridge. It was a vital part of the service of a gun.

"Ram home cartridge!" Mainwaring called.

Sawyer followed the cartridge with a flattened coil of old rope, almost equal in dimension to the gun's bore. Then, hefting up the long pole of the broad-headed rammer, he eased the cartridge and wad down the bore with slow, hand-over-hand strokes, until it thumped in place.

"Home!" Sawyer called, leaning against the rammer to keep pressure on.

"Shot your gun!" At the next order, Martin staggered up with a black iron roundshot in both hands. He waited until Sawyer withdrew the rammer, and then inserted the shot in the bore, another wad atop it.

"Now, Sawyer. Ram home shot and wad!"

Sawyer repeated the ramming process, this time ending with two hard thumps of the rammer, and then eased the long tool out of the gun's bore.

"Run out your gun!" barked Mainwaring. "Take up the slack on those tackles quickly, lads! Now, one to six, together! *Heave!*"

The men had taken up the falls of the side tackles, the pulley-block system that hooked the eyebolts in the side, or cheek of the gun carriage, to ringbolts set in the stone on either side of the gun embrasure. Now, in rhythmic hauling, the trucks or wheels of the gun carriage squealing, the gun was hauled forward to its firing position, the muzzle snouting out through the embrasure.

Mainwaring craned to see the approaching ship. Although it was moving slowly, the narrow barbettes made traversing the guns with the tackles difficult. They would have to wait until the frigate passed through the narrow arc of fire afforded by muscling the gun left or right with the hand-spikes. And the French vessel was no more than a minute or two away from entering that moonlit narrow channel where that arc of death would have to be created.

"Prime!" called Mainwaring, and Slade pulled a long priming wire from his belt, poised it vertically above the vent, and then thrust it into the vent to break open the cartridge within the gun. Mainwaring had his mouth open to bellow for Jackman to bring over his priming horn when Jackman's shape flashed past him, to unstop the great horn and fill the vent and pan with the dark, granular priming powder.

"Well done, Jackman. Slade, you'll still fire the gun. See to those flares, Jackman." He waited until Slade had taken up a linstock and one of the glowing matches, deftly seizing it in the metal jaws of the yard-long rod.

"Mr Howe! Report your gun!" cried Mainwaring. The French vessel – damnably beautiful, backlit by the rising moon, sails arched like the breasts of a lovely woman – ghosted into the line of the gun's fire.

"Gun ready, sir!"

"Jackman! Fire your flares!" called Mainwaring. *McCallum, that damned one eye'd better be open*! came the wild thought.

Jackman's own linstock made a pink arc in the air. With a brilliant pink flash and whoosh, the mounds of loose powder atop the merlon ignited in two six-foot-high flowers of flame, a billowing acrid cloud boiling mushroomlike up above.

"We can hit her now, sir!" cried Howe.

"Blow on your match!" Mainwaring barked. He crouched, peering along the gun, waiting for the ship to enter the tiny rectangle of water visible through the embrasure.

Then it was there. The snaking long arm of the jib-boom, the dark mass of the bows, the ivory curve of headsails.

"Now, Mr Howe!" Mainwaring cried. "*Fire!*"

Mainwaring leaped aside and Slade's linstock arced down. There was a spurt of pink flame, the huff, that shot up from the vent. Then the gun itself fired, with a hollow, ringing thunderclap that deafened Mainwaring. The gun spat out a twenty-foot tongue of pink flame, and a vast ball of smoke that swirled back and over the gun platform, the reek overpowering. The gun had leaped back like a living thing to the full fetch of its breeching line, kept only by it from flinging itself off the barbette altogether.

Almost in the same split-second Howe's gun had fired, another blast and lightning flash, the smoke curling like black wool over the embrasure, round the dark forms of the crew and then swirling away to seaward.

In the murk Jackman was suddenly at Mainwaring's side. "I'll take the gun, now, sir!"

"Very well. See that they sponge out!"

"Aye, sir!" said Jackman. "Adams! Yew'll do to sponge. *Sponge out!*"

At the instant of Jackman's bark, as if expecting it, Adams had taken up the long tool. Now he thrust the sponge head – a tightly-bound cylinder of sheepskin – into the bucket and pushed it hard down the gun's bore, twisting it furiously in a search for embers. A puff of smoke jetted out of the vent.

"Load with cartridge, again!" Mainwaring called. He sprang to the next embrasure along, cursing the smoke, peering for the French ship.

"Christ, sir!" came Howe's incredulous cry. "We *got* her!"

"What?"

The smoke swept clearer and Mainwaring could see the French vessel. But it was no longer ghosting in moonlit majesty towards open sea. The shot from one of the guns had struck the bowsprit at the gammoning, just ahead of the vessel's cutwater. With a great ballooning of collapsing headsails and trailing cordage, the vessel was slewing around, its foretopgallant mast canting aft as the forestay's pressure vanished. The topsails on the fore and the main began to luff in long, rippling waves.

Beside him, Mainwaring could hear Slade and his gun crew working with frenzied speed to reload the gun, Howe's men equally frantic beyond. Mainwaring winced as, before he quite expected it, Slade's gun banged out again, the concussion a physical blow, his ears ringing, the smoke billowing and blinding, setting Mainwaring to coughing and cuffing at his stinging eyes. He leaped to the open embrasure, craning to see. A tall, glittering geyser, silver and plume-thin in the moonlight, was collapsing back into a circle of foam just off the vessel's bows. Now he could see that the frigate's starboard foretopsail yard was canted oddly, the brace pendant streaming out in the wind.

Mainwaring shifted his gaze. The dark mass of le Mourillon was dark no more. Pinpoints of dancing light, lanterns in the hands of running men, were moving on the ramparts. Far off in the inner harbour, the Petite Rade, lights were blossoming on the ships; more now than just the anchor lights.

"*Capitaine?*" It was De Guimond, at his shoulder. "There are lights on the road from la Seyne. I think there are two, perhaps three companies of infantry marching here. And I'm sure they're bringing field guns, by the look of the lights. There was a half-battery of six-pounders in the garrison."

"*Three* companies? Christ save us! How long until they arrive?"

"Fifteen, perhaps twenty minutes, m'sieu'. Less than a half-turn of the glass."

"All right. Keep a close watch on them, De Guimond. You know how they fight better than we do. Alert me when it is clear how they intend to deploy against us. Although I should think they'll simply blaze away at the gates with those damned guns."

"*Oui, m'sieu'!*" said the young Frenchman, and made off, the bloody streaks of dried blood on the back of his white shirt like tiger stripes in the gloom.

Again the guns fired, the twin blasts almost simultaneous, the pink rivers of flame lighting the ramparts with a bizarre glow that froze the figures of the gun crews into statuary poses. As the smoke rolled away Mainwaring could see the French vessel in the gap had swung now so that her stern was facing to seaward. The spray from the two enormous shot geysers was drifting over the ship, twinkling like a snowfall as the droplets caught the cold moonlight. Now he could see that the mizzen topmast was canted at an extreme angle. But there were other splashes in the water, hard to make out in the shadows under the ship's bows. Then he saw.

Boats, his mind said. *They're pulling her clear with their boats!*

The guns fired again in rapid succession, the blast another deafening blow to the ears. Jackman and Howe were increasing the rate of fire as the men fell into the rhythm of the work. But before the billows of smoke obscured his vision, Mainwaring had seen what the French captain was doing: he had quickly lowered the ship's long-boat and was attempting to tow the ship clear of the deadly arc of fire. It had been a quick reaction, and a clever one. The French captain was no fool. The smoke began to clear as Mainwaring listened to the businesslike clink and thump of the gun crews. Then the last tendrils wisped away, and Mainwaring could see.

"Another hit in the foremast rigging, sir!" came Howe's cry. "He's lost his tops'l yard, by God!"

Mainwaring squinted. The ship's boat, like a frantic water-beetle, was out beyond the wreckage of the bowsprit, the tiny oars churning the sea into froth. Painfully, the ship edged inshore and away, the canvas aloft being clewed up to reduce windage for the oarsmen.

"Mr Howe! Jackman! Can you manage one more round, at this angle?"

"Aye, sir, we can," came Howe's call, with Jackman's "Aye, aye, sir!" in the next breath.

"Then hit him again!"

Both guns fired as if on the same match, with a tremendous roar that shook the barbette. The smoke swirled anew, and then was whipped away by a gust of wind. The scene below in the gap brought a gasp of astonishment, followed by a hoarse cheer from the English gunners.

"Sir!" cried Howe. "She's listing heavily to larboard! the rounds must've struck her close together at the waterline!"

Mainwaring stared. It was true. Visibly, the frigate was wallowing deeper in the water, heeling drunkenly to one side. The flying round shot had indeed accomplished what Howe observed, for now in the glint of the moonlight Mainwaring could make out a cavernous gap in the planking of the frigate's hull, below the larboard cathead at the waterline wale. Still the oars flailed from the boat as the boat's crew pulled desperately; but the ship was stricken, and as Mainwaring and the others watched, a deep sound like the sigh of some great animal came over the water to them, and in ponderous slowness the ship's bows settled beneath the dark water, the stern lifting as the bows sank, until all vanished save the topgallant masts, projecting above the swirling foam and wreckage.

Now, too, there was another sound: the voices of men, crying out and screaming in the darkness, as they struggled for life in the inky water.

"Poor buggers!" murmured Jackman, at Mainwaring's elbow.

"Aye," breathed Mainwaring. Then he straightened his shoulders. "Secure your guns, there!" he barked. "Prime and load, and then seat home your tompions and vent covers. Likely we'll need 'em again before very long! That clear, Jackman?"

"Aye, sir!" said the gun captain, moving back to his post. In the next moment he had his crew working briskly round the long twelve-pounder, readying it for its next use.

Howe appeared at Mainwaring's shoulder. "That's an unexpected gift, sir. Gives the Frogs a first-class navigational hazard, right where they'd appreciate it least!" He paused, "What d'ye think they'll do next, sir?"

Mainwaring pondered. "Precisely what I was asking myself, James. I've been half-expecting le Mourillon to open up on us. But now I don't think they will."

"I don't follow, sir."

Mainwaring tapped the black hulk of Jackman's gun, feeling the warmth still in the iron. "The French will know by now that all this has been the work of a British landing party. They'll be determined to root us out as quickly as they can. But they've still got a harbour to defend. Blow this pace to – what's the expression Shanahan has? – 'smithereens', and they've lost one of the key gunnery protections for the inner harbour. I'd hate to be the port admiral in front of an *amirauté* inquiry board saying I blew one of my key defence batteries into shards of rubble because a dozen Englishmen had got into it." He squinted at le Mourillon. "No, we're safe enough from a bombardment, I'd warrant."

"What'll it be, then, sir? More ships risking a run out?"

The American shook his head. "I wouldn't have thought so, James. Not unless the whole of the combined squadrons *must* leave tonight, in which case we couldn't have got in here at a more inopportune time for the French. But they won't otherwise risk a ship against our guns. I'd warrant it'll be a land assault, as De Guimond says. They'll hope to take this place intact, and that means light artillery to bash at the doors and a pack of infantry to rush in at us. They'll retake this place – or try to – before they let another ship suffer the fate of that one."

Howe pursed his lips. "So it'll be a musket-and-cutlass fight instead of a bombardment?"

"More than likely. Wager you a ship's biscuit on it, in fact."

Howe grinned, but sobered quickly. "The odds won't be in our favour, sir. We've no more'n eighteen muskets against—"

"James, it isn't my intention to commit suicide. But it *is* our duty to keep the French bottled up for as long as possible. I have an odd feeling about that frigate. Between you and me, I think the French and the Dons *are* planning to come out, and if not tonight, then within twenty-four hours. That's why anyone coming after us has got to do it quickly."

Howe looked at him. "I'd be interested in how you deduced that, sir. Those ships in there look moored in stone."

Mainwaring smiled crookedly. "Partly a gut feeling. But partly something else. Look inshore, there, at the anchored squadrons. Pretty well lit by the moon, now. What d'ye see?"

"Nought but a substantial number of ships with a lot of lights moving about. Boats thrashing hither and yon."

"Anything else?"

"Ah – no, sir. Should there be?"

"Their masts and rigging, James. Their spars, particularly."

Howe peered. "I don't—" he began. Then he paused. "Their canvas!" he gasped. "They've shaken out their harbour furls! The courses, the tops'ls – damn me, they're all just clewed up to the bunt, ready to let fall!"

"Exactly!" said Mainwaring. "Waiting for the right moment. Or a fair wind. But coming out soon."

Howe stared at the projecting masts of the sunken frigate, around which the tiny shape of the French long-boat circled amidst the floating wreckage. There were still voices carrying across the distance to where Howe and Mainwaring stood.

"And the wind *was* fair, for that one!" breathed Howe. "And she might well have been a picket vessel. Damme, they might *all* be hove up short, ready to sail!"

"Aye, James," agreed Mainwaring. "Which is why I think, without reducing this place to rubble, we are in for a vigorous effort by the French to dig us out of here."

"By God, sir, we'd best—" began Howe.

"M'sieu'!" It was De Guimond, calling from the firing step on the curtain wall across the courtyard. He was waving a cutlass in the air. "They are here, and deploying!"

Mainwaring pulled his own cutlass from the back of his belt and nodded to Howe.

"Come along, James," he said. "The opportunity to sell our lives dearly for His Majesty's benefit has arrived!" With a grim little smile he leaped off down the rampart stairs.

When Mainwaring gained the top of the narrow stair-way to the curtain wall rampart, he was greeted by De Guimond's set expression of determination. Without a word De Guimond led Mainwaring and Howe to the firing step, where the fishermen were crouched at regular intervals, muskets held close at the ready and peering over the lip of the wall into the darkness beyond.

De Guimond mounted the step and pointed with his cutlass. "Look there, m'sieu'!"

The moonlight was bright, now, bathing the flat, dusty field that stretched inland away from the fortification walls in a pale, grey-blue light. The clearing stretched no more than several hundred yards across the coastal cart track to the first of a clutch of whitewashed, red-tiled buildings and a rocky groveland of low, gnarled trees; but it was sufficiently wide and well-lit to show a deployed line of infantry waiting motionless just beyond musket range, the gap in the centre of their formation filled by three field guns and their crews which sat athwart the cart track.

"Good Christ!" Mainwaring exclaimed. "They've sent a bloody little army after us! De Guimond, how many men are we looking at out there?"

The Frenchman laughed without mirth. "There's at least four companies of the *Troupes de la Marine* and a company of the Swiss. And I saw that troop of dragoons – a filthy lot of ruffians, presumably those you saw at the lighthouse – cantering about self-importantly back in the trees. With the *canonniers-bombardiers*, perhaps three to four hundred men."

"Well, bugger me!" Howe said softly. "Who do they think is in here? The entire damned Navy?"

Mainwaring scanned the long motionless line carefully. The men's white gaiters were bright in the moonlight, and here and there light glinted in blue points from a bayonet or buckle. Now Mainwaring could see the smaller forms of the drummers in their dark livery on the flanks, and halberd-wielding sergeants pacing slowly along the rear of the line.

"And there's the *gentilhomme* we shall have to face," De Guimond remarked almost casually.

A figure on horseback had appeared from the trees, trotting delicately forward. The animal was white, and handled effortlessly by the dark figure of the rider.

"And who is that?" asked Howe.

"I can surmise," said Mainwaring. "Our mutual acquaintance, isn't it?"

"Quite, m'sieu'. The Chevalier Rigaud de la Roche-Bourbon."

"*That* swine?" burst out Howe. "Then we do have a fight on our hands, sir. How the devil—?"

"Your guess is as good as mine, James. I would have thought our paths would never cross again." Mainwaring had a fleeting image of a great Spanish vessel being consumed in flame at night off the coast of an island in the Gulf of Panama. "Perhaps his purpose in life is to show up periodically and introduce a distinctly foul element into our lives." He hefted his cutlass. "But a fight it shall be, certainly!"

De Guimond was pointing again with his cutlass. "Look there, m'sieu'. There's action round the guns. They'll open fire in a moment, I'm sure."

Mainwaring set his jaw. "Your women and children. Are they well out of the way?"

"*Oui, m'sieu'*. In the strongest casemate. And next to them – and chained down, the dogs – are the prisoners."

"Very well." Mainwaring took a deep breath. Looking over his shoulder out into the darkness of the open sea where *Barb* had been, he wondered if McCallum had seen the flares. For if any time required the help of the one-eyed Scot and his crew, this was clearly the time. As for *Trusty*, with Hooke, Pellowe and the others—

"They're firing, sir!" called Howe.

The muzzles of the three field guns winked in pink flame almost simultaneously, the reports hard, punching concussions of surprising strength. In the next split-second a splintering crash sounded from below, the curtain wall shaking with the impact of the cast-iron shot.

"Trying to kick in the door, sir," said Howe. "You were right!"

Mainwaring nodded. "So it seems, James!" He spun to De Guimond. "Any chance of a musket shot getting them at this range?"

"The chevalier is too clever for that, m'sieu'. They look closer than they are. Not a chance of an accurate shot."

"Damn!" said Mainwaring. "James, is there no gun on this fortification we could handspike around?"

"No, sir. I had a look at one of those flank twelve-pounders. Too acute an angle, sir."

Mainwaring swore. "All right. Collect the lads off the guns and make sure they're armed as well as possible. We need every musket you can find from that stack down there by the rack. Meet me to one side – *not* in front, mind – of the main doors as soon as you can!"

"Aye, aye, sir!" said Howe, and was off down the narrow stairs.

"De Guimond, they may take a bit to range in on those great wooden doors down there. Keep your lads low but watchful. If you think you've got the ghost of a chance, fire on the gunners. And the instant that line surges forward, I've got to know!"

"*Oui, m'sieu*'! And you—?"

"I'm going below to see if we can shore up those damned gates. What about the flank sally ports? And the seaward one?"

"You've had them securely barred, m'sieu'? They'd have to blast them open, and it's child's play to put a ball into anyone trying it. It'll be a frontal *assaut* on these gates, of a certitude!"

"All right. The moment you—" began Mainwaring.

The guns flashed again and there was a crunching impact against the rampart masonry. A cloud of fragments burst from a spot on the wall immediately before one of the fishermen, and the man staggered back, his musket clattering to the firing step as he clawed silently at his face, which had instantly become a bloody mask. Before a move could be made to help him, he lurched to the edge of the rampart and pitched wordlessly over, impacting with a horrid sound on the *pavé* below.

"Keep them down, De Guimond, except for one watching! And tell me what happens, for God's sake!" cried Mainwaring, a foul taste in his mouth. He turned and went down the slippery stone stairs in a rush. When he arrived on the courtyard, he found Howe kneeling beside the fisherman's limp form.

"Can anything be done for him, James?" he asked.

Howe rose. "No, sir. He's dead."

196

"All right," Mainwaring sighed. "All the lads here?"

"I've left Evans on the rampart, sir, by the guns. I've told him to alert us to any other vessels coming out, boats on the seaward side, that sort of thing."

"Very thoughtful of you." Mainwaring winced involuntarily as several round shot struck home with a thunderous impact against the heavy beams and planking of the gates. Dust clouds curled from the archway, and a thin haze of spinning wood slivers appeared to float in the air.

Howe spat. "That damned wood won't hold much longer, sir! Next two or three rounds and the bastards will pour through at us!"

Mainwaring nodded, his eyes searching the courtyard. "James, those casks and barrels. Move them over here to form a musketry barricade, set back about half-way from the archway!" He ran to a spot, marking out a line with the toe of his shoes in the dust of the courtyard. "Here – to here! Quickly!"

At Howe's bellow the Dianas slung their muskets and moved at a run from where they had been waiting silently by the wall across the yard to the jumble of barrels, casks and hogsheads that formed a rough pyramid beside one of the casemates. Grunting and cursing, they rolled, carried or pushed the awkward wooden containers over the flagstones to Mainwaring's line. In a few minutes they had established a rough barricade almost chest-high, facing the archway and the disintegrating gates.

There was a ringing crash at the gates, and Howe was pointing with his cutlass blade. "That's damned near put paid to the gates, sir! Next round or two, and they'll give way!"

"Ready yourselves, lads!" barked Mainwaring. "Leave the rest of those things where they are! Get yourselves to cover here and prime and load! James, space them out at proper intervals!" He cupped his hands, looking up. "De Guimond! Are ye there, man!"

The Frenchman appeared on the rampart lip as another thunderous crash struck the doors.

"*Oui, Capitaine*! They will be on us in a moment!"

"Yes! Open fire on 'em as soon as they begin their rush! When they get through, fire on 'em from above!"

De Guimond acknowledged with a wave of his cutlass, and was gone, his voice raised in shouted orders.

Mainwaring sprinted back around the end of the barricade and rejoined Howe. The first lieutenant was feverishly ramming a cartridge down a musket barrel, and gestured with his chin to another leaning against the barricade. "Believe that's yours, sir. Dropped it when you came in."

"Thankee, James. Damn me, but this is a far cry from a quarterdeck, what?"

Howe grinned crookedly at him. "Not half, sir!"

Mainwaring thrust his cutlass into the back of his belt and seized the musket, scrabbling with his other hand in the cartridge box at his hip. He glanced at the archway as another sledgehammer blow struck the gates. This time a halo of tumbling, spinning fragments of beams and planking sprang free, thwocking and pattering against the barricade as the Dianas ducked behind their shelter.

"They've breached it, sir!" Howe cried, and at almost the same moment there was a muted cry from De Guimond, and the rampart muskets of the fishermen rang out in a ragged volley, the muzzle flashes sending an eerie flicker playing along the rampart lip.

"They're comin' on, sir!" Jackman cried. "I c'n see 'em! That gate'll not 'old 'em, by Christ!"

"Silence!" barked Mainwaring. "Listen for my orders! Make ready, now! Take your aim on the archway. But not a man fires until I give the word!"

Again, the fishermen fired. Then De Guimond was at the rampart lip, shouting down at Mainwaring, his words now suddenly drowned in the voices of many men: cries of victory, and the short, triumphant barkings of infantry pressing in for the kill.

"Axes, sir!" cried Howe. "They've pioneers with 'em!"

Mainwaring did not answer. Axe blows were raining against the twisted remnants of the gates, and massed figures, a hedge of bayonets showing above the black tricorne hats, were visible behind the flashing axe blades that gleamed brassily in the orange lantern light.

"Listen to me!" cried Mainwaring, over the axe blows and the roar of the men massed outside. "Jackman and every man to his right, fire only on Mr Howe's orders! Slade, and all to his left, on mine! James, you'll fire as we reload, and then we shall do the same! Clear?"

"Aye, aye, sir!" called Howe, his face a white mask of strain. "Bayonets, sir?"

Damn! Mainwaring cursed his thoughtlessness. "Aye! Every man, *fix bayonets*!"

The bayonets slithered out, flashing dully as they clinked and thunked on to the barrels of the muskets. It would make reloading somewhat more difficult; but when the French came to close quarters—

"They're in!"

With a guttural roar, the French marine infantrymen kicked their way through the remaining shards of beam and plank, and pushed in a jostling mass through the narrow archway. As they spilled out into the open, they levelled their muskets at the barricade, still stumbling forward as more men pushed at them from behind.

"Now!" cried Mainwaring. "*Fire!*"

The muskets to either side of him fired in a ripple of sharp bangs, luridly pink pan flashes and sudden gouts of acrid smoke, and then his own punched hard against his shoulder, the pan flash so close and bright the heat seared his cheek. He had only half-seen the figure at which he had fired, and now as the cloud of smoke hung like a sudden curtain across his view, he had no idea what the effect of the volley might have been. Pink flashes were bursting all round him, and balls whizzed past his face like cruising bumblebees or smacked hard into the wood of the cask behind which he sheltered. He was frantically tugging his ramrod clear of its retaining bands as his ears rang with shouts and yells, screams and ear-splitting blasts of muskets fired at point-blank range. In a building frenzy he tore a cartridge from his pouch, bit the end off savagely, hastily primed the pan and cast the musket about as he heard Howe's voice – was it Howe? – shriek "Fire!" Muskets roared, the smoke darkening the feeble light into an almost sightless gloom, and Mainwaring was cursing steadily through clenched teeth as he rammed the ball home, pulled the ramrod clear and threw it at his feet, cocking the weapon and throwing it up to his shoulder to fire, already looking for some target in the reeking cloud.

As if on cue, an eddy in the thick smoke suddenly swirled open, and a knot of grey-clad men appeared several yards before Mainwaring, mouths open in incoherent cries, their bayonets levelled as they saw him and came on in a shambling run.

"*Fire*, lads!" Mainwaring bellowed, wondering if they had heard or waited for him, but then hearing the painful blasts of the weapons, and hearing his own explode and kick his shoulder as he jerked the trigger, wincing away from the pan flash. He had a nightmarish glimpse of a man just beyond his bayonet tip clawing at a crimson hole below one eye, and falling away.

But the wave of men was overwhelming. It surged on over the bodies that writhed and kicked on the flagstones, the same dusty flagstones that were now slick and sticky with blood and horrid fragments of men, the shrieks and pleas of the wounded lost in the steady bellow of the wave of men who trod forward over them, pushing into the mass of barrels and casks.

Now Mainwaring was defending his small portion of the cask wall against a packed horde of marines at bayonet distance, all lunging and thrusting at him, eyes wild, lips in sallow faces twisted in high-pitched cursing. His bayonet and the steel of his musket barrel rang against theirs in a wild, circling duel, and his breath began to come in sobs as he desperately parried, stabbed, parried once more, and then thrust again and again until his arms cracked with pain. There was a hot lancet of pain in one wrist, and he felt more than saw the bayonet rip through his cuff. Now the cask wall was giving way, thumping and crashing open, and he was toe-to-toe with three men, seeing the hate and vicious fury in their faces; into his own mind came the vision of the sobbing children, the raped and murdered mother lying in the casemate, the bloody horror of de Guimond's back, and an uncontrollable fighting fury rose in him. His arms flexed like whip steel, and the musket butt smashed into the jaw of one man, driving him down and away; in the next instant he reversed the musket, and with a grunt of effort he bayoneted a man hard and brutally in the stomach, kicking the screaming wretch away as he pulled the bloody blade free of the grey cloth, only to thrust again and again at the pressing, encircling bodies, glinting bayonet blades and rage-blackened faces. His feet were spread now, and he held his ground bitterly, fighting in a kind of delirium of clubbing and thrusting, hearing the clash and scrape of the weapons, the cursing and shrieking, as a kind of steady roar in his head. His own voice was sounding, too: a high, steady war cry of what words he knew not, and from what unlocked depths within him it had come he knew not.

A man was before him, cutting down at his head with an overhand blow of an infantry hanger. Mainwaring threw up his musket to the cross parry, and the blade shattered against the forestock with a ringing jolt. He had reversed his musket now, steel butt plate first, and he drove it into the man's face, seeing the head snap back, the body falling away. But in the next split-second another man, half-crouched behind a barrel, had lunged for Mainwaring, the bayonet cold and horrid as it sliced through Mainwaring's linen coat and shirt, grazing along the tight muscles of his stomach; and then he was twisting clear, centring his own blade, and with a grunt sinking it to the musket muzzle into the man's belly. The man screamed, his hands clutching at Mainwaring's musket, and with a sob of rage Mainwaring tugged the blade free and kicked at the man until he fell back, eyes goggling.

Some instinct made him turn in time to see another grey-clad marine, hatless and without a weapon, vault in wiry agility over a barrel and thud into Mainwaring, scrawny but powerful, clawlike hands locking round Mainwaring's throat, the man's face a toothless mask of wild, black hair, sallow, unshaven skin, black, hate-filled eyes and a gust of breath reeking of garlic. Mainwaring's knee came up hard once, twice, into the man's groin, and the cursing fury on the rodent face flashed to sick nausea; and then the American had thrown him away like a suddenly limp doll, moving over him as he collapsed to the bloody stones, and buried his bayonet with a bark of triumph in the man's throat as he lay kicking, not listening to the horrid, bubbling scream, not listening to his own savage, steady bellowing, not listening to the stunning level of hideous noise about him of cries and gun blasts, steel clashings, grunts and screams, curses and pleadings, feeling only the red rage within him and the furious need to kill, kill and go on killing.

The explosion was not a sharp report, but more of a deep, throbbing whoomph that snuffed out all other sounds, as if the air could contain no more. Everything in Mainwaring's world vanished in a huge and brilliant ball of flame that washed over the struggling figures, scattering them across the courtyard like a great hand. The same hand caught Mainwaring in mid-bayonet thrust; it tore the weapon from his hands and threw him down and away from the barricade in a painful, tumbling roll.

For an instant, his sense failed him, and he had no idea where he might be. Then sanity returned and he rolled to his knees, smelling the scorched cloth of his coat, blinking as he felt the spattering of soot across his face. He held his hands before his eyes and stared at them, aware that he was breathing in deep gasps. His hands were black and bloody claws which shook as he stared at them, horror rising in his throat until he flexed the fingers and realised he had not been horribly burnt. With an effort of will he fought to his feet, staring round him through a strange, glowing orange haze that filled the courtyard of l'Eguillette.

Then he saw the blackened, smoking bodies, a few still struggling pathetically.

Oh, God, oh, dear God, cried his mind. He turned away, the nausea overwhelming him, and was wretchedly sick on the flagstones, clutching at his knees to keep from falling as he retched.

"Sir? Sir! Are ye all right, sir?" A voice sounded behind him in the eerie silence, and he turned, hating his weak and shaking misery, scrubbing a cuff across his mouth. Jackman was a spectre in a torn and bloody shirt, his face a sooty mask out of which his eyes stared whitely. "Hurt, sir?"

"No," croaked Mainwaring. "I – what in the name of God was *that*?"

As his ears recovered he began to hear the faint voices; voices pleading for help, and more distant ones bellowing orders, fading away, and closer in the awful, ground-hugging murk, from the smoking, humped forms that littered the courtyard around the half-collapsed barricade, groans and whimpering.

Howe appeared, his face a dirty apparition the equal of Jackman's. He was still holding his cutlass, and his shirt was spattered with streaks of gore. He was hobbling in one shoe.

"Explosion, sir. I think the Frenchman up there and his fishermen dropped a powder barrel on – the marines, sir. Went off in the middle of 'em. Saved us, sir."

Behind Howe the Dianas that Mainwaring could make out were struggling to their feet amidst the welter of barrels and bodies, coughing as they stared round them in the smoke. But only a handful were moving; some lay still in twisted, grotesque positions.

Mainwaring stared at Howe, feeling the nausea rising again, feeling the control going.

"James!" he whispered, through clenched teeth. "James, I—" He glanced at Jackman. "All I could do was kill, James. All I—" He turned away and was sick again. As the retching tore at his innards, he felt Howe's hand rest on his shoulder.

"You fought like *ten* men, sir. We'd have broken and run if you hadn't. The lads rallied around you, and wouldn't give way. You held 'em off, sir. You held 'em off!"

The retching passed, and Mainwaring stood upright, fighting to regain control.

"The French troops," he croaked. "The goddamned French, and that whoreson Roche-Bourbon. Where—?"

Jackman was pointing towards the archway. "They've pulled back fer th' moment, sir. Clear of the archway, all of 'em. Them's as were left."

Mainwaring took an iron grip on himself with an almost visible expression of effort. "Jackman, listen carefully. You and as many of the lads as can move push those casks and barrels into the archway opening. Stand clear if their guns begin again. But try and plug it, tight as you can! Then set fire to it. D'ye follow, man?"

Howe spat. "Sir, they're only regrouping! They'll open up with their guns again and blast that to—"

"I don't *care*, James!" raged Mainwaring. "It's *something*! Any way we can hold them up, we shall! *Do* it!"

Howe paused only a split-second before nodding. "Aye, aye, sir!" he said, his own voice cracking with strain. With Jackman beside him, he staggered back to the barricade through the smoke, still as thick as a heavy fog, trying to pull Dianas to their feet.

Mainwaring stumbled forward, looking for his musket. Then he tugged off his bloody and ragged coat and the cartridge crossbelt, and threw them down. From the small of his back he pulled the cutlass, and strode on. Instinct made him look up, and he could make out the half-lit form of De Guimond against the night sky.

"You live, m'sieu'?"

"Yes, damn your eyes, I live, De Guimond! What is happening out there?"

"They are regrouping, m'sieu'! But only one company! The others are arguing with their officers! And they are all obscuring the field of fire for the guns! You have some time before the next attack! Should we not join you there?"

Mainwaring held up a palm in restraint. "In a moment. That infernal blast. Was that *you*?"

"*Oui*. They were overwhelming you. We filled a heavy cask here with cartridges from the guns on the far battery, and put a slow match in before throwing it upon them. Are your men—?"

"I don't know. But I would have done the same. De Guimond, stay there for a moment. But for God's sake watch and warn us when they come again! We'll be setting fire to the wood in the archway, so get clear if it looks sure to reach you up there!"

"I will, m'sieu'!"

Mainwaring spun round unsteadily and made for the archway. Only four figures were working there, spectral creatures with blackened skin and torn, bloody clothing.

204

They were pushing the last of the barrels into a kind of irregular wooden mound almost six feet high.

"In place?" Mainwaring said. "Very good. Set fire to it!" Then he stared at the little group of figures as Jackman knelt with a crude torch made from part of his shirt wrapped round a splinter and applied it to several projecting plank ends. He had lit the torch from one of the guttering wall lanterns, and now the wood of the barrels began to catch the flames quickly, whooshing into bright tongues that drove the Englishmen back with the sudden heat.

Mainwaring stumbled and almost fell across the body of a dead man of the *Troupes*, and then looked at Howe.

"James," he said, raising his voice over the roar and crackle of the building fire. "Is – this all we are left?"

Howe nodded, his face drawn and tight. "Yes, sir. Besides Evans, there's Jackman, Slade, Sawyer, myself, and – and yourself, sir."

"The others?"

"Dead, sir."

"Sweet Christ. Sweet Christ." For a moment Mainwaring could think of nothing else to say. He stared at the four watchful faces, seeing the shock and horror there. Then he saw something else, and he marvelled.

Discipline. Steady, obedient discipline, waiting quietly for his next order.

He turned away, certain they had seen the misting in his eyes. He cupped his hands, looking up. "De Guimond?"

The Frenchman appeared.

"We – I think the best thing is for you and your brave fellows to join us here. Will you?"

De Guimond gave him and the four silent figures a long look. Then the cutlass swung up in a graceful formal salute.

"Of a certainty, m'sieu'!" And he turned to call to his fishermen.

"Evans!" Mainwaring barked. "Rejoin us here!"

"Aye, sir!" came the Welshman's call.

Mainwaring turned back to the four men who stood leaning now on their muskets, their eyes grave and watchful.

"The fishermen will join us. We'll stand together for the end." He paused, keeping his voice steady by effort of will. "I'm sorry that this did not work out as I had hoped. You've done everything duty could ask of you, and more. I'm proud of you." He coughed. "When they come in at us again, we'll have a chance to take some of the bastards with us, lads. That I promise you."

"Sir?" It was Howe. "What about the women and children? When the soldiery get through with us—"

Mainwaring met his look and nodded. "You're right, James, of course. Damn my forgetfulness!" His eyes lifted to De Guimond, coming down the stairs at the head of his clutch of fishermen.

"De Guimond!" Mainwaring called. "I am most regretful that we must do without your company, charming as that would be. Please tell your fishermen to fetch their families out of that casemate. The seaward sally port is clear, and beyond it is the jetty with the longboat we brought in here. I'll trouble you to take it out, to safety."

De Guimond was before him now, staring at him. "*What, m'sieu*? But our place is here—"

"Your place is helping these brave men and their families to get to that boat, as quickly as you can, De Guimond! Pull out to the outer harbour approaches. I'm sure you can all cram into the craft. Find one of our ships – there are two – and tell them I sent you. They'll look after you!"

"M'sieu', I cannot," began De Guimond.

"You can and will, sir! Now, by God, tend to your countrymen, or I shall do it for you!" said Mainwaring tightly.

De Guimond's brown eyes warmed with a look of deep admiration. He repeated the graceful cutlass salute, the clumsy weapon in his hands as light as a rapier.

"Very well, m'sieu'. And I salute you."

"And I you, De Guimond. More than you know. Now, for God's sake, *go!*"

De Guimond turned and spoke rapidly with the fishermen. As they listened, they shared a long look with the Dianas, a look that said much across the barriers of language, and then ran for the door of the casemate. They

206

flung it open and emerged with the women and children, a wide-eyed silent throng. With De Guimond leading them, they moved quickly to the low sally-port door out of which Mainwaring and his men had burst seemingly ages ago, and were soon ducking into it. A few cast anxious looks back at Mainwaring and the others, in particular one woman whose eyes sent a last message across the dim courtyard to Mainwaring before she, too, vanished from view.

Finally, De Guimond was the sole remaining figure. He straightened to the Position of the Soldier, gave the effortless cutlass salute once more, his face full of pride and sorrow at once.

Then he was gone, the low door slamming shut behind him.

Mainwaring turned to Howe and the others. Behind him, the fire in the archway roared and billowed, the yellow hedge of flames licking up fiercely round the roof of the archway, the smoke lifting in a thick column into the night sky. The flickering light played over the exhausted faces of the men as they met Mainwaring's gaze.

"That fire will hold the swine back for a few minutes, lads," said Mainwaring, a strange calm coming over him. "I'm sorry we couldn't have gone in the longboat as well. But if the women and children were to have a chance . . . " He did not finish.

"Better them than us, sir," said Slade. The wiry little man grinned at him, a black-faced elf. "Beggin' yer pardon, sir."

"Yes," said Mainwaring, simply. He looked at the archway. In a few moments the men who would kill them would move closer to the fire, and once they had kicked or pushed it away, would rush in at them in overwhelming numbers. Clearly there was no alternative to what was about to happen; for the escape of De Guimond's people to be successful, the attackers – and above all, Roche-Bourbon – had to believe that no one had left.

Mainwaring smiled to himself. So the bastard on the white horse had won, after all.

"Very well," he said quietly. "Prime and load, lads. We'll form a skirmish line just to one side of the line of fire from the archway. Then, when they come through—"

"Sir?" It was Howe, craning to look past the rushing flames, stopping in the loading of his weapon. "There's – there's something odd going on out there, sir. Look!"

Mainwaring turned, following Howe's gaze. Through the flickering hedge of flames now sinking lower even as he watched, he could dimly see figures beyond, lit by the light of the fire. There was a ragged line of the grey-clad *Troupes*, perhaps a half-company in all, eyeing the archway and apparently waiting for the order that would send them forward again. But behind them, Mainwaring could see sudden movement and action: action that included the galloping past of the white horse, the dark figure astride it gesturing with a long sword that caught a quick glint of the firelight as he passed.

"Damme, James, they're *leaving*!" burst out Mainwaring. "All but a score or two of 'em! What in the devil—?"

Howe's ramrod clinked back into place. "Another threat of some kind, sir?"

Mainwaring nodded slowly, mystified. His heart was suddenly beating with excitement. "Perhaps. By God, let's find out! Evans?"

"Sir?" said the Welshman.

"I need you back on your perch. Get back up on that wall, quick as you can! Find out what is going on out there! Lively, now!"

"Aye, aye, sir!" Evans sprinted for the rampart stairs, his cartridge box banging and rattling against his hip as he ran.

"Fire's a-goin', sir!" twanged Sawyer. "They'll be in after us, quicker'n a 'coon up a tree!"

"I could not put it better," said Mainwaring, his jaw muscles tight. "Ready yourselves, now. Form a line – here. They'll be able to get through in another minute or so."

Howe had hefted up his musket into the 'Make Ready' position with all the ease of a grenadier. Now he pointed with his chin at the archway. "Look there, sir. Pioneers moving up to hook away the fire."

"All right. Ready yourselves!" said Mainwaring. He had taken up a musket from the courtyard and briskly primed and loaded it. Now he drew the weapon back to full cock, and looked at the faces of the others. A few feet apart, they stood in a forlorn little line in the middle of the lamplit, smoky courtyard, litter and death all around them. The shards of the barricade, the twisted bodies now silent and still, with here and there the recognisable form of a Diana, attested to the savagery of the fight. They had fought well, all of them. They had followed him without question, and had done their duty. If his plan had failed, and the French and Spanish were about to put to sea and bring to an end England's hopes in the Mediterranean, it would not be the fault of the men of *Diana*. Mainwaring knew that he alone was responsible for their deaths, and for the failure of what he had attempted to do. He wished he could have said more to them, and particularly to those who now lay dead on the dark and bloodied flagstones of the courtyard.

He shifted his musket to free his right hand and turned to Howe.

"James? I've no wish to intrude in your thoughts, but I wish you to know that you've been a friend, a true shipmate, and a fine officer. I could have asked for no one better." He took the first lieutenant's hand in a warm, firm grip.

"Thank you, sir," said Howe. His face seemed carved in pale stone under the soot and blood. "I am – I feel the same way, sir. Thank you."

Solemnly, Mainwaring went along the line and shook the hands of the others, seeing in their steady eyes a respect and warmth that humbled him. He could not utter the words to tell them how bitterly he regretted bringing them to this death, and at the same time how desperately proud of them he was.

Wordlessly, he resumed his position and faced the archway. The grey-clad *Troupes* were already there, perhaps twenty men, their bayonets levelled and glinting in the flickering light as they edged forward, waiting for the few men with long billhooks standing closer to the flames to pull away the last bits of burning wood and clear a path for the rush. Mainwaring knew that the French could see them, and the marines' faces were lit as much with a leering

209

anticipation of the final kill as by the flickering firelight. The marines licked their lips and grinned at one another, a feral bloodlust in their dark eyes so clear that Mainwaring could perceive it where he stood.

Evans arrived back breathlessly from the ramparts, his bare feet slapping on the flagstones. His face was a mask of astonishment.

"Bloody marvellous it is, sir! By the lighthouse—"

But Evans' voice was drowned by another sound; a sound that stunned Mainwaring and the others.

A wild volley of musketry thundered from somewhere beyond the archway, musket blasts that were joined by deep-throated hoots and fighting yells.

"Good Christ!" burst out Howe, in astonishment. "What—?"

As Mainwaring and the others stared, the line of French marines wavered, men crumpling here and there, others turning, crouching, throwing up their muskets and hastily firing at an unseen target off to the right. Then a wave of figures burst over the French: burly, strong-muscled figures in seamen's clothing, with cutlasses flashing down and boarding axes swinging like reapers' scythes. They fell upon the French like a pack of baying hounds and cut them down where they stood in a storm of slaughter.

And leading them, a huge basket-hilted sword swinging in wild arcs round him while he bellowed strange cries, a powerfully-built man with grizzled, curly hair and a piratical eye-patch.

"*McCallum!*" gasped Mainwaring. "It's *Barb*! The landing party from *Barb*!" He levelled his musket at the archway. "*Come on!*" he cried.

Through the archway, vaulting over the still-smouldering embers, Mainwaring moved at a dead run, the other Dianas behind him. Then they were out, fierce cries of escape and joy coming unbidden to their lips, and they rushed alongside the men of *Barb* at the handful of French who still stood.

In a few quick, bloody seconds it was over. The French lay in tumbled heaps of dead, or were vanishing into a low tree line at a run, pursued by scattered musket shots to urge them on their way. Panting and unbelieving, Mainwaring and the others were surrounded by a grinning, back-thumping mob of British seamen, with the one-eyed McCallum, his huge sword scarlet from tip to guard, fixing Mainwaring with the widest grin of all.

"McCallum!" laughed Mainwaring, feeling lightheaded and dizzy. "The flares! Ye saw the flares!"

"Aye, lad!" beamed the Scot, his face flushed and his single eye burning. "We saw them, right enough, and put in as quick as we could. But ye made enough noise with yer fightin', that we couldna missed where ye were!"

Mainwaring shook his head in thankful wonder. "The longboat. With the women and children. There were fishermen in it who had helped us, and a French officer who did as well. You found them?"

"Aye. Or more rightly, he found us! Him and his boat-load o' bairns appeared out o' th' night as we were standin' in, an' made it clear we were tae put in after ye, an' no mistake aboot it. We clambered into it, tae pull in. They wouldna hear o' leavin' you. He's guardin' it now, by that small hidden jetty. It meant we could bring more of th' lads. A guid thing fer you, I'd say. Yer own boat's sunk!"

Mainwaring gripped the Scot's arm, feeling the steely muscle there. "Better for us than you know, McCallum. We'd not have lasted a minute. But there were more French than this! They all went off, when—"

"Och, I know, I know," said McCallum, holding up a protesting paw. "We thought a wee diversion was needed, so to speak. So we went ashore at the lighthouse – a bit of a climb up those rocks, I can tell ye – and built a sort of bonfire, ye might say, in the lighthouse itself. We also did a wee bit o' shootin', and the Frogs must have thought a bigger problem than you was afoot out there!"

"Well, bugger me!" gasped Howe.

Mainwaring's expression sobered. A wave of nausea and fatigue washed over him, but he willed himself to resist it.

"McCallum, we've got to get clear of here. The French commander is a vicious bastard who won't be fooled long by your diversion. We'll have to be away in the boat before he returns!"

"We canna hold it against him?"

"Not a chance. He's still got three field pieces and well over two hundred men." Mainwaring pointed at the archway gaping behind them. "With those gates gone there'll be no holding them."

"Aye," McCallum nodded. "Weel, ye've still got command. Just say what ye want done."

"Thank you." Mainwaring was thinking quickly. "Evans, what was it you were about to tell me?"

"The French ships, sir! And the Dons, I think, too. They're slippin' and movin' for the gap, sir. I think they be puttin' to sea, *all* of 'em, sir!"

"Bloody hell!" Mainwaring spat into the dirt. "I knew they would! Are you *certain* of that, Evans?"

"Aye, sir! Clear as a bell, it was, and easy t' see 'em as they swung when they hove short, sir. The wind's backed considerable, but they can brace up an' still reach out. An' that's what they're about, look you, sir!"

Mainwaring turned to McCallum. "What about *Barb*? Where is she?"

"Safe enough for the moment, I think," said McCallum, scratching his chin. "She's standin' off a wee bit, as is your lad Hooke with *Trusty*. An' I'd think they'd have no trouble gettin' tae weather o' any Frog as came after 'em."

"Then we'd best get to the boat. Unless—" Mainwaring turned to Howe. "What d'ye think, James? A last round from those rampart twelve-pounders?"

Howe shook his head. "Would hardly do any damage, sir. We were damned lucky to sink that one frigate. If we start firing, it'll bring that bastard on the white horse back like the furies of hell."

"You're right." Mainwaring eyed the hulking fortification. "There's only one thing left to do before we run for the boat, then."

"What's that, sir?" asked Howe.

"In a moment, James." Mainwaring turned to McCallum, stepping close to the Scot.

"John, you've got to get those lads back to the boat as quickly as possible. You say it's tied up at the small jetty on the seaward side?"

"Aye. An' yer Frenchman's watchin' it there, as I said."

"Right, then," said Mainwaring briskly. "Move to it quickly, now! Roche-Bourbon – the French officer in charge of the mob that attacked us – is quick and crafty. He'll soon determine that your lighthouse fire was a ruse, and will come back here at the full gallop, certainly with those dragoons he had!"

"And what of ye?" said McCallum. "Ye canna—"

Mainwaring indicated Howe and Jackman with a look. "Three of us will stay. I'm going to get into the magazine. There we'll set a slow-match. You'll have to wait for us to get to you at the boat. Hopefully we can get out through the seaward sally port."

"Christ's guts! D'ye mean *blow it up*?" McCallum's single eye gleamed in astonishment.

"Aye, John!" said Mainwaring. "But we've another problem. There's a dozen or so French prisoners on one of the casemates, inside. Give me three or four of your lads to deal with 'em."

"Done," said McCallum. "Fulham, take those messmates o' yours an' go along with Lieutenant Mainwaring."

"Aye, aye, sir," said a burly seaman with dark hair clubbed into a tarry pigtail. He knuckled a forelock to Mainwaring. "What is it ye have in mind, sir?"

"Go along with these Dianas, Fulham. That's Slade, Sawyer, and the grinning Welshman is Evans. Slade, you'll be senior hand. Release the French prisoners out of their casemate on to the roadway, here. Unharmed, if you please. But relieve 'em of their shoes. Then get to the boat as quickly as you can. Clear?"

Slade exchanged a grin with Fulham. "Aye, aye, sir! Come on, yew lot. 'Ave a glim at th' Froggies we put in th' bag!" said the little Cockney, and the men doubled off through the archway after him, their kit clinking about them.

213

9

Mainwaring looked towards the distant cape. A bright pillar of flame licked skyward in the inky night, and he wondered where Roche-Bourbon was between here and there at that moment.

"Now, John," he said to McCallum. "Best you return directly to the boat. Out oars and be ready to pull the very devil out of here. With a fuse burning in this place's magazine and a whole bloody *fleet* ready to come barging out—"

"The picture's clear, sir!" said McCallum, and Mainwaring noted that it was the first instance when McCallum had called him that. "But d'ye need help settin' the charge?"

Mainwaring shook his head. "No, John, with thanks. But for God's sake don't pull out and leave us!"

McCallum grinned, the bright eye alight with humour. "Och, I'd no do that. Ye give a lad too much enjoyment t' be left behind, an' that's sartin!"

There were several barked commands behind Mainwaring, and he turned to see a clutch of hatless and dishevelled – and barefoot – prisoners in *Troupes* uniforms gingerly picking their way over the rough, rocky ground outside the archway. Pushing them along roughly at bayonet point was Slade's party, which was largely barefoot as well and not sympathetic to the tenderness of the landsmen's feet.

"What d'ye want done wiv 'em again, sir?" called Slade.

"Show 'em the road to la Seyne – that way – and send 'em packing!" Mainwaring shouted back.

"Aye, aye, sir!" replied the Cockney. They began to push the cowering little knot of men along the shoreside cart track, like large border collies worrying a group of craven sheep.

"Not very imposing soldiery, that lot o' Froggies," said McCallum.

"Not that particular lot, John," agreed Mainwaring. "Far too busy mistreating women and children. All very vicious when they had the upper hand." He cupped his hands. "Let 'em go on from there, Slade! Ye've got to be in the boat yourselves!"

Mainwaring nodded to McCallum as he saw Slade and the others give the French a last shove, and then turn and run for the water side of l'Eguillette. "Now it's your turn. I trust we'll meet again in the sternsheets of the boat?"

"We'll wait for ye, sir! No fear o' that!"

Mainwaring grinned. "I'll see you eat your bonnet if you don't!" He turned to Howe and Jackman. "Come on, James. Time to set one more surprise for our garlicky friends!"

With Howe and Jackman at his heels, Mainwaring ran lightly back through the archway and on to the lantern-lit courtyard, where the dead still lay in their twisted and grotesque shapes. Mainwaring shivered, forcing the image of the killing and his own bloodlust from his mind, and peered around the shadowed walls at the row of ochre-coloured doors set in the casemates.

"The whoreson magazine, Jackman!" he muttered in exasperation. "D'ye know *where* Evans found the damned thing?"

Jackman scratched the back of his head, thinking. Then he turned, pointing to a thick, ironbound door in one corner of the fortification.

"There, sir. Leastwise, 'twere from there that the fishermen brought the cartridges."

"Come on, then!"

At a run they crossed to the door and thrust back its heavy bolt. As the door swung ponderously open, they saw angled, whitewashed walls and a single candle lantern set behind glass in a wall sconce. There was an odd odour that Mainwaring at once identified as mouldy felt.

"Hanging curtains. Watch your step, lads, and don't drag your feet! Place 'em carefully. One spark and we'll come to earth somewhere west of Gibraltar . . . "

Mainwaring pushed aside a damp, hanging partition of the black felt and found himself standing in a vast chamber

215

down either side of which tall framed timbers held stacked powder barrels, reaching to the arched ceiling.

"Good Lord!" Mainwaring breathed. "If all this *does* go up—!"

"Sir?" It was Jackman, at a low work table. "Pouch with a coil o' slow-match 'ere, sir." His eyes were white in his soot-blackened face, the shadows of his cheeks thrown into stark relief by the dim orange light of the lantern.

"Good. James, take my musket and set it down very slowly and carefully. Jackman, give me a foot – no, a foot and a half – of that slow-match. Christ, hope I remember how quickly that burns! Give me a hand here, James."

Moving with extreme caution, Mainwaring lifted down a small gunpowder cask and set it on the planking. With Howe helping, he soon had a chest-high pyramid of the smaller powder casks piled in the centre of the narrow space between the towering racks of larger casks.

"Right. Now for some priming!" breathed Mainwaring. He realised with a start that he was streaming with sweat. He pried the bung from one of the casks and shook out enough of the powder into a dark, granular pile until the space within the cask was sufficiently large. Carefully, he rotated the cask until the bung hole was near the top as it lay on its side. Then keeping the cask in that position, he laid it very carefully at the foot of the pyramid.

"Now, Jackman. The slow-match, please."

Jackman handed him the length of match, and with infinite care Mainwaring inserted it into the barrel and then draped the match down the side, ready for ignition.

"Very well," he said, letting out a lungful of air. "Now how do we *light* the damned thing?"

"One of the slow-matches on the barbette, sir?" offered Jackman.

Mainwaring shook his head as he crouched down. "No. Likely all burnt down by now, in any event. There's but one way; I'll have to crack open that sconce lantern."

Howe stared at him. "An open flame? Damme, sir, we'll go up like a firework!"

"Then suggest another way of doing it."

Howe looked at Jackman and then shook his head.

"Exactly," said Mainwaring. "James, take my firelock." Mainwaring moved to the smoky-glassed sconce and opened it, reaching gingerly for the lantern.

"Gently is the word," he breathed, and carried the lantern over to the stack of casks. "James, I want you two to leave and ensure the seaward sally port is clear. Then one of you post yourself by the archway. Roche-Bourbon and his hounds may be closer than I'd like to think."

"Aye, sir," nodded Howe. "Jackman, you get to the arch. I'll take the sally port." He paused. "Good luck, sir."

"Thank you," said Mainwaring. "As soon as this is lit, I'll be out of here at the full gallop, so be ready to move. If I botch it, we'll all be so much stone dust. Away you go."

"Sir." Howe grinned unconvincingly at him and then was gone, the rattle of the casemate door-latch echoing hollowly as they went out.

Mainwaring took a long last look around the dim chamber. Then he drew a deep breath, eased it out, and carefully slid aside the glass pane fronting the guttering tallow candle. Moving with deliberate slowness, he pulled the candle off its base pin and took it out. Shielding the flame with his free hand, he turned to the hanging slow-match.

Now, pray you are indeed 'slow', he said to himself. Holding his breath, he lifted the flame to the match. There was a heart-stopping sputter and flash, and a sulphurous smell, then a steady red glow that began eating its way up the cord.

His heart pounding in his throat, Mainwaring kept himself from rushing as he placed the candle back in the lantern. Then he padded over to the casemate door, set the lantern down, and went slowly out, careful not to slam the heavy door shut. The cool air washed over him, and as he eased the latch into place he realised that his shirt was soaked in sweat. He expelled the air from his lungs in a rush and sank against the door for a moment, gathering himself.

"Sir?" called Jackman, stepping out of the archway shadows. "Did ye—?"

"Quite." Mainwaring gulped for air. "Come on!" He broke into a trot across the courtyard towards the far angle of the fortification, dodging over the dim, lantern-lit surface with its litter of bodies and past the hateful rack where the fishermen and their families had been tormented. Now Jackman was coming at a flat-footed gallop from the archway.

The sally port! Where in hell *was* it?

Howe appeared out of the shadows of the angle of the wall, the open, rounded entry to the sally port gaping behind him. "It's clear all the way through, sir!" he said, as Mainwaring panted to a halt. He handed Mainwaring his musket, and then both men turned as Jackman slapped in alongside them, puffing and blowing.

"A life at sea ain't one t' make yew a runner o' sorts!" he gasped.

"The roadway?" said Mainwaring. "What sign of the French?"

"Thought I caught sight o' that damned white horse atop a rise in th' moonlight, towards the lighthouse, sir. A-gallopin' this way, it were. An' a line o' lanterns bobbin' along wiv 'im. Mayhap it's them dragoons or whatnot, sir."

"Possibly so. Damn Roche-Bourbon to hell! All right, follow me. And Christ save us if that one-eyed Caledonian isn't waiting for us!" Mainwaring hefted his musket, ducked into the darkness of the low, arched passageway, and set off into its depths. As before, it was a dank, cobwebbed burrow, rough and hurtful to the feet as the three men stumbled through it. Their laboured breathing was magnified in the confined space, and mingled with the scuffing of their shoes and the clink and thump of their kit. The passage seemed far longer than when they had come in; was this in fact the correct tunnel? Or were they caught in some ghastly wrong turn that would see them still entombed within all this claustrophobic masonry when the slow-match reached the—

"The door, sir!" puffed Howe at Mainwaring's shoulder. Ahead in the inky black, a thin blue streak outlined the straight sides and curved top of the seaward exit door.

"Thanks to a kind Providence!" muttered Mainwaring. He put his foot to the rough wooden planking of the ironbound door and pushed. It was unlatched and swung open to the moonlit night with a creak of rusty hinges and a sweet rush of sea air.

In the next moment all three men were out on the narrow, rocky beach, looking quickly round at the scene of the anchorage with its distant garlands of lantern lights against the purple mass of the shore, the moon casting a silver pathway across the narrows between where they stood and le Mourillon fort, the sunken frigate's mastheads like black fingers reaching out of the silver. Off to the right, they could see the line of the little jetty, where the long white hull of the longboat rode, crowded with figures, murmuring and anxious-sounding. A handful of men were standing on the jetty itself, including one with curly hair and a huge, basket-hilted sword which he waved in greeting.

"Lieutenant Mainwaring! Thank Christ!" boomed the Scot. "This way!"

Mainwaring and the others stumbled along the short stretch of beach and then clumped out along the jetty.

"John, we've no time to lose!" Mainwaring said in a low, even voice. "I've set the charge, but Christ knows how long, or how short a time, it'll take the fuse to burn. We'll have to pull hard for open water!"

"Aye, sir!" said the Scot. "But we'll no be the only ones at sea. D'ye spy *that*, sir?" The long sword pointed in towards the inner harbour.

"Good Lord!" burst out Mainwaring.

Their topsails glowing bone-white in the moonlight, a mass of ships was moving in slow, towering majesty towards the gap between the sunken frigate and the dark mass of the Eguillette where they stood. Scores of lanterns glimmered in the darkness on high transom rails, and white Bourbon ensigns drifted in delicate waves from mastheads and ensign staffs. At first, Mainwaring could not make out how many ships were moving; it seemed as if the entire surface of the inner harbour was in motion, the tall shapes heeling slightly as the beam winds came in to fill their braced-up canvas, and white gleamed under the forefoot of each dark bow.

"Damn my eyes, sir!" said Howe beside him, his voice filled with awe. "It's the whole of the bloody combined squadron! The Frogs *and* the Dons!"

Mainwaring eyed the narrow stretch of moonlit water before them. "They're going to try to pass out to this side of the wreck. It's a beam wind. Braced up, they may do it! Damn!"

McCallum was shaking his head. "Dinna blame yerself", sir. Ye did all a man could do t' keep 'em in there!"

Mainwaring's lips were a tight line. "Thankee, John. But we've still bloody well failed!" He spat into the water and then looked at the pale faces crowded in the boat, all turned anxiously on him. He could not see her, but knew she was there. "Come on, John. Either we be run down by the naval might of France and Spain or sit here until the magazine blows. We'd best get out to *Barb* if we can. Do ye see *Trusty*?"

"No, sir," said McCallum. "She must've beat in out o' sight behind Cap Cépet. I couldna see her when we put in."

"Very well. Christ grant they've an eye on what's happening. Into the boat, all of you, quickly!" Mainwaring pointed to the tiller bar. "Take the helm, John. Let go your lines!"

At Mainwaring's bark, the men at the boat's bow and stern line cast off the lines and sprang for the boat. Mainwaring stepped in, fumbling his way over the hunched, crowded bodies until he half-fell into the sternsheets beside a grinning De Guimond, who was holding a small clinging child on his lap.

"I am glad you are safe, m'sieu'," beamed the Frenchman.

"And you, De Guimond," said Mainwaring, managing a crooked smile. "But I see we will have company in a moment that may make things a good deal less safe for all of us!" he added, looking at the ghostly mass of approaching ships.

McCallum clambered in and wedged down beside the tiller bar. The boat was dangerously overcrowded, but there was no helping it. They had to get to sea, and away.

"Stand by your tiller, Mr McCallum. Out oars, lads, if ye can! Shove off, for'rard, there! Can ye bear us off aft, here, Slade?"

"Sir!" The little Cockney grinned at him. Was the man never afraid? With a reversed musket butt he pushed the longboat's stern slowly away from the jetty.

"Give way, *together*!" barked Mainwaring. "Stroke . . . stroke . . . easy, now, lads. Mind the passengers . . . stroke . . . " He swivelled in his seat. The great ships loomed up against the backdrop of the shoreline and the starlit sky, and seemed impossibly tall from the vantage point of the boat. They would reach the narrow gap – and Mainwaring's boat – in perhaps ten minutes. Precious little time to be able to pull away. At any second sharp eyes in the bows or tops would spot them. Perhaps if Mainwaring kept the boat closer inshore, they might be able to escape notice until the last possible moment.

Mainwaring swore to himself, looking back at the pale faces of the huddled women and children. How could he tell them that their chances of surviving the night were so desperately slim?

"Call the stroke, will you, John ? Steer there, close inshore for the Balaguier fort. It's our only chance, I fear!"

"Aye, sir. Inshore 'tis. Pull together, now, lads . . . stroke . . . stroke . . . " McCallum's voice was strong and confident; it gave the sound of stability, and the people in the boat needed that.

Even with the packed conditions in the boat, with seamen at the oars sitting amidst the fishermen, women and children, all of them barely able to move, the men put their backs into the pulling, and the heavy boat began to move ahead in the darkness, the open face of the Golfe de Giens and *Barb* the hidden but beckoning safety somewhere beyond the stem in the darkness. But the lead ship of the huge formation astern, a frigate of about twenty guns, was moving briskly along the beam wind, its masthead pennant snapping. It was as Mainwaring had suspected; the ships *were* steering to pass through the remaining channel in the narrows between the wreck and the Eguillette shore. In all the great vessels, Mainwaring could see the yard being braced up to let the ships pass close along the la Seyne shore. In a great column the ships would slip past into the wider waters of the

Grande Rade, and then out to freedom in the Golfe de Giens itself.

And there, Mainwaring thought gloomily, *England will begin to lose it all. Because of Mathews' narrow little unimaginative mind. But most of all, because of what I failed to do.*

"Oh, Christ!" muttered Howe, at Mainwaring's other elbow. "Look aft there, sir!"

"What is it?"

"That leading sloop-o'-war, sir. By the way they're handling her, I've a feeling they've seen us!"

Mainwaring twisted in his seat. The vessel was still a good firelock shot inside the wreck, but even at this distance and in the moonlit gloom, there was something that Howe's trained eye had seen; perhaps a minute adjustment to a sheet or brace, or the glint of a swivel being trained round.

"I can see nothing, James. Are you certain?"

"Aye, sir. Almost a feeling, more than anything."

"Very well," said Mainwaring. "Keep watching them." He turned to McCallum, keeping his voice low. "If he's right, John, we haven't a chance. They'll run us down in half a league!"

"D'ye think they know what we are, sir?" asked McCallum. "After all—"

"John, I think it's damned well likely. Good Lord, we *sank* one of their ships and drove off an attacking force; now they see an overloaded boat skulking away from the place to seaward. I know the kind of decisions I would make if I paced that quarterdeck. And so do you, I'd warrant!"

Mainwaring looked at the frigate again. Then his eyes narrowed and he felt a cold knot seize his stomach.

A gun! said his mind. *They've run out a bow chaser!*

"Sir!" Howe cried. "They've got—"

"I know, James! *Pull*, lads!"

McCallum's eye swung to him, wide with alarm. "What is it, sir?"

"They've run out a gun, John. If I'm not mistaken, they're about to—"

A flash lit the surface of the sea inshore, a flash in the bows of that leading frigate that was footing along smartly towards the narrows. As the heavy *crump* of the gun's report reached the wallowing longboat, a noise like ripping cloth sounded in the air. In the next instant, a tall, glittering geyser of spray leaped up like a monstrous fountain from the sea several hundred yards ahead of the boat, collapsing back with a hiss.

Screams and wails burst from the packed figures in the boat, and the men at the oars broke their rhythm as hands clutched at them in terror.

"Steady, there!" barked Mainwaring. "Stand to your oars, damn you! Keep the stroke! Call it for them, Mr McCallum!" He swung on De Guimond. "Tell your people to be quiet and be still, or we'll not escape for certain!"

De Guimond immediately began to call out forcefully in quick, emphatic French, and the hubbub and turmoil in the huddled mass quietened.

Another flash lit the night, and again there was the ripping sound in the air. This time the deep report of the gun was drowned by the sharp slap of the roundshot into the water barely five feet away from Mainwaring's hand where it gripped the gunwale. The geyser shot up in immense, glittering beauty, and then collapsed over the boat in a drenching welter that sent the shrieks and wailing raging anew.

"Silence them, De Guimond!" cursed Mainwaring. "*Pull*, lads! Don't lose the stroke! John, veer us from side to side, so their shot—!"

He stopped, staring. Dead ahead of the bows of the longboat lay the point of land on which the Balaguier fort stood. Behind it, curving round out of sight, were the sheltered waters of the Baie du Lazaret.

As he stared, a vessel braced up hard on the larboard tack appeared into view from behind the dark mass of the Balaguier, laying over to the wind, its speed building: a full-rigged vessel, small in size, standing in with her jib-boom centred on the narrow astern of the longboat, and moving along under the freshening wind with phosphorescence gleaming under her bows. Even in the dark of the moonlit night, the Jack that fluttered out from her foretruck could be made out clearly.

"Sweet Christ!" breathed Mainwaring. "It's *Trusty*!"

Another flash blossomed astern, and again the air was ripped by the passage of a round shot that brought another enormous glittering tower of water leaping up twenty yards off the longboat's starboard bow. If McCallum had not swung the tiller . . .

Now the strain was beginning to tell on the oarsmen, and they groaned and cursed as they hauled on their looms, the women and even children reaching to push or pull in help, all working to get the boat somehow to safety from the death threatening astern.

But as they rowed in frantic effort, heads were turning in the longboat to gape in astonishment at the onrushing shape of *Trusty* until Mainwaring's bark brought them back to the oars, and they pulled on, staring at Mainwaring's face as if to see there a mirror of what was happening ahead.

"By the holies, its *Barb*!" suddenly burst out McCallum, pointing forward. A short distance astern of *Trusty*, another vessel had appeared from the Baie du Lazaret. Its great lateen winging out to leeward, the shape of the hurrying xebec stood out like a small ivory carving in the moonlight against the dark velvet of the sea. And it, too, was shaping a course for the narrows, the phosphorescence aglow under its low bows as it came on.

"Damn me, what a sight!" cried McCallum. "Come on, my girl! Come on! Come—"

Again the flash lit the sky astern. But this time, as the thump of the report struck Mainwaring's ears, it came simultaneously with a tremendous hammerblow against the longboat's transom that flung Mainwaring forward to his knees. The spray of the shot's impact fell like torrents of tropical rain, and odd bits of wood were in the air, one striking the back of Mainwaring's head with painful force as it spun away. The air amidst the deluge of salt water filled suddenly with shrieks, wails and curses, and Mainwaring felt the boat sink away from under him, and he was in water to his armpits. The water itself was churned to a froth by the struggling, desperate figures all round him that clutched at him and each other in a wild, frantic panic.

Blindly, Mainwaring struck out, trying to push the struggling bodies clear. He kicked off his shoes and tore away the linen shirt, the fabric disintegrating in his grip. A terrified child, her face turned in pale horror to the sky, her hair streaming back in the water, was suddenly before him. He seized her hands as she grasped weakly at him, and swung her round on to his back, locking her small hands about his throat.

"The boat!" he heard himself crying out. "The boat! Stay with the boat!"

The wild chaos in the dark, threshing water was overwhelming. Piteous cries and desperate shrieks filled his ears above the splashing, the little girl on his back sobbing continuously now, her fingers digging tightly into his neck. An oar was in front of him, and he swam on with it until he found a man and woman, arms locked round each other in a final embrace and coughing as they sank. He roared something at them and thrust the oar under their arms, pulling their heads up and cuffing at their faces to rouse them, and then swam on with furious energy.

Abruptly the white island of the overturned boat's hull, gleaming like a beluga in the moonlight, was before him. He clutched at figures struggling in the water around him and thrust them towards the boat, in some cases forcing their hands on to the craft to where they could get a grip of sorts. His breath coming in great gasps, he fought his way through the throng, again and again pushing or pulling people to the boat, where they clung to it and each other in an extremity of exhaustion and horror.

"Look, sir!" It was Howe's voice, coming from the far side of the boat. Now Mainwaring could see him, clinging to the craft with one arm while supporting two shivering children with the other. "*Trusty*, sir! She's going in!"

Mainwaring shook the water from his eyes. The shape of the little ship went rushing past with a roar of foam at her bows, the masts and rigging towering above them, a small boat tugging at its line astern. Men were moving quickly over the ship as it sailed on, lit now by the grandeur of the moonlight: men with flickering torches in their hands.

"Damn my eyes, they're firing her!" Mainwaring croaked. His hands found the splintery wood of the longboat's planking, and he clung there, the girl shaking and crying against him, as he watched the scene unfold in a kind of numb awe.

Trusty lay over to the wind, surging on no more than two hundred yards from the narrow gap into which the French frigate was also sailing, behind her a closely-packed column of towering vessels all bracing their yards for the beam wind and steering for the gap as well. A strange glow was showing through the slanting stern lights of *Trusty*, from within Mainwaring's own cabin; and now a flickering light was beginning along the little ship's sides, as one by one the peculiar bottom-hinged gunports fell open to reveal a brilliant glare of flame within. A thin pall of smoke was drifting, low and sinuous, off to leeward of the ship, keeping pace with it. And now flames were licking at the bases of the masts, as the dark shapes of men flitted past them.

"Hooke! Pellowe!" Mainwaring breathed. "For God's sake get clear, lads!"

Trusty surged on, and now in the French frigate canvas was rippling as the threat rushing in at them became suddenly evident. But the French vessel had nowhere to go: to one side sat the dark shore with the Eguillette's looming walls; to the other, the wreckage of the sunken frigate blocked a leeward escape. From astern, unaware of what lay ahead, the steadily advancing columns of the great French and Spanish line-of-battle ships made no escape possible in that quarter.

Perfectly done, thought Mainwaring. *Isaiah's timed it perfectly!*

Now the flames were licking up *Trusty*'s masts and the lower canvas, the courses, became sudden writhing masses of brilliant, licking flame. The whoosh of their ignition carried across the water to Mainwaring, mixed now with the crackle and popping of burning wood.

"Jesus!" From somewhere among the huddled figures clinging to the boat, Jackman's wondering murmur reached Mainwaring. "Jesus, look at *that*!"

Trusty was now barely fifty yards from the frigate, her flames illuminating the French vessel in a lurid orange light as shrieks and cries of panic echoed now from it. The frigate had swung from its track, but lay trapped, its topsail canvas gone aback. And now *Trusty* rushed in. The flames reached the topmasts, and three glowing crucifixes, black crosses surrounded by haloes of flame, floated above the flaming hull as it closed with its doomed enemy in final transfiguration.

The ships struck with a grinding crash and a vast shower of sparks and flaming segments that cartwheeled down into the sea. *Trusty* slewed around alongside the other hull, and now flames leaped across, the French topsails vanishing in a sheet of flame, the sea around turned to a molten pool of light by the enormous fire. Amidst that molten light splashing showed as desperate men, many themselves trailing flames from burning clothing, leaped from the decks of the frigate. Within minutes the tarred wood of the French ship was burning with a deep roaring sound, rivers of flame pouring upwards now out of its gunports, the enormous column of fire from both ships reaching up a hundred feet above the locked mastheads.

In the next instant, a hollow blast punched across the water to Mainwaring and the other watchers with the force of a blow to the face, and the frigate disintegrated within a searingly bright ball of flame that boiled upwards, laced now with black, curling and ballooning up into the night sky. Tumbling, burning fragments filled the sky and arced up and out in firework slowness, to fall hissing into the sea.

"Magazine went!" came Howe's voice. "God, what a—"

But Howe's words were drowned in a different sound. A blast, like that of the frigate's magazine, but of such deep, sonorous intensity that it literally sucked the breath from Mainwaring's lungs, and the dark water all around him leaped up in strange, frothy wavelets. A hot gust of wind whisked across the sea face, and behind it a roaring that seemed like a single continuous report from a twenty-four-pound gun.

As Mainwaring stared, the dark grey mass of the Eguillette fort appeared to expand upwards and outwards in painfully slowed motion; an expansion that released into the night a vast, flattened bubble of flame that was speckled and marked with falling stone fragments and the black lacings of smoke. The bubble resolved itself into a huge, glowing cloud of fire that changed from searing yellow to orange and finally deep, angry red as it boiled upward, vanishing then into more cartwheeling pinpoints of light that arced in slow dignity towards the land or sea. Now, all around the foundered longboat, rubble began to splash and patter down, thwocking against the boat's planking, voices crying out here and there as swimmers were struck by the falling pieces. ·

In the gap lay the locked and burning hulls of *Trusty* and the French frigate as the explosion of the fort rose above them. They had swung now so that no passage through the narrows was possible for anything save a small craft. The flames still licked in long tongues skyward from their mutual pyre as the fireball from the Eguillette died away. The light of the burning was obscured by a low-lying, thick cloud that drifted from the dark, smouldering craterlike shape of the Eguillette across the narrow waters of the gap. But the flames still revealed the chaos of collision and luffing canvas of the great, trapped squadrons behind the sudden barrier of wreck, explosion and flame. And now the next vessel astern of the frigate in what had been short moments ago a stately column of naval power had flames licking up her foremast, and was turning towards shallows on the Eguillette shore, a stricken monster. There she struck with an audible rending crash, the flames taking only minutes to turn her, too, into a leaping pyre of licking, smoke-laced flame.

Still shaken and stunned, Mainwaring stared at the appalling scene of destruction, finding it hard to form a thought. What had—?

"Ahoy! In the water, there! Can ye hear us?"

Mainwaring thrashed round, locking the little girl's hands against his throat so as not to lose her. He saw McCallum, blood streaming from a wound on his forehead, lift his head and try to speak, but then slump back against the boat.

"Here!" croaked Mainwaring. "We're here!"

Like a graceful gull, her clewed-up canvas lit in a medley of colour from the moon and the flickering flames inshore, *Barb* lay hove to scarcely a hundred yards away. A boat was pulling strongly towards the overturned longboat, a man in the bows holding high a lantern as he called.

But it was not that boat which caught Mainwaring's eye. It was another ship's boat, pulling firmly out from the direction of the gap and the burning wrecks. A ship's boat, crowded with men, but visibly carrying in its sternsheets a burly-looking man with the look of a veteran seaman, and a shaggy thatch of hair off which the moonlight gleamed – and a youthful figure with blond locks turned silver by the same moonlight. The boat was steering for them now, as they saw *Barb*'s boat.

"Isaiah. Stephen," murmured Mainwaring. "Dear God!" He found he could not form more words. There seemed to be an enormous lump in his throat which got in the way.

Barb's boat was closer, now, the voices of those in the water calling out to it. Now Howe was there before Mainwaring, taking a firm grip on McCallum, strong arms already lifting into the boat the children the first lieutenant had held. Now they were reaching down and pulling the unconscious Scot with great gentleness into the boat, and reaching for the women and children as the swimming men brought them to the boat's sides.

Then, "Your turn, sir," a man in the boat was saying. But Mainwaring reached for the small hands that had clutched at his throat, and very gently pried them apart. With one hand he stretched up and gripped the boat's gunwale, and lifted the little girl while she looked from him to the boat with large, frightened eyes.

"Not before you take this one, and all the others. They've given so much. No need to ask more of 'em."

As the men lifted the little girl to safety, Mainwaring turned and saw the still form that had clung to the boat, previously hidden by McCallum's body. It was the form of a beautiful, workworn woman, seemingly asleep, but whose cheek was as cold as marble as Mainwaring's fingers brushed it. With infinite tenderness he loosened the grip of her hands on the splintered wood, and cradled her

229

against him with one arm while the men on the boat looked at him oddly.

"God knows they've given enough – already!" he whispered. He kissed her cold brow, his eyes clouded with tears that turned the distant flames of the burning ships into a dancing blur of light.

10

Richard Brixham tugged at one laced cuff of his brocaded town coat and smiled genially at the young man who sat across from him. Brixham had spent a lifetime in the Caribbean wearing simply what was practical rather than what was fashionable. Now that life in London provided endless opportunity to dress well, and he felt the pressure of a certain *noblesse oblige* upon receipt of his knighthood from His Britannic Majesty, George the Second, Richard Brixham was delighted to take that opportunity. He was a distinguished-looking man with a kindly face and dark, sea-coloured eyes that varied from blue to green depending upon the light; tall and still straight and slim, he was physically hardy from years of long work and an outdoor existence. To have liquidated his plantation holdings successfully at such excellent terms in the City, to be contemplating a life of ease far from the disease- and pirate-ridden lands of his toil, and to have, without apparent effort, insinuated himself into Court where he found himself actually on speaking terms with his shy but intelligent sovereign, was all proving enormously pleasurable. That he had been able to enjoy the establishment of his London household with his daughter Anne – and thereby introduced that headstrong hellion to proper society rather than leaving her to the deplorable habits she had been developing in the West Indies – had added immeasurably to his bounty. So as he regarded the square-shouldered and serious young man who sat fidgeting across from him in the small waiting-room in the Admiralty – a young man for whom he felt a good deal of affection – he was fairly brimming with good humour.

"My dear Edward, you needn't look quite so ferociously glum. The King will not *eat* you, you know."

Edward Mainwaring tugged at his tight white neckcloth and tried to smile at the old gentleman. He was dressed in a russet-coloured suit of velvet that had cost a preposterous sum – he would not even have considered its purchase on the basis of his lieutenant's pay and wore it now only because Brixham had insisted upon paying for it – and fine white hose above tiny dress pumps that cramped his feet and looked, he thought, ludicrously feminine. His hair had been neatly dressed into side curls and a bar-taut queue, although he had fought and won over the issue of powdering it, and on his lap he dandied a gilt-edged tricorne of glossy brushed beaver, again a purchase of the Brixham purse. He was intensely uncomfortable and sweating, and had been morosely dwelling on the likelihood that they would have to perch on the hard little ladder-back chairs for hours more before anything might occur.

"I'm sorry, Sir Richard," he said. "I don't wish to be poor company. Feel rather like a damned trapped rat, if the truth be known."

Brixham laughed gently. "Well, you *would* go clanging about the Mediterranean staging preposterous happenings that drew attention to yourself. You should count yourself lucky to be getting away with merely an audience with His Majesty. Think if the mob had taken you to its heart more than it already has! My boy, your life would be quite intolerable."

"Togging out in all this foppery is intolerable enough, sir. With respect," said the American.

"I quite understand. Well, you needn't be too gloomy. Anne will be here in—" he looked at his pocket watch, "a few more moments. And presumably His Majesty will see us within the hour." Brixham paused. "He's quite a soldier, you know. Strong interest in things military, and naval as well, I should think. Likely what prompted him to want to see you. It's quite extraordinary for him to have come to the Admiralty, although I suspect that's because he's far more comfortable around fighting men than courtiers. We might, you know, have found ourselves simply part of the throng at St James's."

"I do appreciate that, Sir Richard."

"Yes. Well." Brixham's expression softened. "Look here, it's your concern for your men again, isn't it? I had thought

232

that first lieutenant of yours had everything well in hand."

Mainwaring looked up from the hat. "To the degree that he would be free to make his own decisions, I trust him completely, sir. But you'll recall I told you that on arrival in *Barb* at Villefranche, my report caused Admiral Mathews to relieve me of my duties and confine me to the ship. I was then sent back to England in the *Basingstoke* sloop, which carried despatches announcing that the squadron had sailed for Toulon. The last I saw of Howe and the others, they were still in *Barb*, and I've deuced little idea where they might be, or if—"

Brixham held up a calming hand. "Gently, my boy. Patience. I'm sure things will be clarified and resolved."

Mainwaring looked unconvinced. "With respect, Sir Richard, I'd like some more evidence of that. With the loss of *Diana* I face an obligatory Court. Admiral Mathews made quite a few displeased noises when we limped in, and I have no illusions about what will be construed from *his* report!" Mainwaring was about to run his fingers through his hair, remembered the dressing at the last moment, and returned to fiddling with his hat. "The Navy will undoubtedly find something unpleasant to do with me, and I've resigned myself to that. The matter that most concerns me is what has happened to my lads. Christ, if they've been drafted into some slime-bilged scow commanded by one of Mathews' lisping toadies—!" He did not finish.

Brixham looked sympathetic. "You mentioned some French fishermen and their families who helped you, and whom you managed to take off with you. Were there many?"

Mainwaring's expression changed, to an odd mixture of pride and pain.

"No. Perhaps twenty-five souls, all told."

"And they actually helped to defend the fort?"

Mainwaring nodded. "Aye. And willingly. The French troops had mistreated them: burnt their homes, tortured them, even undertook to shoot them. They were willing enough to help."

"And you put them ashore at Villefranche?"

"Yes. The Savoyards said they'd care for them. They offered a commission at the drop of a hat to the officer I brought out with them,' said Mainwaring.

"And that was this fellow – er—"

"De Guimond. A fine man. I hope he has a distinguished career ahead of him. We owed him our lives."

Brixham nodded. "And you say you were ordered confined soon after making your report?"

"Yes. At first in *Barb*. The commander of it was – is – a crusty, one-eyed Scot who came to our rescue inshore. He took a splinter in the head, but recovered. I've no fear that he would misuse my lads, but they'd be drafted out of *Barb* in a clock's tick, with the shortage of hands." Mainwaring clenched his fists. "I *must* find out what has become of them: help them, if I can. Point out that if any blame attaches to any in this, it is mine alone. My orders led to it all."

Brixham's mouth formed a slight smile. "You must admit it is somewhat extraordinary to lose two commands in less than the same number of weeks."

Mainwaring looked up with a hard light in his eyes, but softened when he saw Brixham's expression. "I suppose. But presumably an unbiased Court could see that there were extraordinary circumstances present as well. I doubt whether I'll be that fortunate," he concluded glumly.

Brixham toyed with his gold-headed cane. "You lost some of the French civilians, I gather?" he said quietly, after a moment.

Mainwaring studied his shoes. "Yes. When the longboat took a round shot. Several of the adults and a child. Drowned. And one – woman took a splinter in the head. Never knew what hit her."

Brixham heard the hoarseness in Mainwaring's voice, and nodded silently.

"It is a difficult thing to feel responsible for the deaths of others," he remarked, after a moment. "Even when the fault was, in fact, not yours."

Mainwaring's eyes were full of pain when he raised them to the older man's.

"But the fault was mine, Sir Richard," he said, in a half-whisper. "I ordered *Diana* in to where the gun batteries ashore destroyed her, trapped by the boom. I concocted the plan of going in to Toulon itself, rather than simply standing off. Those wretched fishermen and their families owe the death and loss they've suffered to *me*. I'm quite aware of what I've done," he finished bitterly. "Do you want me to go on?"

Brixham pursed his lips. "No," he said gently. "But I would wish my future son-in-law to listen to something I had to say to him."

"I'm sorry?"

Brixham leaned forward, resting his hands on his cane. "War is a ghastly business, Edward. It is a nightmare, for all its calls to glorious arms and hymns of valour. No one knows that more than the men who have to do the fighting. But in this world, here and now, the country needed – and will continue to need – men who will do just as you have done. Men who will see that the country they serve, and which relies upon them, calls on them to fight His Majesty's enemies with every bit of cunning and imagination, and every bit of determination possible. To see their duty, and from within find the strength to carry it out *whatever the cost*." He paused. "There are far too many men in the King's service who see only what can be gained for themselves in a particular situation; too many who look only for the safe course, and trust to sickness or bravery to carry off the selfless fools that bar their way to effortless promotion."

Mainwaring smiled grimly. "You seem to understand the Royal Navy perfectly," he said.

"Only as a spectator. But mark me, Edward. The shirkers and the sycophants I have described may look to 'interest' to further their careers. Let them. They are *not* the Royal Navy, not the *true* Navy. The real Navy is you, and men like you. Men like your Hooke and Lieutenant Howe, and that one-eyed Scot you described so well. Men of inner fortitude who care only that their duty is done, and the men in their command looked after, to the last of their strength."

Brixham's dark eyes bore into Mainwaring's. "Edward, we are a free people because of such men. And you are one,

235

my boy. I wouldn't allow Anne to be near you, were you not." He smiled. "So you need not fear what any damned Court will say. And you didn't kill those people, into the bargain. The *war* did. You should hate the confounded war, Edward. But don't turn that hate against yourself, where it manifestly does not belong!"

For a long moment Mainwaring stared at Brixham and then nodded slowly. He stood and walked to the far end of the little room, and when he turned he felt unbidden tears burning in his eyes. He kept his face expressionless, but reached wordlessly for the older man's hand. Brixham rose, and as silently took Mainwaring's in a warm, firm grip.

"Sir Richard. Lieutenant Mainwaring. If you will be so kind as to follow me?"

A cadaverous figure in the austere black dress of an Admiralty clerk had arrived at the waiting-room door. With an air of bored disdain he led the two men back into the main lobby of the building and then down a long, gleaming hallway to another door which he opened and stepped aside.

With Brixham leading, the two men walked in. Mainwaring's eyes took in the long, polished table, the tall windows facing on to what he presumed were stables of the Horse Guards, the rack of charts on the wall, a sonorously-ticking upright clock, and a compasslike wind indicator set high on one wall, its face an outline of the coasts of Western Europe. His mind told him that he was standing in that most holy of holies for his profession, the Board Room.

A group of magnificently dressed gentlemen were standing partway down the length of the table. One, a pale-featured man with blue, protuberant eyes and ruddy cheeks, strode briskly towards them.

"Ah, Sir Richard! So this is your young firebrand, *nicht wahr*?" he said in a light voice that bore only a modest trace of a German accent.

Richard Brixham bowed gracefully.

"Your Majesty. May I present Lieutenant Edward Mainwaring, late of Your Majesty's vessels—"

"*Ach*, I know, I know," said the King. "He has a habit of having my ships blown up. I've read your report, Lieutenant. You seem to have made a remarkably fortunate shot with the twelve-pounders of that battery."

Mainwaring fumbled his way into a bow.

"Er – yes, Your Majesty. We – ah – were fortunate, sir." He felt his face flame red.

"My experience of guns, Mainwaring, suggests that the further one is from them, whether in front or behind, the safer one is. Would you agree?"

"I believe that would be so, sir. If – if one has the luxury of choice, sir."

George the Second's watery eyes warmed with amusement. "Well put. And I gather you fired the French three-banded firelock. That would be," and here the King thought for a moment, "the *modèle* 1728. A smaller ball than our trusty 'Bess'. How did it handle?"

Mainwaring's eyebrows rose. "Er – very well, sir. Lighter than the 'Bess' as well, sir. Snapped reliably and was sturdy enough in the bayonet push, sir. I had no idea—"

"That your monarch might know a bit about the military arts? In truth, Mainwaring," and here the King lowered his voice, "I get more pleasure from the company of some honest grenadiers than from all these soft-handed gentlemen behind me, *verstehen Sie*? Now, Walpole was a chap one could talk to, but this Carteret fellow—" he stopped, seeing Mainwaring's expression. "But none of that concerns you at this moment. I believe I must ask you to advise me on a serious naval matter, Mainwaring."

"If I can be of help, I shall, sir," said Mainwaring. His neckcloth felt like a band of steel around his throat.

"As I would expect," said the King. "I have a problem of a very junior officer who has brought considerable upheaval to the smooth functioning of our fleet and our ships."

"Sir?"

"Tut, tut, let me finish. Who entered the Navy from, I believe, the American colonies, and has since his entry contrived to get himself into circumstances which, for one reason or another, created a deuced lot of expense!"

"Sir, I—" attempted Mainwaring.

"And who, in his most recent activity, managed to destroy not one but *two* of our ships, within a remarkably short period of time."

"Please, Your Majesty, if I may explain—"

"But while doing so, led a landing party into the principal Mediterranean naval port of our cousin Louis, where he sank a vessel which then blocked the channel, destroyed one of the principal fortifications protecting that port, inflicted heavy damages on at least half a dozen of the French and Spanish men-o'-war in that harbour, *and* produced such a final blockage in the channel that the French and Spanish squadrons were not able to sail from that place for *six weeks*, thereby allowing our vessels to deploy to counter them suitably."

Mainwaring was silent as he saw the expression on the King's face, and on the faces of the men who stood behind him.

"And who," went on the King quietly, "thereby prevented an unthinkable disaster from overtaking our naval forces in the Mediterranean, the consequences of which would have been injurious in the extreme to our Crown and our realm. Are *you* this man?"

Mainwaring flushed. "I – am, sir."

The King's smile was warm and genuine. "*Richtig*! Then we have no choice but to impose a suitable punishment, Lieutenant Mainwaring." He paused.

"You are hereby 'made post', as I believe you put it, Mainwaring. You are promoted to the rank of post captain, at the most junior level of seniority. My concern expressed to Their Lordships has brought them to give you an excellent command. You're to have *Pallas*, forty-four guns, which we are told is a fine, well-found vessel. And, at the urging of our favourite whist partner, Sir Richard, here, we have given orders that those of your former crews and officers who wish to sail with you shall be allowed to do so. What do you have to say to *that*?"

Mainwaring opened his mouth to speak, but could not find the words. His monarch stepped forward and took his hand in a surprisingly strong grip.

"Then you'd best not say a word, before we change our mind, *ja*?" And Mainwaring found himself exchanging a grin with him.

"Sir Richard!" said the King. "We have not had the pleasure of speaking with your delightful daughter for some time. She is here, *nicht wahr*?"

Edward Mainwaring turned as the King pointed. In the doorway stood a dark-haired young woman in a delicate white gown, her hair piled in elegant powdered curls atop her head, an ivory and lace fan fluttering in one hand. But there was no mistaking the wide, happy grin that seemed to flood the room with sunshine as Mainwaring stared at her, his heart racing.

Sir Richard Brixham was exchanging a knowing look with the King.

"She is indeed, Your Majesty," he said.

"Then let us welcome her," said the King, with a warm smile. "We are sure that she and *Captain* Mainwaring will have much to discuss . . ."